THE
COMMANDANT

**LIBRARIES
LEABHARLANNA**

CORK CITY COUNCIL | COMHAIRLE CATHRACH CHORCAÍ

You can renew items through the online catalogue at
www.corkcitylibraries.ie, or by telephone.
Please return this item on time as others may be waiting for it.
Overdue charges: 50c per notice + 30c per week.

Is féidir iasachtaí a athnuachan trí bhíthin na catalóige ag
www.corkcitylibraries.ie, nó ar an nguthán.
Muna gcuirtear iasacht ar ais in am, gearrfar costaisí
50c do gach fógra, maraon le 30c in aghaidh na seachtaine.

Class no./Ur. aicme: _____ HIC _____

Tory Top Library
Leabharlann Bhothar na mBuaircíní
021 4924935
torytop_library@corkcity.ie

_rd_

STEERFORTH PRESS
HANOVER, NEW HAMPSHIRE

Copyright © 2014 by Patrick Hicks
ALL RIGHTS RESERVED

The first chapter of this novel appeared, in a slightly different form, in *Epiphany*.

For information about permission to reproduce
selections from this book, write to:
Steerforth Press L.L.C., 45 Lyme Road, Suite 208,
Hanover, New Hampshire 03755

Cataloging-in-Publication Data is available from the Library of Congress

ISBN 978-1-58642-220-2

First U.S. Edition

1 3 5 7 9 10 8 6 4 2

ALSO BY PATRICK HICKS
This London
A Harvest of Words (editor)
Finding the Gossamer
The Kiss That Saved My Life

CORK CITY LIBRARY
WITHDRAWN
FROM STOCK

For the Unknown

What have you done? Hark, thy brother's
blood cries to me from the ground.
—Genesis 4:10

PART I

BEGINNINGS

The records show that some 710,000 souls died at the small concentration camp known as Lubizec. But to call Lubizec a "concentration camp" is incorrect because it was not designed to hold people as if they were common criminals or a threat to the Nazi state. No, it is more historically accurate to call this tiny area of barbed wire and train tracks an "extermination camp" or, if we are being more honest with ourselves, a place of overwhelming mass murder. Lubizec was a factory of death with one purpose: the swift and unrelenting slaughter of human beings. It was a place of mass annihilation, and it rested far beyond the frontier of mercy.

What remains of the camp today is on the southeastern border of Poland, and there is practically nothing left aside from a cement memorial where the gas chambers once stood. Few people visit Lubizec not only because it is so remote, but also because there is a serious misunderstanding about what happened there. Auschwitz is remembered because survivors managed to limp away from that wicked place and bear witness, but hardly anyone knows about Lubizec because it was an extermination camp. Of the 710,000 souls that entered its gates, only forty-three survived to talk about what they saw. This lack of survivorship is almost certainly why the world isn't as familiar with the camp as it should be. We simply don't have the stories to make it real. It is also very difficult to imagine 710,000 people and then see each of them being dead. How has this influenced the world? What might their children, and grandchildren, and great-grandchildren have gone on to do? Although these murders continue to echo into our future, the scale of this crime is, for most of us, simply beyond comprehension.

Even in the immediate aftermath of World War II, little was known about this place deep in the woods. Auschwitz was preserved by the Russians as proof of genocide, and the entire world became aware of it when newsreels and testimonies were released to the public. Lubizec, however, was plowed into the ground by the Nazis after the startling events of March 1943. The rebellion and escape surprised everyone, including the commandant, and it was decided to level the buildings and pretend that the place never existed. We have no photos of Lubizec, and this has made it a footnote in history books rather than a focal point. There are rumors of Nazi scrapbooks and some related photographic materials floating around but, as yet, nothing has been authenticated and determined to be from Lubizec itself. Much of what we do know comes from Chaim Zischer's chillingly blunt, *The Hell of Lubizec* (1954). Zischer writes about the murder of his family with such clinical detachment we quickly feel it was the only way for him to write about what he saw, and in fact, shortly before his death in 2009, he found it impossible to believe he was the last eyewitness to the camp. He was worried that Lubizec would be forgotten about, and it has to be admitted the writing of this book is partly prompted by Zischer's passing.

It is indeed odd to realize that Lubizec has now slipped into history, entirely and completely. There is no one left who saw carbon monoxide being channeled into the gas chambers, there is no one left who saw people being herded off the trains towards an engine that was ready to crank into a higher gear, and there is no one left who saw the commandant walk through the camp with his infamous ledger and pack of cigarettes. When we think of places like Lubizec, we are used to seeing black-and-white photos, which offer us comfort that such events took place long ago, deep in the past. But if we try to view this camp in color and allow ourselves to feel the sandy dirt beneath our shoes, to see the swastika flapping like blood on a pole, to see the guards strutting around in their charcoal-gray uniforms, if we do this, we might feel the camp lift itself out of the pages of history.

One thing is certain. All across the planet we are losing our eyewitnesses to the Holocaust and this book is an attempt to make Lubizec feel real (or as real as words can make anything feel). In so doing, the author hopes to remind people of these extermination camps and give voice to the voiceless. Little is known about Lubizec, but by talking about this one single camp perhaps a larger discussion may arise about other death camps like Bełżec, Sobibór, and Treblinka, which aren't lodged in the public imagination as fully as they should be. Perhaps this book will act as a doorway into somewhere else, and in that dark, terrible space, maybe we will be provoked to remember anew.

So how did this little spot in Poland become a site of mass murder?

This is where we shall begin.

It started when a huge drum of barbed wire was tossed to the ground—it wobbled like a monstrous coin to a stop. Hammers and crosscut saws were brought out of trucks. Men shouted and laughed as they marked off camp boundaries with little flags. They set up a phonograph and put the needle down onto some classical music. Fence posts were pounded into the sandy ground.

Lubizec was built five kilometers from the sleepy village that gave it its name and it was also near a major rail line, which meant it was secluded enough to keep prying eyes away but close enough to rail traffic to bring victims in. From the very beginning it was a place of secrets. It was a place hidden deep in the woods.

The first commandant was a doughy man named Wilhelm Fischel. He had the trees leveled, he built a series of guard towers, and on October 24, 1941, he accepted his first shipment of prisoners. They were mostly Polish men who refused to accept German rule over their country, and they were forced to build barracks for the SS who, at that time, were living in olive-drab tents. Other buildings sprang up, a latrine was dug, and rail tracks from the village of Lubizec were extended into the camp itself. Fischel had a small clapboard office built for his private use, and he made sure the SS had a bar stocked with excellent beer imported from Munich. All the while, more and more prisoners were stuffed into Lubizec and the food supply was kept intentionally low.

As they died off, Fischel had them buried outside the barbed-wire perimeter in a massive trench. Space inside the camp became an increasing problem as more prisoners were packed in. Fischel solved the problem by ordering each of his guards to shoot five prisoners a day. He didn't care how these selections were made as long as it kept the numbers down.

Things got much worse in April 1942 when it was decided by the higher-ups in Berlin that Lubizec would cease to be a concentration camp and it would become, instead, a death camp. Fischel began to drink more heavily around this time. He sat in his office and showed absolutely no interest in running the camp. He got sloppy with vodka and didn't care how his guards went about the killing—they usually hauled prisoners off the trains and began shooting them as if they were scurrying rabbits. Women clutched their children as guards opened up their guns, and as the sun grew hotter and hotter, and as sweat began to prickle everyone's scalp, the guards decided to let the new transports die of thirst in the railcars instead. It was easier this way. They kept the doors bolted shut while they waited in the shade. When the cries finally stopped, that's when they rolled open the doors.

Bodies were everywhere. They were dumped beside the rail tracks, scattered around like rag dolls. A thick meaty stench filled the air, but still Fischel drank on. His men called him "The Pickled Hermit," and word got back to high command that there was a problem at Lubizec. Whole trainloads couldn't be processed because the camp was so disorganized, and this infuriated SS *Hauptsturmführer* Odilo Globocnik who was in charge of exterminating the Jews of Poland. He drafted an order to replace Fischel with someone else, someone who knew how to manage problems—someone who was loyal to the Party and understood what it meant to have an ordered system.

Hans-Peter Guth arrived on May 27, 1942. He was in his early forties, handsome, in shape, and well rested. His copper-blond hair was misted with gray, and he liked to keep it clipped short. It was raining softly when his Mercedes pulled into the village five kilometers outside of camp. The dirt roads needed to be graded smooth, and the car bumped along through deep puddles of brown water. He ordered his driver to slow down so that he could see everything.

"Good Lord," he said, making a sour face. "What's that *stink*?"

The car lurched through ruts as they turned down a narrow road towards the camp. Old-growth pine trees launched themselves into the sky and rabbits darted away from the car—they scurried over decaying needles as Guth pulled out a cigarette and tried to light it. The wind made this difficult, so in frustration, he flicked it onto the road. Train tracks ran beside the car in blurry parallel lines of steel, and he saw what looked like sacks of wheat every few yards. He squinted and realized they were bodies.

"What a fucking mess," he said, shaking his head. "It looks like a war zone."

The car continued down a tree-lined road. Sunlight and shadow flickered on the dashboard, the springs bounced and creaked, and as they rounded a corner, the bodies increased. Flies were everywhere. They drove through huge banks of them. Once-beloved humans were putrefying in various stages of wet decomposition and the smell of rotting flesh curdled the air. Guth covered his nose. The smell of aftershave was still on his fingertips and he breathed in.

"Astonishing," he said, shaking his head. "Just astonishing."

His car—long, shiny, the color of coal and midnight—turned and drove next to the tracks for another kilometer. The bodies increased and they looked like cast-aside marionettes, as if their strings had been cut. The camp hove into view and Guth looked through the windshield as they bounced down the unpaved road. The Mercedes came to a rolling stop in front of a red-and-white pole barricade that looked vaguely like a huge candy cane. Inside the camp, men shuffled around with shovels and Guth watched as a guard hit them with a rubber truncheon. The stink was overpowering. It crawled into his nose and made him blink a few times. He cleared his throat and tried to focus.

The driver got out, ran around the black snout of the car, and opened the door with a quick snap and a Hitler salute. "Welcome to Lubizec, sir."

The commandant got out and stretched.

Sunlight glinted off the chrome of his car and the engine clicked as it cooled. Guth did a slow turn on the sandy gravel and glanced at the dead—the inconvenience of them—and he wondered how to solve the problem of their presence. Flies circled his head in a buzzing peppery cloud and he shooed them away with a leather glove.

"Fischel ought to be hanged for this."

He looked down the rail tracks, which disappeared like a long iron needle into the trees. Swollen bodies were everywhere. Maggots jittered in open wounds. Ravens orbited overhead; they cawed as dark clouds began to roll in. Rain was on the horizon.

"It's like a battlefield around here," he said, using his foot to nudge an arm out of the way. "Or like something out of Dante's *Inferno*."

An SS guard stumbled around the corner with a bottle of vodka and wobbled on unsteady legs. His uniform wasn't buttoned properly, it was cockeyed, lopsided, and this made Guth angry for the first time all morning.

"You there."

The man with the bottle tried to come to attention but he stood like a wet shirt on a hanger.

"Are you drunk?"

There was a burp, then a giggle.

Guth's face hardened into marble. He turned to his driver and said, "Take my things to the office and telegram my wife. Tell her I've arrived safely." There was a brief pause as he looked around. "There *is* an office in this place, yes?"

"Of course."

"Good. Good. Now send that telegram."

The drunk realized who was in front of him and dropped the bottle. He offered up a sloppy Hitler salute as clear liquid glugged and flopped onto the sandy ground. The candy cane pole barricade was still down, and although Guth had not yet entered the camp, he could see inside.

Another guard came out of a wooden building and yelled at a prisoner who was moving too slowly. He had the gray man in dirty clothes lie on the ground as he pulled out his pistol. The guard took careful aim at the man's head—he straightened his arm and locked his elbow. *Crack.* It was a cool and clean shot, echoing. The guard was as dispassionate as if he had kicked a stone down the road and was pleased to see its trajectory. The guard holstered his weapon and began to stroll away.

"You there," Guth half shouted. "Yes, you. I'm talking to you."

The guard adjusted his SS cap and walked over as if he had all the time in the world. It began to rain and large splats of water darkened his gray uniform. Thunder rumbled in the distance.

"What are you doing?"

The guard looked at the swollen bodies dumped everywhere around them and began to stammer. "I was—I was—sorry, sir. I—I don't understand the question."

"If you're going to shoot these creatures, don't leave their bodies lying around. Clean that mess up."

The guard paused.

"Do it now."

The guard turned on his heel but Guth whistled for him to stop. "One more thing."

"Sir?"

"Shave your face. This isn't a holiday resort."

And with that, the barricade was raised and Hans-Peter Guth entered Lubizec.

During the next few weeks the bodies of mothers, fathers, sons, daughters, students, rabbis, shopkeepers, musicians, and poets were gathered up. A long trench was dug. Guth stood back as exhausted, thirsty, and ragged prisoners shoveled down into the sandy soil. Limp bodies in various stages of decomposition were fitted like herrings into the raw earth. Lime was scattered onto their chests and heads as still more bodies were dragged over. Guth sometimes pointed at prisoners who worked too slowly or paused to wipe sweat from their foreheads, and whenever this happened they were tossed into the trench and shot.

While it is tempting to speculate on what Guth was thinking during all of this, we should never lose sight of the prisoners working at a fever pitch around him. We need to imagine a thin man (perhaps, let us say, a man who had been a doctor before the war) and we need to imagine him stumbling around over chests and arms and legs. His shoes sink into the layered dead. He trips often and has to hold out his arms—like a tightrope walker—to balance himself. Now let us imagine that his job is to arrange these bodies just so, and he knows that if he slows his frantic pace for any reason, or if he stands up to stretch, or if he pauses to catch his breath, he will be shot. What would this man think as Guth strolls along the lip of the trench, ledger in hand, the blue sky framing his silhouette? What would he think as Guth yells out, "I want everything clean and tidy. Ordered, yes? Good. Good."

We can only guess what this hypothetical prisoner was thinking because no one survived this early period of Lubizec's history. They were all murdered. This is a problem because when historians talk about the early days of Lubizec the only testimony we have comes from the Nazis themselves, and this is what makes the beginning of Lubizec so heartbreaking to bear. We want a character we can believe in, we want some nugget of truth to ponder, we want a glimmer of light amid the overpowering darkness of this extermination camp, and, more than anything else, we want to hope.

These are all perfectly reasonable desires for a world living safely beyond the gravitational field of Lubizec, but we are talking about a death camp and our expectations of narrative arc have to be readjusted and retooled in the face of so much murder. The year is 1942 and the war is far from over. In fact, the Nazis are in total control and they are tossing lives into the abyss at breathtaking speed. Although we may want the story of Lubizec told from the perspective of the victims, at this early stage in the camp's history this is impossible to do. Stories of survivorship will come later, but for now, we can only approach this death camp through the eyes of the perpetrators. All other viewpoints have been erased. Snuffed out. Covered in lime.

We therefore know that Guth wanted everything "made cleaner" and that he banned alcohol in the SS canteen until "after 2100 hours."

"This isn't the front line," he told his guards one night. "Here you have it easy because no one's shooting at you." He paused and raised a finger. "Write home to your mothers and sweethearts tonight. Tell them you're safe. Tell them you love them."

Guth had the wood line widened to create better fields of gunfire as well as strategically defined boundaries of left and right vision for the guard towers. He put distance markers out in the forest so that his men could see how far their bullets might travel if an escape ever happened. He reinforced the barbed-wire fences and put a solid guard rotation into place so his men would get proper amounts of sleep. He ran drills. He inspected weapons. He laid out clear expectations of on-duty and off-duty behavior. He also made sure his men ate decent food, he got them beds instead of cots, and he had a wide moat of landmines placed around the camp. The prisoners were forced to dig these holes, and on ten separate occasions landmines went off killing inmates, but it was never determined if these were accidents or suicides. To the guards who ran Lubizec it hardly mattered, though. Dead prisoners were dead prisoners. We can only imagine what it must have been like to sow these angry explosives into the earth, but for the prisoners, it must have felt like they were building an invisible wall around themselves, that they were burying hope itself deep in the ground. We have no account of what these men were thinking because, after this wide moat of landmines was completed, they were all shot. Students, rabbis, shopkeepers, musicians, fishmongers, tailors, doctors, and poets. Every single one of them. Shot.

Guth spent more time in his office, but unlike Wilhelm Fischel, he wasn't a hermit. Far from it. He was on the phone constantly, drafting blueprints and making sure building materials were delivered to the camp on time.

One detail that horrified Guth about Lubizec was his discovery that whores were brought in every weekend. Apparently under Fischel's command, local women and huge cases of champagne were brought into camp.

"We're not running a brothel here," he said to his guards one morning on the parade ground. The sky was salmon pink, smudged with blue clouds, and his men stood at rigid fixed attention with their shadows stretching away from them. They looked like a packet of bullets. Crows cawed and a tractor puttered in the distance. Guth took in the smoke of his cigarette, held it inside his chest for a long moment, and then spewed it out into the world.

"Things are about to change around here," he said, pointing to the empty rail tracks. "See that? In one hour a train will arrive with pallets of bricks. These bricks have a very special purpose. Since the world began spinning, no one has done what we are about to do in this place. It will be a triumph of logistics, and when you're all old men sitting around talking about the great war in the east, you'll be able to look back on this moment of your life with pride." He raised a finger and smiled. "With pride."

Exactly one hour later a train huffed through the forest. It pulled up to Lubizec with steam erupting from both sides. After it squealed to a stop, prisoners were beaten out of the gates and ordered to unload bricks—"*Schneller, schneller.*" The sun was out and everyone felt their hair follicles open up with sweat. Guth handed a rolled-up blueprint to his subordinate, Heinrich Niemann. He was a giant of a man with a weird meandering scar on his chin. His fingers were meaty and Guth found this in keeping with the boxing information that was in Niemann's file. Apparently in the early 1930s he was a regional Bavarian champ. He certainly had the fists for it.

"When it arrives we'll install it over there," Guth said lighting a cigarette. He puffed and marched over to an imaginary X. "Right here." He tapped his foot in the patchy grass. "Here. This is where the engine will go. And I want you to erect the showers just there. It all needs to be done in a week, but if you get it done in six days I'll throw in a crate of champagne. Get it done in *five* days and you'll get another crate. Understand?"

He walked across the sandy earth in his polished boots and didn't pay any attention to the prisoners who were straining to move impossibly heavy loads of bricks. One prisoner with a shock of black hair and long gangly legs—huge kneecaps—lost control, and his bricks spilled to the ground in a clattering clunk. A guard came over and began beating him until the man was hunched into a ball. The blows sounded like a carpet being smacked clean of dirt.

Guth looked around and did a quick calculation about what still needed to be done. He walked over and spoke without anger.

"Stop that."

Years later, when one of the guards was asked about Lubizec, he cited these few seconds as an example of Guth's mercy. He said his commandant "didn't like to see the Jews suffer." Whether this is true or not is for the reader to decide, but we do know that Guth returned to his office after this incident and emerged often to make sure the gas chambers were built properly. He got out a level and made sure the brick walls were plumb. He made sure the cement was mixed into a thick paste that resembled oatmeal and he made sure prisoners smoothed out the concrete floors with long metal skims. As promised, the engine arrived the next day and it was pulled into place by a large bulldozer.

Guth watched all of this while he smoked cigarette after cigarette. He said nothing as prisoners orbited around him in a frenzy.

At night he closed his office door and pulled out a silver flask.

His wife and two children were moving into a nearby house but they hadn't yet arrived so he slept on a cot near his desk. He looked at charts, maps, train schedules, duty rosters, water table levels, food consumption rates, electrical needs, and he calculated the weight of two thousand bodies. He used a slide rule. A mound of cigarette butts sprouted up from his ashtray, and sometimes, when he was deep in thought, he sat back and spun his wedding ring. The stickier the problem, the slower he spun his ring until—"Ah, yes"—he leaned forward and scribbled the answer.

This, we should note, is the face of evil, this studious man working late into the evening. In any other setting he would just be a building site manager, but Guth was a true believer in Nazi ideology as well as an excellent administrator. With his typewriter and pen he was able to kill hundreds of thousands of people. We must never forget that killing took on many forms in the Holocaust and that these crimes weren't confined to a single place like a gas chamber. Guth was very good at his job. His desk became a weapon of mass destruction.

We have a telegram dated June 25, 1942, where Guth tells his superiors how proud he is to be associated with "Operation Reinhard" and that Lubizec is ready to join the ranks of Sobibór, Bełżec, and Treblinka as a model camp. He called in several guards and they toasted each other with tall glasses of brandy. They sat back and smoked cigars while, outside, the prisoners who built the gas chambers were all lined up and shot.

Sometime the next day *SS Hauptsturmführer* Odilo Globocnik called Guth and congratulated him personally.

"You are a credit to us all," he said. "When can you begin?"

Lubizec became a death camp on July 4, 1942, and Guth decided it might be fun to play some American big band music as the first train rolled in. He found a record player and put on Glenn Miller's "Don't Sit Under the Apple Tree" to commemorate what he called Germany's own version of Independence Day. The guards stood on the newly constructed platform next to the tracks—the smell of sawdust was strong in the air—and they waited as a black cloud of soot plumed up from the horizon. It looked like a foaming geyser of oil as the train passed over the rails until, at last, it hissed to a panting, complaining, shrieking, stop.

It was one of the hottest summers on record and the guards mopped their foreheads with handkerchiefs. They drank water from canteens and laughed. They tapped their feet to the swinging music.

When the doors finally clattered open, the people inside were saturated with sweat. The men had taken off their shirts and many of the women were stripped down to their undergarments. A layer of damp coated everyone and deep inside the oven-hot cars were several infants that had died of thirst. What happened next is horrifyingly familiar to anyone that has studied a death camp. The victims were ordered off the train and promised a cold shower as well as plenty of pumpernickel bread. Guards made announcements about how they were in a transit camp and that they would be resettled to a "Jew village" a few kilometers down the road. There was a murmur of relief.

It is good to pause here and remind ourselves that these 726 souls were not merely statistics. They were mothers and fathers, brothers and sisters, aunts, uncles, husbands, wives, sons, daughters, and grandchildren. They each had a story. They were each packed with memory. They were each a vital part of the universe itself. But when the guards raised their clubs they were driven into oblivion.

As we continue on with the story of Lubizec it is easy to become numb to its horror because the brutality of the place pushes us towards finding a coping mechanism, towards wrapping a shell around our hearts, and this often means it can be easier to imagine a faceless mass moving into the gas chambers instead of individual people with individual lives. But these people could have been our family members or neighbors. On that muggy day in July, they were all scared, worried, and nervous—as anyone would be—so rather than view these 726 souls as unknown characters lost to history, it would be better to imagine our own families on that wooden platform. Our parents are there. Our siblings too. All of our loved ones are soaked with sweat and terror. We glance around at each other and wonder about this strange new place called Lubizec.

"Where are we?"

In front of us is a handsome man in a uniform. His copper-blond hair is cut short and his boots are polished to a high shine. "Welcome to Lubizec," he says. "My name is Commandant Guth."

And then? Then we are herded into the camp.

LIFE IN A DEATH CAMP

Lubizec was divided into two separate areas. It was bisected across the middle by a large fence that had twigs and leaves woven into it and this "natural curtain," as Guth called it, split the camp into zones of life and death. Camp I consisted of long wooden barracks for the prisoners that were intentionally built without running water, heat, or flooring of any kind. The barracks were designed to be as uncomfortable as possible and they were stuffed full of triple-layered bunks. Instead of mattresses, hay was used. A few puny windows were added to let daylight in and roll call took place in front of these buildings. Although the ground was stamped hard from use, stubborn tufts of grass grew up here and there.

Immediately beyond the roll call area was the entrance to the camp. An iron gate had been installed and even though it was mostly locked, the hinges were well greased. Unlike places like Dachau and Auschwitz where the words *Arbeit Macht Frei* (Work Sets You Free) greeted each prisoner upon arrival, Guth wanted something else for his camp, something simple and ironic. And so, after a few days of thought, he had a large metal sign pounded out that simply read *Willkommen* (Welcome) in large black letters. It hung over the gate and faced the rail tracks, which were surrounded by a gauze of barbed-wire fencing. Beyond the camp, purple wildflowers waved in the wind.

The living quarters for the SS were on the south end of Camp I. The guards enjoyed a well-stocked kitchen, a small post office, a barber-shop, and they also had a vegetable garden full of green beans, onions, and potatoes. Beer was served in the canteen after 2100 hours, but only when Guth felt that it was deserved.

Camp II took up the northern half of Lubizec and it was here the killing took place. It required one hundred prisoners to keep it going and there was a long wooden hut for cutting hair. The only brick building in the entire camp was also here: the gas chamber. It had four separate units, it was painted a creamy pale white, and there were huge flowerpots in front of it. Sometimes roses greeted the victims. Other times it was marigolds or geraniums.

There were seven guard towers in total, each equipped with a powerful searchlight, and at night these giant cones of light roved the ground like animals on a leash. They sniffed here and there before moving on. Guards complained about moths fluttering around these powerful lights but there was nothing Guth could do about it.

"Nature is nature." He shrugged.

As for the mass graves, they lay to the northeast, along with enormous pallets of quicklime.

Guth was pleased with the first week of operations. "Delighted," as one guard put it. The bodies had been buried and everything was running smoothly. He called over his second in command, Heinrich Niemann, and pulled out two cigars from his uniform. The sun was like a bullet wound. These jackbooted men stood in twilight with the tips of their cigars glowing hot, then dim. Smoke billowed from their mouths as fireflies floated above the grass. Frogs sang from a nearby creek as Guth tapped ash into the air. He nodded to the cantaloupe-colored sky.

"Beautiful, isn't it?" Without waiting for a response he added, "We can go door to door in fifty-two minutes."

"Door to door?"

Guth nodded to the rail tracks. "Door of the train to the door of *that* place," he pointed to the silhouette of the gas chambers. "We can process twelve hundred units in fifty-two minutes."

Niemann hummed in understanding. "I see. Door to door. That must be some kind of record."

"I'd like to be faster."

"A tall order."

"We can do it. Imagination is the only thing slowing us down now."

What is striking about this exchange isn't necessarily the callous nature of the men but that they saw absolutely no moral emergency in what they were doing. For them it was just a job, it was just a tweaking of numbers, and this is what horrifies us to the core about Lubizec and makes us want to turn away. For men like Guth and Niemann, though, mass killing was just a job. It was routine. Scheduled. There was no anger involved. There was only planning and execution.

They continued puffing on their cigars, and when the searchlights snapped on, sending huge cones of bleached light into the air, they glanced over their shoulders. The world was a deep blue with a few stars coming out, and in that moment of approaching night, Guth said he was going home. His family had just moved into a house not far from the camp and he was keen to see them again. It was one of the perks of being a commandant: having your family close by.

"See you tomorrow," he said, turning on his heel. He paused and spoke with his head half turned. "And Niemann? Thank you."

He walked towards his Mercedes and drove away from the glowing searchlights. A deepening dark covered the world as he bounced over the rough dirt road. His tires maneuvered around potholes and skittered into watery ruts. Gravel pinged off the undercarriage as Guth pulled onto the main road and pointed his headlights towards the village. Little cones of light shot into the leafy darkness.

In the backseat were wrapped presents for his wife and kids.

Wooden boxes still needed to be unpacked and there was a ghostly presence in the air of something lost. The previous owners had been made to disappear ages ago, shortly after the war began, and the house had stood empty for nearly two years. There was a mustiness in the air. The smell of attic.

Guth dropped his SS hat onto a marble table as his kids came around a corner with whoops of joy.

"Daddy, Daddy!"

His daughter, Sigrid, hugged his waist while his son, Karl, embraced his leg. Guth shuffled down the wood-paneled hallway with outstretched arms and pretended to be a lumbering giant. He lowered his voice.

"Who are these little people? How did they get in my castle? I must *eat* them."

And then this man, who, in a single week, had organized the murder of eleven thousand people, bent down and gave his children lavish kisses. He held them and didn't mind how they stepped on his polished boots or how they argued about who was going to wear his SS hat. He made sure his pistol was snapped into its leather holster.

"You're here at last," he cooed. "Now tell me about your journey. Tell me, tell me. I am one big ear."

Sigrid and Karl pulled him into a dining room that had a giant chandelier and an enormous marble fireplace. Ostrich feathers hung incongruously in the corner and there was a lush Persian carpet on the floor. Boxes of china plates and silver platters and crystal were stacked against a wall, and he looked at himself in a darkened window as his children tugged him forward. His wife came around the corner in a rose-colored dress and stood beside the fireplace. Her curly blond hair tumbled down to her shoulders. She held out a whiskey for him.

"What've you been up to?" she asked.

We only know about these private scenes of home thanks to Sigrid's memoir, *The Commandant's Daughter*, published in 1985. Her recollection of life in "the Villa" not only offers us an unusual picture of her father at rest, but it also documents her struggle to understand what it meant to be raised in the shadow of a death camp. We quickly learn that Guth was affectionate, sometimes moody, and that he often talked about how lucky he was. We also know from *The Commandant's Daughter* that Guth's wife, Jasmine, never called him Hans-Peter. She didn't particularly like that hyphenated name and referred to him instead as Hans. Our understanding of life in the Guth household is further deepened by having Jasmine's unpublished diary from this period of time. By reading both books against each other, we have the unusual opportunity of seeing how a particular moment in time transpired, and as we progress through the history of Lubizec these two primary sources will help us to understand Guth both as a father and as a husband.

Guth was different at home. We know that much. But whether the man inside the Villa was the real Guth or the man running a barbed-wire kingdom was the real Guth, we will never know. What we can say with great certainty is that he slipped into the role of murderer as easily as he became a loving father at home. These two worlds never seemed to overlap in his mind, and this makes it all the more baffling that he could love his family and yet commit acts of such pure wickedness. Had Guth been a recluse who locked himself in his office and went about the business of obliterating lives it would be easier to comprehend his crimes, but this isn't the case. He went home and took care of his family. Many Nazi officers were like this. They killed—then they played with their children.

"I saved dinner for you, Hans."

"Oh?"

"Potato dumplings, red cabbage, and pork hock."

He rubbed his hands and sat down at a long table. He snapped open a linen napkin and placed it gently into his lap. He rubbed his hands again and smiled. "Oh, it's good to be home."

Jasmine rang a little brass bell and this made a Polish woman appear in the doorway as if by magic. She stood with her hands balled up against her generous belly. With a nod from Jasmine, the Polish woman backed out of the room and returned a moment later with a large silver tray. She lifted the domed top and said a single word: "Enjoy."

Guth picked up his knife and fork and was ready to cut into the pork hock, but Jasmine touched his arm. He immediately folded his hands and bowed his head.

The four of them said the Lord's Prayer, and when they finished, the Commandant of Lubizec picked up his silverware again and went back to work. He cut into the veiny meat and speared it with a fork. He ate. He cut. He reached for a glass of red wine and swallowed it down.

A clock gonged in the hallway and this made Jasmine glance at her wrist. "My God. Is it nine already? You kids should be in bed."

They groaned and complained and whined as Guth swirled bits of pork hock into cabbage juice. Jasmine tapped her fingernail on the table and, slowly, Sigrid and Karl came over to kiss their father good-night.

They thumped up the wooden stairs and could be heard stomping above the dining room. The crystal chandelier jiggled.

"Quiet!" Jasmine yelled up to the ceiling. "Get your pajamas on. And brush your teeth."

We know what happened next because Sigrid—rather than going to bed—crept downstairs to watch her parents. As she says in *The Commandant's Daughter*, she missed her father and wanted to be around him. She also talks about being in awe of his charcoal-gray uniform and she wondered about the pistol he carried on his hip. She knew he was in the SS but beyond that, her father's life was a deep mystery. She tiptoed down the stairs on bare feet. The hallway was dark and the dining room looked like a lighted stage.

Guth brought his wine up to his nose and took a deep sniff. He closed his eyes and drank it in. "Gorgeous stuff. Where'd you get it?"

"You still haven't answered my question, Hans."

He unbuttoned his collar and the silver threads of his SS insignia caught the light. He rubbed his face and said, "We've gone over this a *thousand* times. Lubizec is a transit camp. There's nothing more to tell."

He snapped his fingers for the dishes to be cleared away, and when the Polish woman emerged from the doorway he studied her rough, gnarled hands. His plate had globs of fat shimmering in little pools. Curly shreds of cabbage were left behind and the potato dumpling was untouched. His knife and fork made an X.

"Thanks," Jasmine said. "You can go home now."

Guth leaned back when she was gone. He yawned and stretched. A heavy silence fell between them and it began to rain, slowly at first, then more quickly. The rain was soon coming down so hard it sounded like static.

"Has the new radio arrived?" he asked.

Jasmine shook her head. She went over to a liquor cabinet for a wineglass. She gave it a little twirl of inspection and sat down again, motioning for the wine bottle with a flick of her finger. She poured out a measure and stared at the red patterns of crystal light that shimmered on the tablecloth.

"Sometimes I think about those people . . . the ones in Berlin. The ones at the mental hospital where you worked. Did they really need to be put down?"

Guth picked a bit of meat from his teeth and nodded. "They were crippled in the brain. We can't have half-wits and idiots running around the country."

"Well, I'm glad you're not involved in that eugenics program anymore. Lubizec is a fresh start for you." She took a long sip and eyed him. "It's a transit camp. Right?"

He glanced at the kitchen door. "Do we have anything for dessert? I'd like some strawberries, maybe some cream."

Jasmine reached for his sleeve. "Hans, what's that awful smell coming from the camp? I had the windows open this afternoon and when the wind came up it was *terrible*. I had to turn on the ceiling fans. I even had to spray perfume around the house to get rid of it."

"It's garbage. We've buried most of it now."

She looked doubtful, but he took her hand and brought it to his lips. And then, with a mischievous grin, he asked if their bed was ready.

They climbed the stairs slowly, not holding hands, and undressed each other in the pale moonlight. Guth pawed at his wife. He was clumsy.

Day-to-day operations were running smoothly and this pleased Guth enormously. He got up at five-fifty each morning and went downstairs for twenty minutes of calisthenics. He kept a logbook to make sure he did the same number of sit-ups, knee bends, and push-ups every day. His shower was brisk. Cold. Invigorating. Breakfast was at six-thirty and he made sure to eat plenty of fruits and nuts.

He never touched eggs or anything fried in lard. Most mornings he sat alone and watched lemony sunlight spill into the wood-paneled dining room. Dust floated in moats of light and birds sang outside as he sipped tea. Shortly before seven Sigi and Karl came rumbling down the stairs and whenever this happened he gave each of them a bear hug.

He then snugged his SS cap onto his head, he looked at himself in the hallway mirror, and he opened the front door with a quick snap.

"See you for dinner," he said.

There were usually two transports a day. The first arrived into Lubizec at eight when dew was still on the grass and the air had a wet chill to it, and the second pulled in at one o'clock when the sun was bright and warm. Whenever a transport showed up in the middle of the night, which happened often, the train stood on the tracks outside camp. The people sealed inside had to wait until the next morning and it was only then that the train was allowed to move forward down the remaining stretch of track.

The smell of sweat, piss, shit, and death filled the air when each transport pulled in with a slow grinding of brakes. The heat was so intense in the afternoon that waves of it could be seen rolling up from the cars, and the rusty metal bolts on the doors were hot to the touch. The victims jumped out, stiff legged, sore, tired, wobbly because they hadn't walked for a long time, and when the platform was clotted with people, Guth would climb onto a specially made wooden box. A guard would blow a whistle for everyone to be still.

Guth cleared his throat and began to speak. What he said never varied, and years later, survivors like Chaim Zischer and Dov Damiel could repeat it word for word.

"Welcome to Lubizec. I am *Obersturmführer* Guth, commandant of this little transit camp. We're very sorry your journey wasn't convenient but we're at war and cannot spare more pleasant accommodation for rail travel. You will be given bread and cups of tea shortly. I give you my word as an SS officer that everything will be better now. Much better. We'll take good care of you."

Prisoners known as the "Green Squad" would then carry luggage into a large wooden hut. They moved quickly, in a "kind of scuttle," as one SS guard later called it, and they said nothing for fear of being beaten. These ragged men weaved in and out of the crowd as they tried to stay away from the guards. Unlike prisoners at other camps, these men didn't wear striped uniforms nor did they have tattooed numbers because it saved Guth the hassle of having to buy specialized clothing or having to make any special provisions for them whatsoever. He saw no need to separate the prisoners from the new arrivals because to him they were all equally worthless. A man that survived one transport could easily be replaced two weeks later for a newer, stronger one. As a result, the prisoners all understood that death waited for them sooner or later. It was just a matter of time.

As for the people on the platform, they were made to run into an area of camp called the "Rose Garden." It wasn't a garden, and it certainly never had roses, so the reason for the name has slipped into the unknown. This, however, follows the standard Nazi ideology of deception and euphemism. It was easier to tell prisoners they were going into a rose garden than to tell them the truth, which was far more horrifying. Even though we have no idea how it became known as the Rose Garden, it serves as a subtle reminder that language itself has a secret archeology. If we could dig down far enough, we might discover that the name originates from a joke. Perhaps some new arrival asked an SS guard where they were being taken, and perhaps this guard said something offhanded like, "You're going to a rose garden." It is a short leap to assume that other guards found this humorous and they too began to use the phrase. And so, as transport after transport rolled into Lubizec, and as a river of people were channeled off the trains and diverted towards their deaths, the joke turned into fact. "This way for the Rose Garden." What started off as black humor became useful for its deception and haziness. Words blunted a terrible and impossible reality.

The victims were made to run beneath the massive WELCOME sign so they wouldn't have time to think about what was happening, and Guth was very clear about this because he believed a revolt had less of a chance of succeeding if the victims were whipped on.

"They should be shocked and nervous at all times," he wrote in a letter to one of his superiors. "They should be disoriented. Always. The moment they get their bearings is the moment we lose control."

This meant the guards, which up to this point were merely standing on the platform with their hands cupped gently behind their backs, turned into demons. They picked up whips and truncheons. They pulled out pistols. They began to shout so hard their faces turned red. Some of the victims sensed this was the end and began ripping up the last of their money. It was a small protest, but a protest nonetheless. *You may kill me*, they said without words, *but you won't take everything.*

It would be good to pause here and remember that Lubizec and the other Operation Reinhard camps didn't have a selection process. Once a train pulled into its kingdom of barbed wire, almost everyone was sent to the gas chamber. Occasionally, very occasionally, a strong-looking man might be plucked from the running river of people, and he would be forced to become slave labor, but this happened so infrequently that 99 percent of the people who entered Lubizec were dead within an hour. It was not meant to be a work camp. It was meant to kill people as swiftly and relentlessly as possible. It therefore becomes difficult, perhaps even impossible, to explain what Lubizec was like because we run into a fundamental failure of language. In order to describe a place we need to talk in terms of presence, but the only way to describe an extermination camp is through absence. We can say that A happened, then B happened, then C happened, and we can certainly look at the daily operations of the camp, but it is the holes, the gaps, the missing lives, the not-*there*-ness that deserves our attention. How do we represent this though? How?

We can therefore talk about how the men and women were separated, and we can explain how the men were forced to undress in a cramped area, and we can talk about how they unbuttoned their shirts, and we can imagine their trousers sliding to the ground in pools of fabric. Perhaps we can sense their embarrassment as they stand around cupping their penises. Some of them may still have their socks on but when the whips come out—hitting indiscriminately here and there—these socks are pulled off. Maybe their mouths are as dry as steel wool.

Some of the men might whisper the *Shema* or *Adon Olam* to calm themselves in the pale luminous dust of morning.

All we know is that these men are rushed down a walled path called the "Road to Heaven" and they disappear from us, forever. Only their clothes remain.

Words like *fear* and *pain* can certainly be used to describe what these men were feeling but what does this mean when we view Lubizec from a safe psychological distance? At this very moment you might be on a sofa or sitting in a coffee shop. Raspberry-flavored iced-tea might be within reach and at any moment you can look away. You can perform a magic trick and make Lubizec disappear. So what do *terror, hunger,* and *pain* mean to any of us under such cozy circumstances? How can words describe this camp at all?

They cannot.

Words fail us. Language fails us. Our own imaginations fail us.

Even the word *Holocaust* is too small. In Greek it means "wholly scorched," but how can this tiny cluster of ink summarize the sound of a steel door being screwed shut and poison being dumped into a room? No, in order to capture what happened between 1939 and 1945, a whole new language needs to be created; it needs to be a language of destruction and absence. Perhaps the best way to understand the Holocaust is to imagine a giant book and then watch it get erased, word by word. If you flip through the pages of this book—this very book you are holding right now—if you thumb through it and imagine each individual word getting erased, as if it were a life, then, perhaps, maybe, we might have a language that begins to explain what happened. (As a point of reference, this book holds over 81,000 words, but if each of these words were to represent a human life, that is still only a tiny percentage of the *millions* who disappeared under the Nazis.) Thus, in order to describe the Holocaust in any meaningful way, we need a language that isn't there. We need to think of absence. We need to imagine words being erased. Murdered.

The men were gassed first. And while they were being sealed into concrete airtight rooms, their wives, daughters, and mothers were being pushed into wooden barracks to have their hair cut off. The barbers had strict orders to make only three snips with the scissors. No more, no less. The women were rushed in naked, they were forced to sit down on benches, and then these barbers would snip in quick rapid jerks. Curls fell to the floor, like a carpet of leaves.

Dov Damiel, a survivor, was interviewed about this in 1977. He says when groups of women rushed in, he was forbidden to say anything. Not a word. The only sound in the room was the furious clipping of scissors. These women knew something horrible was going to happen and many of them asked how they would die.

"By firing squad? Electricity? Tell me."

When these women spoke, their voices sounded like powder. They stood around, covering their nakedness as best they could with their arms. Many of them had pale skin and varicose veins. Some wanted the barbers to slow down so that they might have a few more minutes of life. Many sobbed.

The guards paced the floor and shouted, *"Die Haare schneller schneiden. Schneller, schneller!"*

When interviewed about this in 1977, Dov Damiel said he tried to pat the women's shoulders and offer one last act of kindness but, as he says, "The Nazis, they make us move so quick. One woman, she sits down and I have to cut, cut, cut, and then another takes her place. Blond hair, black hair, gray hair, red hair, curly and straight, it all falls when the scissors go to work. It was such a violation taking these women's hairs and I still hear their cryings in my head. 'Please cut slowly. Please . . . I want to live.' They begged me these things but what can I do? I am only one man caught in a web."

We don't have a single story about what it was like to run into this room naked, to have your hair cut away, and then to be pushed back out into the sunlight. Hundreds of thousands of women went through this at Lubizec, but none of them survived to tell us what it was like. Their stories have all been erased.

Anyone unfamiliar with a death camp may wonder why the Nazis were gathering their hair in the first place, but the answer is simple as long as we are satisfied with a technical response like: "It was useful for the Third Reich." Enormous sacks of hair were gathered up and shipped to Hamburg where they were made into blankets. These blankets were then given out to submarine crews. Hair, like gold or wheat, or life itself, was just a commodity to the Nazis. It was there to be harvested.

"*Schneller schneiden*," the guards yelled.

From this room of flashing scissors, the women were then herded down that walled dirt path called *Himmelstraße* (the Road to Heaven). They were forced to run so they didn't have time to absorb where they were going. Running meant they were always on edge and it meant they couldn't think of escape. The guards whipped them, constantly. They used heavy leather cables and took sloppy aim at shoulders, heads, and buttocks. If someone tripped and fell into the sand, a guard would flail away until that woman staggered up and joined the others. In this way, fear and speed drove everyone into the gas chambers because they all wanted to escape the hail of whippings. Once the door was screwed shut, it hardly mattered if a revolt was planned. By then it was too late.

Guth, however, didn't want his guards behaving like "silverback gorillas." Brutality was necessary to keep everything in order, but he didn't like to watch it, possibly because it reminded him of the trenches of World War I. So, after he delivered his speech at the train platform, he strolled back to his office with his hands in his pockets. He didn't like watching the victims undress, nor did he like the haircutting, but he usually appeared when the naked masses were driven up the Road to Heaven. Guards later said it reminded them of cows or pigs being pushed into pens.

The gas chamber was the only brick building in camp and Guth had it painted white because he thought it might appear less threatening, more medical. There were flowerpots near the entrance and immediately above the door were the words, *Bad und Desinfektion* (Shower and Disinfection). Inside the building were four separate chambers and they were rotated so that at least one was in constant use. Behind the whitewashed building was a massive engine with an elaborate system of pipes that was connected to the bunker. The gas chamber doors were heavy and required two guards to push them shut. Three winged screws (one on top, one in the middle, one beneath) were spun home quickly. A glass peephole was in the middle and the last thing many victims saw was an eye looking at them—it glanced left and right. A moment later, carbon monoxide spilled into the room and a cloak of heavy poison fell upon them.[*]

Chaim Zischer, who managed to survive all of this, said that screaming happened all the time at Lubizec.

"It was constant from the moment a transport arrived, until the moment it was processed. There was always screaming at Lubizec. It was horrible. Horrible. These cries were made from deep within the lungs and it kept on going and going. This noise only stopped in the gas chamber. It was like a switch had been flicked, and then the silence was total. You could actually *hear* the silence. Imagine all that noise and then . . . nothing."

When the mass killing ended, the prisoners of Lubizec became busy with other tasks. A "camouflage unit" was ordered to rake footprints out of the Road to Heaven as well as clean up any blood that might have been splattered onto the wooden walls. Other prisoners were forced to inspect clothing for diamonds that might have been stitched into seams. Another group pulled gold teeth from corpses, and lastly, some one hundred prisoners began hauling bodies to the graves. They laid them out—head to foot—and when the bodies were all knitted together in the earth, quicklime was caked onto them.

Guth was pleased with the clockwork motion of his camp, and whenever he had a free moment he disappeared into his office. He put on a little Mozart and lost himself in numbers. If a problem was

---

*Unlike Auschwitz, which used Zyklon-B (hydrogen cyanide) to murder the innocent, the death camps of Operation Reinhard used carbon monoxide from engines. We will discuss this more in the following chapters, but for information on the gas chambers at Auschwitz-Birkenau, please see two harrowing eyewitness accounts from survivors: Filip Müller's *Eyewitness Auschwitz* (1979) and Shlomo Venezia's *Inside the Gas Chambers* (2007).

particularly sticky, he might sit back and twirl his wedding ring. At other times, he pulled out a slide rule and did math on a large piece of paper. When the sun began to set over the guard towers, he loaded up his briefcase and drove home. Trees swayed in the wind. Rabbits darted out from the murky woods. Guth followed the dirt road away from camp and felt his heart swell with love for his children.

He wondered, vaguely, what was for dinner. He pressed down on the accelerator.

— 3 —

THE VILLA

Commandant Guth took up horse riding at the end of the summer. He first learned to ride in the early 1930s to impress the higher-ups in the Party and, to his great surprise, he ended up enjoying it. Living in the heart of Berlin made this new hobby difficult because there were so few places to ride properly, but the Polish countryside was lush and wide open. It was built for a man and his horse. He didn't like galloping through tall, wet grass or jumping wooden fences but he did enjoy the lazy pace of a horse threading its way through birch trees.

He bought a muscular white animal from a local breeder and got himself a saddle—an American one that seemed very cowboy. It had fine leatherwork, strong cross-stitching, and he paid to have his name embossed in heavy gothic lettering. HP GUTH. It cost a small fortune but money was flowing into Lubizec. It was like a money pump had been turned on because gold, diamonds, and currency from France, Norway, the Netherlands, and Russia were funneling into his camp. It was tempting to skim off the top, of course, but he always bundled everything up and made scrupulous records of what had been found. The Reich Office gave him a huge raise because they were pleased with how much he was sending back to Berlin. This new salary, along with the massive country house at his disposal, made him feel like a feudal lord or baron.

"These are good days," he wrote to his mother. "I haven't been this happy before."

Thanks to Jasmine's unpublished diary, we know Guth rode to work most days and that he enjoyed the solitude. It calmed him, it soothed him, and he liked how the rolling motion of his horse brought him home at dusk. Sometimes he looked down at the leaf rot and pinecones beneath him, and other times he studied the circling hawks overhead. Misty sunlight surrounded him as he plodded home, unbuttoning his SS collar. Sometimes he stopped by a bubbling creek and watched the crystal-clear waters.

We might wonder how Guth could oversee the machinery of mass annihilation and then go home to his family. It's easy to use words like *monster* or *beast* when we talk about him but we should remember he was a human being that walked the earth. By calling him a monster we remove him from our species, and although this might be precisely what we want to do, to dismiss him as an aberration, we need to remember that a man committed these crimes. Not a monster. A man.

It's hard to understand people like Guth. We imagine that for him coming home from Lubizec was like taking off a great woolen cloak of wickedness and hanging it on a peg. There it hung until the next morning when he robed himself in it again. He opened the front door, stepped back into the world, and returned to killing. Guth went to work with the same indifference as a butcher or exterminator. No doubt he slept well at night. He worried about his kids and was affectionate with them. His worldview was crystal clear and he saw absolutely nothing wrong with mass homicide. He went to work, he did his job, he came home and hung up his uniform.

The path beneath him was firm and sure as he rode through the trees, his conscience unbothered. The leather saddle creaked beneath him as he clomped up the cinder driveway towards the house and sauntered into the stable, where he turned the reins over to a Polish boy (he never could remember the kid's name) and he muttered something about buffing the brass until it sparkled.

"Like a diamond."

He jogged up his small hill and came to a patio. Huge banks of sparrows were wheeling and tumbling through the air in choreographed bursts of speed and peppery black. His wife sat in a chaise longue watching the sun dissolve into the lake. He joined her. A band of oily pink simmered on the dark water as he sat in a pinstriped deck chair. Fireflies came out as burning green dots. They winked like little stars in a shifting constellation.

Guth pulled out a silver cigarette case, one that had someone else's name on it. A Jewish name.

"Hans. What *is* that smell?"

He lit a match and ignored her. The flame illuminated the lower half of his face.

"It's been two months since we arrived and that stink's still in the air. What's going on in that camp of yours?"

He rubbed his forehead and exhaled slowly. "We don't have water pipes installed yet and the prisoners need to bathe. We're at war . . . remember? I can't snap my fingers and make copper pipes appear."

She made a face. "That seems like more than unwashed bodies."

"Well then," he said, pointing to a lilac bush, "do you want more of these around the house?"

"No, I'd like the truth."

They watched the fireflies glow and fade for a moment. The world beyond the patio was shadowed in dark but a large carpet of warm light spilled out of the house. It was inviting.

The wind batted Jasmine's hair and she removed a few strands from her mouth. "It's just that . . ."

"What?" He was obviously annoyed but he took a little breath and asked the question again, this time with more patience. "What?"

"I've heard things. In the village. People say horrible things about what's happening in that camp."

"Oh yes, the trustworthy Poles," Guth said, picking a burr off his trousers. He stood up and straightened his uniform. "Don't believe everything you hear. It's a transit camp, nothing more. It's a place of arrivals and . . . departures." He pointed to the reading room and smiled. There was a bow, as if he were being a gracious host. "Shall we go inside? I hate talking about work."

She looked at her fingernails for a long moment, as if weighing up a thought. "Yes," she finally nodded. "It's good to have you home."

The Villa was lush and ornate. Antique furniture was in every room along with carpets, cabinets, and bone china. Guth moved past these collected things and called out for his son and daughter.

"Karlie? Sigi?"

He breezed past an enormous oil painting of Hitler. Flowers were everywhere and a radio murmured in the corner, its dials glowing in circles of light. Guth drew in the last of his cigarette and stubbed it into an ashtray—a puff of smoke, like a skinny phantom, floated up from his fingertips.

"Karlie? Sigi?"

A clattering of feet came from the kitchen. Karl appeared first with a handful of tin soldiers. He dumped them onto the table and began to make shooting noises. Sigi walked out in a dark swishing dress and leaned against a wall. A book was tucked into the nook of her arm. She looked bored.

Guth asked about their day. He leaned in close. He smiled.

Karl held up a soldier and talked about killing dirty Communists while Sigi stood back and waited for her younger brother to finish. He spoke quickly, with long pauses and exclamation points.

"I! . . . used my soldiers! . . . and we attacked! . . . the Soviets!"

"I see."

"Yes! And . . . and . . . and . . . it was hard!"

"Did you get Stalin?"

"No! . . . He . . . he ran away!"

When the little boy no longer talked about machine guns or planes or bombs, Sigi stepped forward and explained her day. She was in the middle of reading yet another book by Karl May and she liked how he brought the American West to life. She especially loved his stories about Old Shatterhand and how he did everything with his Indian friend, Winnetou. Together they roamed the wilderness and sometimes they were chased by mountain lions.

"Karl May is a good German writer but"—Guth raised a finger in warning—"don't get too dreamy about his idea of America. It is a country of mixed races and Negroes."

Sigi nodded and walked across the carpet. She curled into a wing-backed chair and went back to reading. Karl was sent upstairs to put on pajamas while Guth sat down to roast beef, apricots, and peas. He poured seltzer water into a crystal glass and watched it effervesce into stillness.

We have access to these snapshots of domestic life thanks to Sigi's book. More specifically, she mentions how her father ached for love and, at least from this account, we are led to believe he liked how Jasmine looked at him when he was buttoning up his uniform. *The Commandant's Daughter* is bloated with stories of a doting father and there are many photos of Guth standing beside his children with his long arms draped around them. He looks happy. He is smiling. It is very odd seeing him in a sweater. It's also very hard to balance these images against the murderer we know him to be and it makes us wonder how he could switch so easily between his two selves. It's almost as if we are dealing with two different men, a Jekyll and a Hyde.

Through this book we also gain a deeper understanding of Guth's relationship with religion. Jasmine was a practicing Catholic—we know that much—but we also know that Guth formally signed a document in 1934 stating that he was no longer a *Gottgläubiger* (a believer in God). The Party had never been too excited about religion in the first place because it believed the survival of the Fatherland was the only true faith for any good German to practice. In spite of this, Guth still attended Mass every Christmas, but he probably did so to appease his wife. Although there were several crucifixes in the house and one image of the Sacred Heart, it's hard to imagine he gave them a second glance. To Guth they were just old icons of a dead spirit world. They meant about as much as Santa Claus or the Easter Bunny.

"Hans," Jasmine said. "You forgot to say grace."

Guth opened his mouth as if to argue but he folded his hands in prayer. He made a steeple of his forefingers and pressed them against his lips. They said the Our Father together and in that moment Guth was obedient, submissive.

When the prayer was over, he picked up his silverware and went back to his undercooked beef. His knife squeaked on the bone china plate and, after a few hesitant chews, he reached for Jasmine's hand.

"I see the Polish girl still isn't cooking food long enough. Maybe we should replace her?"

"No. The children like her, Hans. And the dinner she made for us earlier was just fine."

"Boooom!" Karl said at the base of the stairs. He was playing with his tin soldiers again. "Boom-crackle-rackle!"

"Why aren't you in bed?"

Karl shrugged and went back to making explosions. A tin soldier was tossed high into the air. It hit the ceiling.

"Stop that. I asked you a question," Jasmine said. "Why aren't you in bed?"

A shrug.

She pointed to the stairs. "Off you go."

"Do I have to?" he half sang, half whined.

Guth cleared his throat and this brought the boy to full attention. He gathered up his soldiers and thudded slowly, very slowly, up the stairs, one after the other.

"Faster," Guth said without raising his voice.

The boy's footsteps were soon moving around his bedroom. A door slammed. The house was silent except for the ticking of a grandfather clock and, from the other room, the mumbling radio. The window was open and a night breeze fluttered the drapes. A rotten-egg smell floated around the table and Jasmine made a face. She got up, latched the window, and pulled the drapes across in one fluid motion.

"Agh. What *is* that?"

He speared an apricot and used it to mop up some beef juice. "We're back to that again, are we?"

"Don't be dismissive. Not with me. I'm not one of your guards."

He picked up a linen napkin and wiped the O of his mouth. "I told you," he said, reaching for the seltzer water. "It's a transit camp. I can't tell you more, I'm sorry. It's official business. You know I can't tell you more."

"Can I see the place?"

"Good Lord, no. No one's allowed within a kilometer of the camp without being shot, not even you, my dear."

The grandfather clock ticked heavily in the background.

"Are the prisoners treated well?"

Guth was confused. "Why should that matter?"

"Rumors. In the village."

He pushed his plate away and reached for her hand. "I crunch numbers. Other men take care of discipline."

"So these rumors are—"

"Rumors, my lovely. Just rumors. Don't worry about all that stuff."

"I have a right to know."

He squinted as if to challenge her. "No. You don't. Not when it comes to Reich's business."

They looked at each other for a long moment before Guth glanced at his daughter. She was still reading.

"Are you eavesdropping on us?" he asked. His tone was sharp.

Sigi shook her head.

"Don't lie. You must never lie." His face hardened and he pointed his chin upstairs. "Go to bed."

She closed her book and stood up.

"You must never lie," Guth said again. "Always tell the truth, especially to family."

In *The Commandant's Daughter*, Sigi mentions how her father never raised his voice. Instead, he was able to make a room tremble by speaking slowly and drilling holes into the air with his eyes. This hard gaze now followed her as she went upstairs but, according to her account of this particular evening, she sneaked back down on bare feet. She was curious to know about the smell and what her father did in the camp. These thoughts wouldn't have concerned her at all except that her mother had been wandering around the house and was now obsessed with the tangy stench. "What in God's name *is* that?" she asked, squirting perfume here and there. Sigi began to wonder too. It became a big mystery and she thought about creeping into the woods like Old Shatterhand to find out more. She would bring a compass and head out into the wild.

That summer was one of the hottest on record, so the stink would have been overwhelming and ghastly, especially when thousands of new corpses were stuffed into the ground each day. As the body count continued to grow, quicklime seemed increasingly useless. "It was like throwing salt into the sea," one guard later said. Other accounts mention how the ground heaved up and down by half a meter or more because the gasses under the soil began to expand and contract. An unholy essence lifted up from the ground and blood began to seep *up* towards the surface. It was against the laws of gravity and common sense but somehow the thick motor oil of these bodies wicked up into the sandy soil. Bloated earthworms began to appear in biblical plaguelike proportions and a low popping sound came from the ground as if the earth itself refused to hide the dead, as if it were choking on what had been given to it, as if the ground were spitting up evidence of crime. Guth worried about the water table being contaminated and he ordered crates of seltzer water trucked into Lubizec because he didn't want his guards getting sick from bacteria in the ground. The huge number of decaying bodies stacked in the earth did much to explain the invisible stink that floated out from the camp but, as Guth stood near the mass grave with his eyes stinging from the rot of human flesh, he knew something had to be done. But what? Other camps like Auschwitz and Chełmno were experimenting with cremation. Treblinka was having a similar problem. So too were Sobibór and Bełżec.

"So these rumors about the camp are . . . ?"

"Just rumors," Guth said again, shaking his head. "That's all they are. Which reminds me, the groundwater has been fouled by something, so only drink seltzer water from now on. I'll have more cases delivered tomorrow."

Jasmine squinted. "Fouled?"

"My men are looking into it."

"Is it from that camp?"

Guth drank until an ice cube rested on his upper lip. He slouched back and pulled out his silver cigarette case. "Reich's business. I can't discuss the camp with you. You know this. Just let me come home and relax, darling. That's all I ask."

He lit a match, but instead of bringing it to the tip of his cigarette he studied the wavering flame for a moment. He glanced at the ashtray and spoke quietly, almost to himself. "Yes, that might be a solution."

"Solution to what?"

"Nothing." Guth smiled.

He blew out the match and looked at the burning orange tip of his cigarette. He puffed a few times and then, very carefully, tapped a small body of ash into the tray.

He looked up and seemed pleased. "What's for dessert?"

— 4 —

THE GOOD MEN OF BARRACK 14

While Guth spent his days making sure the machinery of his camp was well oiled and that it hummed along with merciless efficiency, the prisoners of Lubizec were worked to the bone. They sorted luggage that had been piled as high as a house, they dragged bodies, they stacked clothes, and they did all of this on the run. At night they were locked into their barracks—the padlock clicked shut; bolts were driven home—and while they settled into the exhausted dark, they often felt as if they were floating above the camp itself. This cramped world of bunk beds was both part of Lubizec and separate from it. The SS could certainly enter these sleeping areas whenever they wanted to but they rarely did, and this made the barracks the only place in the camp where the prisoners felt a little safer, a little more at ease. The prisoners loved the night because it freed them from the nightmare of the day. To crawl into bed was to realize they had survived yet another twenty-four hours. To live was to fight. It was an act of defiance.

They lit candles without saying a word. Little flames twitched and jerked against the darkness as first one man coughed, then another. They pulled out crusts of crumbly rye bread from their jackets and stuffed them into their mouths. They chewed. They swallowed. Crumbs were picked off clothes and eaten. Flickering shadows danced on the wooden walls until they were chased away by a searchlight—it slashed through one of the windows, blinding everyone for a moment, before it went away to another barrack. The faint sound of polka music could be heard from the rear of the camp. The SS laughed. They drank beer. Sometimes radio broadcasts of Hitler's voice could be heard.

The men ate their crusts of bread and shared with each other. Although it was not wise to talk about their lives before Lubizec, they sometimes mentioned the streets of Warsaw or Lublin or Radom, and they talked about buying a bag of plums and going home to their families. They talked about walking up the creaky stairs and seeing their wives and children in the kitchen. They resurrected these loved ones, these faces that had existed before the Nazis stormtrooped their way across Poland and shattered lives apart as easily as if they were smashing a mirror to the ground. These men sometimes held up broken fragments of their past and turned them around in their minds. They talked of love, and wives, and sons, and grandfathers, and lighting candles on the Sabbath. And whenever the burden of this loss washed over them to the point where they needed to close their eyes and breathe deeply or risk bursting into sobs, that's when they stuffed another chunk of crust into their mouths.

They chewed. They swallowed. They ate.

It was common for a man to chuckle at something his wife had said and it was equally common to watch this same man bow his head and study his frayed shoelaces. It was dangerous to think too much of the past because it crippled you, it sapped your will to live. Whenever this happened, the men of Barrack 14 nudged each other and passed over ribbons of dried meat.

"Eat," they said. "Eat."

They distracted one another with talk of meals they once enjoyed. Apricots, roasted potatoes, beef cuts the size of a fist, pierogi, ice cream, pączki, blueberries, mushrooms, salmon, pickled red cabbage, chocolate, candied oranges, gefilte fish. They licked their lips. They created dreams together and whispered words into the candlelight to keep the hallucination going. Shadows flickered and danced on the walls.

"Green beans."

"Butter on warm bread."

"Jelly. A jar of it."

"Tomatoes."

"Yes. Large ones that're red and juicy. The kind where seeds dribble down your chin when you bite into them and they make that *crunch*. I can almost hear that crunch."

"My wife used to make green tomato relish," said one man. His voice cracked. "I'm never going to eat that ever again now. She's gone. Just gone."

A man nudged this prisoner who was wandering too deep into the past. "What else would you eat?"

"Her relish. I only want her relish. It was so tangy, so sweet. I never appreciated it until now but . . ."

"What would you put it on?"

"Chicken, I guess."

"Tell me about the chicken. Forget the relish."

These husks of men who had been rounded up with their families and pushed into railcars, these men who tried to care for each other, they imagined a world without barbed wire. They dreamed of escape.

Chaim Zischer and Dov Damiel found themselves among these shadows in late September 1942. They didn't know each other before they were shoved into Barrack 14 but now they were forced to share a bunk.

Years later, in 1983, for the fortieth anniversary of the rebellion and escape, Chaim Zischer was asked about his time in Lubizec. The Israel Broadcasting Authority traveled to New York and interviewed him in his apartment. In the video, Zischer sits in a green leather chair and, just behind him, is a massive bookcase that has many titles about the Holocaust as well as a number of framed photos of his grandchildren. A mug of coffee steams next to him. He leans forward and pushes a wisp of gray hair away from his forehead. Liver spots dot his arms and he looks strong, healthy. His eyes are little flames.

When the interviewer asks about his first day in camp, Zischer glances down and clears his throat.

"All of us, we all saw Guth give that speech of his near the train, and then . . ." He pauses and starts over. "First, they robbed us of everything. Suitcases, money, clothes, wedding rings, watches. Everything. An SS guard tapped my shoulder with the snout of his pistol and told me to start stacking suitcases. My wife and son were carried away into the Rose Garden with the rest of the crowd but I, I was forced to stay behind. I was told to stack suitcases. It was the last time I would see my family."

Zischer goes on to explain that his wife was wearing a pink coat and he watched this color shrink away. Her form turned through the gate that said WELCOME, and then she was gone.

"It was the last time I saw Nela and my son, Jakob." Although his voice is blunt and matter-of-fact, he rubs the lower half of his face and his eyes mist over. "That, *that*, was my first ten minutes in Lubizec. *That.*"

As you watch Zischer in this interview, your eye is slowly drawn to the coffee mug and the steam rising next to him. It is easy to imagine the steam as ghosts floating up and you quickly sense that Zischer lives in two different time zones. His body may be in the here-and-now but his mind flits back through the decades, back towards the camp, back towards the shouldering crowds. Watching Zischer is like watching a man travel through time. His body may be in the present but his mind is not. When he looks at the camera he isn't seeing a film crew from Israel. No. He is back on a platform, sorting luggage, and he is watching a pink coat and a little boy disappear from him forever.

"Why do you think you survived?"

Chaim Zischer cocks his head. "A good question. One that I have asked myself many times, over many years. Anyone who speaks Hebrew knows my name means 'life.' Maybe I was destined to live because of this?"

There is a scowl, as if he is reprimanding himself for saying something so stupid. "That is, if you believe in destiny, which I do not."

He goes on to explain that he still marvels at the beating of his heart and the movement of his hands and the bellows of his lungs. He doesn't use the word *miracle* at any time during the interview but he does shake his head on a number of occasions, as if he is still trying to comprehend the odds of his own survival. Zischer leans forward and says that both he and Dov Damiel arrived into Lubizec at the same time—late September 1942—and that it was dumb luck they pulled themselves away from the gravitational field of the gas chambers.

"It was a black hole, those gas chambers. Thousands of human beings arrived each day and they were all sucked in. You know how stars and planets get devoured by a black hole? How everything spirals into its drain of fire? That was Lubizec. Relentless. All powerful. Final. It pulled people in from all over Poland. It was unstoppable."

He mentions that he wasn't any smarter or faster or wiser or better than those who were murdered. He and the others who lived were just blessed with a greater share of luck. That's all it was. We may want to pinpoint certain qualities that explain why these men, and not others, survived, and we may want to see their steely-eyed determination to break out of Lubizec and tell the world about what they witnessed as making them somehow stronger than those who were killed, but Zischer is adamant they were just luckier, not more in love with life. This is an unsatisfactory answer for us. We want some mysterious ingredient that explains their survival. Zischer, however, does not want to be seen as special, quite possibly because he doesn't want to think of himself as being somehow better than those who were murdered.

"It was chance. I could be dead now and someone else could be alive. It is 1983 right now and I live in a possible world where I am still alive. It could have gone the other way in the 1940s just as easily. Because of this, I often feel like a corpse on vacation."

He takes a long sip of coffee and shakes his head as if he wants to change the subject. He smoothes back his graying hair and adjusts his bifocals.

"In Barrack 14, we cared for each other as best we could. If we didn't watch out for each other—if we allowed these killers, these Nazis, to make us into animals—it would have been a victory for them. So there you have it. We wanted our barracks to be a place of goodness even though evil surrounded us. To do such a thing made us feel human. Do you understand what I am saying? It is only by helping that you are truly alive. If you can do this, especially on the cliff of death, it separates you from the beasts."

"I see."

"I'm not sure you do. To us, it felt like goodness itself was caged inside Barrack 14. It was a prisoner like us, on the verge of dying. It needed to be nursed back to health."

There is a pause. A very long pause.

"Were all the barracks like this?"

"No. No. Absolutely not. But in Barrack 14 we decided that sharing food and making our space one of righteousness, as much as we could in a place like Lubizec where there was no righteousness, *this* was the only way we could survive day to day. Men still died . . . nothing could stop that, not even God himself . . . he was on vacation during the Holocaust . . . but we lit candles in the dark. We pulled out bread and apples and herring. We shared these things and got variety into our stomachs. Maybe this working together saved me? I do not know." Zischer shakes his head and closes his eyes. His large Adam's apple bobs up, then down. "Many good men died in Barrack 14. At night I see their faces."

Although it may surprise the reader, there was an adequate amount of food in Lubizec because the transports brought in a steady stream of chocolate, bread, canned fruits, nuts, and dried meats. Prisoners only had to hunt through pockets and suitcases of the freshly murdered if they wanted to stuff their mouths. The prisoners of Lubizec certainly didn't get fat or put on weight, but they weren't on the verge of starvation, as was the case in the concentration camps.

"The transports were endless. Rivers of people were channeled down the Road to Heaven and they always brought food with them because they thought they were going to a work colony in the east. They had no idea what Lubizec was about. So after they were gassed, we ate their food."

"Did this make you feel guilty?"

"No. No. No. No."

There was also no shortage of clothing in Lubizec. Prisoners only had to root around for a new shirt, or sweater, or hat, or a new pair of shoes. Because it wasn't a concentration camp like Dachau or Bergen-Belsen or Sachsenhausen, the prisoners didn't have to wear pinstriped uniforms. They could shuck off one set of clothes for another. There was no need to do laundry. Just dig around in the mountain until you found something clean. However, if a prisoner was caught changing clothes, he was badly beaten—not because it was illegal but because he was taking care of personal hygiene when he should have been stacking suitcases or sorting goods. Once again, it is important to remember that Lubizec and the other Operation Reinhard camps were not designed to detain people or use them as expendable slave labor. They were designed to kill them. And this meant there was a surplus of just about everything because in Lubizec the dead always outnumbered the living.

Chaim Zischer and Dov Damiel may not have suffered from crippling hunger but they *did* have to worry about whippings, beatings, gunshots, and they were often thirsty because the guards never allowed them to drink water. They and the other prisoners were also infested with fear. It was like living with a cocked gun behind your head. When would it go off? Now?

Maybe now?

In ten minutes?

Tomorrow?

When?

Not surprisingly, there were a number of escape attempts from Lubizec. If someone managed to avoid going down the Road to Heaven (the survival rate for this was roughly one percent), the most popular escape attempt was a mad dash to the barbed-wire fence. The guards often amused themselves by letting a prisoner climb halfway up the fence before they cut him down in a hail of bullets. The body hung on the spikes, limp and bloody. Startled ravens from the forest circled up from the trees, they did a slow orbit in the blue cloudless sky, and then they settled back onto branches.

A few prisoners studied the rhythm of the camp and realized the only way out was the same way in: by train. There is a story that one prisoner, Władysław Sadeh, managed to get out by hiding himself under a carriage and when the train backed out of Lubizec with its steel wheels spinning faster and faster he went with it. It was twilight, it was raining heavily, and the guards never looked beneath the carriage. The train clattered through the trees and on to freedom.

Zischer is adamant that Sadeh made it out and there are reports that he managed to find his way up to neutral Sweden in the hopes of warning the Allies about what was happening in Poland. A few people in the coastal town of Trelleborg remember a "mad Jew" approaching city hall and demanding passage to the British Consulate in Stockholm, but the trail ends there. It vaporizes into rumor. We have nothing more.

When the Israel Broadcasting Authority asked Zischer about this in 1983, his face tightens and he raises a finger as if to drive home a point.

"I knew Sadeh. He was a tough man and I am telling you he escaped. We never saw him again."

"What do you think happened to him?"

Zischer shrugs. "Who can say? War is a thick fog. It covers the truth."

"Did others try to escape by hiding under the train?"

"Three others, yes. They tried the next day but they were foolish . . . stupid really . . . they left at the same time. It wasn't twilight, and it wasn't raining like it was for Sadeh. The Nazis, they saw them clinging like monkeys to the bottom of the train and they—" Zischer pauses and pretends to shoot a machine gun. "The train ran over them."

"And then?"

"Security around the train was immediately tightened. Guth saw this as a puzzle that needed solving. To him it was just an interesting puzzle. Nothing more."

"What did he do?"

"He got long poles with mirrors on them. In this way the guards could look under the train before it left and no one escaped after that. No one. Guth made sure of it."

The interviewer for the IBA shuffles some paperwork and there is the sound of a fire engine whining down a nearby street. The shriek rises, then fades. Zischer doesn't glance up at the alarm. He keeps staring ahead.

"Next question: You were badly whipped in your first month at Lubizec. You almost died but the men of Barrack 14 saved you. Tell us about that."

Zischer scratches the back of his head and almost smiles. One gets the impression he is used to answering this question and, in fact, many of the sentences he uses in this interview are similar to those that appear in his memoir, *The Hell of Lubizec*. He says that like many of the innocents who arrived into Lubizec, he hid valuables in his suitcase and took the further precaution of sewing his grandfather's pocket watch into the waist of his trousers. It was a family heirloom that dated back to the 1820s and he wanted to keep it safe. He didn't want the Nazis stealing it and they would have because it was made of gold. It gave Zischer strength to feel the small circular disc press against his waist and he went to bed each night with the knowledge that part of his family past was still safe. Part of it lived on.

And then one of the guards, *SS Unterscharführer* Rudolf Oberhauser, discovered the watch when he saw Zischer fiddling with his trousers. The tall man with beady weasel eyes marched over, pulled out his pistol, and cocked it against Zischer's forehead.

"What are you hiding there?"

The watch was found, Zischer was tied to a wooden sawhorse, and he was whipped twenty-five times for "hiding property that belonged to the Reich."

The world was a blur of pain as the hippopotamus-hide whip came down onto his back. It felt like cactus needles and broken glass were digging into his spine. With each heartbeat, his skin pulsed and bled. He was on the verge of blacking out. The world moved like a kaleidoscope.

And when he was finally untied from the sawhorse, he slumped to the ground.

"You must work, Chaim," came a voice. It was Dov Damiel. "You must work or say goodbye to this world forever."

He somehow managed to stack suitcases and, whenever he stumbled, or fell, or tripped, the arms of the other prisoners caught him. Damiel's voice hovered in his ears. "You must work or they will shoot you."

When he was finally allowed to stagger back to Barrack 14, he was pushed into one of the top bunks and his fellow prisoners examined the open slash marks on his back. Pus was forming and they sponged it out as best they could with prayer shawls.

In the interview with Israel Broadcasting Authority, Zischer's voice is steady but he is obviously on the verge of tears.

"These men, they saved my life. They hid me in a top bunk for two days and nursed me back to health. They brought me food and water and hid me under blankets. This is how Dov and I became friends. He risked his life and I will never forget this." Zischer taps his forehead. "I will never forget this."

He explains how he got the chills and shook so violently it made the whole bunk rattle. At night, the men of Barrack 14 gave him food and cleaned out his wounds. They wrapped him up.

Zischer adjusts his bifocals again. "I ask you, if we Jews weren't good to each other, who *would* be good to us?"

There is a long pause and the camera pans in closer.

"I wouldn't be here today if it weren't for those men. Those men saved my life. They saved my life in a place where life was not meant to be saved."

At this point in the interview Zischer moves off on what appears to be a tangent, but it is a useful tangent for our purposes because it opens a doorway into what we will discuss in the next chapter.

"No one slept at Lubizec. Not really. You fell into your bunk, exhausted. Shattered. I do not remember having any dreams while I was in that place. When you live in a nightmare, your brain seems to shut down during sleep. It turns itself off like a television going blank. It is the only freedom you have."

He then spends the next five minutes trying to explain how the barracks were a miasma of stale farts and diarrhea. Two buckets of piss were in the center of the wooden barrack and the stench of body odor, cheesy feet, and sweat saturated everything.

"It is very hard to explain the stink of Lubizec. It was atrocious. Awful. There were so many rotting bodies we had trouble breathing. When the wind changed directions, when it blew into our faces, it felt like we were drowning. Even the SS had to stop working when this happened. People today have no idea how badly Lubizec stank. No wonder Guth had the bodies burned."

It is worth noting that even when Lubizec exhumed the dead and started burning them in massive open-air pits, even then Zischer had to sleep with a rag over his nose.

"I tell you this," he says, leaning forward. "And I want everyone who sees this interview to think about what I am saying. I wouldn't be here if it weren't for the good men of Barrack 14. We cared for each other at a time when the rest of the world did *not* care about us Jews."

His face tightens.

"Each night I went to sleep knowing that the men in wooden bunks around me were all I had left. They were my brothers and I was their keeper . . . at least as much as I *could* be their keeper in a place like Lubizec. But what I don't understand are the people living beyond the barbed wire. How could they go about their daily lives knowing that Lubizec was in their backyard? They could see the columns of black smoke. They saw the trains coming in full and leaving empty."

He points at the interviewer, as if challenging him.

"Go to Poland. Ask the people living around Lubizec what they remember. Ask them what it was like to live next door to a factory of death. Go on. Ask them."

— 5 —

NEIGHBORS

It has been suggested that living around Lubizec would not necessarily mean people understood what was happening inside the camp. Some have claimed that because Lubizec was so far beyond all previous experience (and, indeed, so far beyond all previous human imagination) that those living around the camp were simply unable to recognize that an extermination center had been set up in their backyards. In other words, they didn't recognize it because the very idea of a death camp was unknown to them. How could they understand what was happening in Lubizec when camps like it had never existed before? How could they recognize a death mill?

This, however, ignores the obvious signs that something awful was taking place in the woods and it also absolves anyone living close to the barbed wire of any degree of critical thinking. To live within five kilometers of Lubizec was to realize that something was very, very wrong. Something new and terrible had been unleashed in the woods.

We know that farmers who worked the fields routinely saw trainloads of people clattering towards Lubizec. One farmer, Józef Novodski, had clear memories of harvesting wheat while one train stopped on the tracks near his fence. He rumbled by on his tractor and saw arms reaching out of the barbed-wire mesh windows. When asked how he felt about this, Novodski shrugged. "I had a tractor and my wheat. What did I care about Jews being resettled?"

The train sat there for hours as Novodski trolled back and forth. Hands waved out of the train but he didn't look at them. Instead, he lowered his cap and kept on harvesting.

"I would have been shot if I did anything," he told one historian. "It was best to keep your nose down, and, anyway, the train took off soon afterward. It returned a few hours later. Empty."

Novodski isn't alone because many farmers saw trains pass their fields. Hands reached out from the mesh windows and the people inside begged for water.

Farmers near the camp talked about hearing the pop of small-arms fire and everyone could see black smoke curling into the sky. It floated up like a smudge of tar. One person described it as a geyser of smoke. Another called it a black fog that dimmed the sun. Rumors began. Tales were told. The burning happened once a day—usually at twilight—and it had an odd smell, like bacon or overripe grapefruit. The villagers around Lubizec also noticed something orange and greasy coating their windows.

"It was so difficult to clean," one woman said.

It had the consistency of wax and had to be scraped from the windows with a razor. Months later everyone began to realize they were scraping a thin layer of human fat from their windows.

By late September 1942, the bodies of Lubizec were all torched and this sent heavy oily smoke drifting across the countryside. These pyres of human flesh made the whole sky hazy. Sunsets were smeared with bright red colors because of the particulate in the air.

We know from one boy, Jerzy Mrożek, that trains crept across the countryside and that most people paid little attention to them because they had become so commonplace, so normal. In 1992, when he was interviewed for a documentary about living so close to Lubizec, he recalled how the trains usually had ten cars and how chalk numbers were scrawled above each door. His parents told him to pay no attention to these trains, but he was an inquisitive boy and he sneaked into the woods where he hid in a fallen oak. It was a shell of a trunk so he was able to climb in and peek out of a hole the size of an apple. He watched one train roll by at a slow speed and he saw frightened faces looking out from the barbed-wire mesh. As the steel wheels spun by, they sounded like two swords grinding together. He took out a small notepad and wrote down the chalk numbers that chunked past him.

124. 147. 132. 143. 157. 136. 147. 153. 150. 157. 156.

Mrożek waited inside the damp tree as the train rolled away. All was quiet again. He watched a beetle cross his arm—its hooked legs paddling against his skin—and he looked at the bright greenery of the trees around him. Their leaves were fat; they ate sunlight. The whole world was full of bark and sap and glowing life.

A few minutes later he heard the distant screaming of German, along with several gunshots. The cracks echoed across the country-side as he continued to hide in the damp log.

Thirty minutes later the train reversed past him. It was empty and the chalk numbers had all been scrubbed off. The steel wheels spun by, faster and faster, and they made that sword-grinding sound again. The smell of chlorine filled the air.

He sneaked home through leafy bushes and added up the numbers he had just written down. The total was 1,602.

Mrôżek asked his mother, "What's happening to the Jews?"

She swatted him with a wooden spoon and told him to never, ever, go near the camp again. And he didn't. Like everyone else he began to ignore the trains. He played with his friends as cargo of people clattered by, unseen.

But if this young boy of twelve could ask such a simple question, it only stands to reason the adults around Lubizec were also wondering what was going on.

"Trains go in full and come out empty."

"There's gunfire. Don't forget about the gunfire."

"What *are* they burning in there?"

These must have been hushed questions for the people of Lubizec as they went about the business of farming and woodworking. In the vegetable markets, and in the bars, and outside Saint Adalbert's Catholic Church, they must have whispered about the camp. And yet, immediately after the war, they claimed to know nothing. Nothing at all. It's like it never existed.

As the decades rolled past, and as the horror of Lubizec became a more distant point of memory on the horizon, many people who lived around the camp slowly began to open up about what they saw. This probably has much to do with their advancing age and a wish to tell their stories before it became too late, but, equally, when Poland gained its independence from the Soviet Union in 1989, the borders of the country opened up and this meant foreign scholars and filmmakers were more apt to travel there. And travel they did. They brought cameras, and ledgers, digital recorders, maps and charts, and above all else they brought a willingness to hunt for stories that were in danger of being lost forever.

Oskar Kszepicki was one of these people who never talked about the camp. He sealed his experiences deep inside the kingdom of his skull and he never mentioned Lubizec—not even to his family—until, at last, an historian from the United States Holocaust Memorial Museum knocked on his door. It was January 2004. Kszepicki was eighty-five years old.

As a young boy in the 1920s, Kszepicki became fascinated with steam engines and he loved to watch them chug through the pine trees. He stood near the tracks and pumped his fist up and down in the hopes the conductor might blow the whistle. Sometimes the man did this and it filled Kszepicki with such joy to watch the train clatter faster and faster over the tracks, sending up huge banks of smoke. It surprised no one when Oskar Kszepicki ("Oski" to his friends) became a conductor, and soon he was driving trains from Kraków to Lublin. When the Nazis invaded he found himself moving tanks and troops and huge pieces of artillery around the countryside. Coal too.

And then one day he was asked to drive a special train to Lubizec.

"What's the cargo?" he asked.

"You'll see."

"More tanks? Troops?"

"Oh God, no. No, no. Something else."

And so it was that Oski found himself carrying passengers in a way that stunned him. When he was interviewed in 2004 by that historian from the Holocaust Museum, he spoke matter-of-factly but occasionally he had to stop and take a long drink of water. He pulled on his left ear as if trying to block out a sound he didn't want to listen to. The historian, David Zimmer, set up a small camera and it is clear that Oski Kszepicki is wrestling with ugly images from his past. He swings between smiling and wanting to cry, all the while pulling on his left ear. From this thirty-minute interview we know he stopped his train many times to let other freight trains loaded down with tanks and artillery pass by. His cargo of people could wait in the blazing heat or the blowing snow because they weren't weapons for the war. They weren't considered valuable.

While his engine breathed quietly on a side track, he could hear screams from the back and if he turned his ear towards the wind he could hear people begging for water. The constant screams, especially from babies and young mothers, distressed him so he sat near the valves of his engine and went about the business of making sure the firebox was stoked with coal. He was pleased to have a modern engine that fed coal directly into the hopper by way of a mechanical auger. Shoveling coal wasn't necessary because technology was making his life easier. But that didn't mean his job was easy. Far from it. Sweat always rolled down his face and he was covered in grime. His hands were badly calloused from years of pulling stiff levers but he was content with this because it meant he could touch the warm metal without protective gloves. He knew that hundreds of human beings were trailing behind him in locked cars and he knew exactly where they were going, but he chose not to think about it. He stared ahead and didn't think of the future.

The Germans always gave him a bottle of vodka—"to make the job easier"—and at first Oski had no interest in becoming a caricature of a Polish drunkard, but when he pulled into Lubizec for the first time he uncorked the bottle. By the third day he was used to drinking and powering the train. It was easy to drop the bottle into a fire bucket and go on pulling levers. He only had to worry about dehydrating from the overpowering heat and making sure that he slowed the train down in time. He took a sip of water and a sip of vodka. He alternated like that. Water, vodka. Water, vodka. He'd stick his head out the side and blast the whistle when he approached a road. Sometimes he might glance back at the cars and see hands grasping the air like they were trying to squeeze water out of nothingness. This made him turn back to the bottle of vodka. He focused on the trees that blurred past him. Sometimes he worried about the Polish Underground dynamiting the line ahead and his engine tumbling off the tracks—but this never happened. He just kept going down the line.

When he reached the woods surrounding the death camp he came to a stop and listened to the clicking huff of the engine. He let out two long blasts of the whistle to signal that he was ready to approach the platform. A green light flickered on up ahead and, when he saw this, he let the massive steel wheels spin back to life. The train rolled down the tracks and came to a grinding, hissing, complaining, stop.

Oski Kszepicki never jumped down from the train. He cleaned the regulator rod or fiddled with safety valves or jiggled the ash grate as people were ordered out of the cattle cars. The train rocked slightly as hundreds of people jumped out at once. Shrieks of anguish filled the air and sometimes he blasted the release valve to drown out their noise. His engine had a life of its own and he went back to caring for it. The hot belly glowed with nourishing fire when he opened the iron grate. Heat pushed against his trouser legs and he felt the pores on his forehead open up. Sometimes he leaned out the window of his driving cab and watched people on the platform. They moved like bees in a box and there was so much noise. Corpses of infants were thrown out of the cars along with packages and suitcases. Ragged people held on to their children. They looked up at the gigantic WELCOME sign above the iron gate of the camp. The commandant stepped onto a specially made wooden box and delivered a speech.

"It was always the same," Kszepicki told the historian. "It never changed."

"And what did you do during this speech?"

"I greased the rods or looked at timetables. Sometimes I cleaned my hands with a rag."

"Didn't you . . . didn't you feel *guilty* about bringing these people to their deaths?"

At this point in the interview Oski Kszepicki shakes his head. Nothing is said for a long time.

"I could have been replaced. Another would have done my job."

"But *you* did it. Not someone else. You."

Here Kszepicki stands up and leaves the room. The video camera stops recording. It starts up again later (we don't know how much time has elapsed) and Kszepicki is back in his leather chair. His eyes are bloodshot and puffy as if he has been crying. The historian asks him to please finish the story. Kszepicki goes on to say that once Guth finished his speech everyone was marched through the gates. Guards beat people with rubber truncheons, which made them move faster.

"They were driven on like cattle. With whips," Kszepicki added. "They were given no time to think about their situation."

Luggage was strewn across the platform as prisoners in little teams began to clean everything up. Another team pulled the dead out of the cars. These corpses were thrown into a wooden cart and taken away—where to Kszepicki couldn't say because he never went into the camp itself. Hoses were unspooled and the cars were washed out. The chalk numbers were scrubbed off with wire brushes and everything was made clean again. Chlorine was splashed into the cars and the terrible reek of a chemical cleaning agent filled up the air.

At a nod from one of the SS guards, Oski Kszepicki, that same little boy who once loved trains, would pull a long lever and his train would shudder back towards the village. At a roundhouse near a vegetable market he would set off towards Lublin, Kraków, or Warsaw. The train that had been packed with human beings thirty minutes ago was now completely empty, and the cars were left open to air everything out. The stink of chlorine trailed behind it.

At this point, David Zimmer, the historian, asks Kszepicki a simple question. "In your opinion, did the people around Lubizec know what was happening inside the camp?"

Kszepicki speaks without hesitation. "Yes. Absolutely. The farmers, they watched my train pass with a full load and I returned later, empty. Where am I taking these souls? They must have asked that question. Where? Even if you were blind to these trains, there were those bonfires of human flesh."

"The people knew what was going on then?"

"Oh, they knew. They knew. Everyone knew."

Guth didn't concern himself with the villagers living beyond the boundary of his camp because for him they were simply Poles that had been conquered by the Third Reich, they were second-class citizens. Serfs. Peasants. Laborers. It's true he wanted to hide the meaning of Lubizec—but not from those living near the barbed-wire fence. No, he wanted to hide its purpose from the arriving Jews in order to keep them calm. If they realized the true intent of the camp before reaching the gas chambers his schedule might be thrown into chaos. And he wasn't about to let that happen.

It slowly occurred to Guth that greater deception was needed, especially within the first ten minutes of arrival. After the victims were pulled off the train they stood on the platform and grew more nervous as each minute passed. They looked around and began to suspect they weren't really at a train station at all. But where were they? After one particularly messy incident when a rabbi was shot for refusing to obey orders, the crowd almost revolted and Guth realized that the victims needed to feel safe, at least for the first few minutes of their arrival. But how?

The idea came to him as he studied his clipboard and paced up and down the empty platform. His boots clicked off the wooden planks and he made notes about loose nails that needed to be pounded back into place. He looked up and began to nod.

"Yes, that might be a solution," he said.

He shouted for his deputy, Heinrich Niemann, and they marched off to his office where they made a long list of improvements. Later, when Niemann was interrogated by the U.S. Army about his role at Lubizec, he said the idea was the "mark of a genius." The officer who transcribed Niemann's testimony was horrified but he took excellent notes about what was said. Captain Joe Ehrenbach, from Brooklyn, was a Reform Jew but he didn't tell Niemann this until after the interrogation was over. It is easy to imagine Captain Ehrenbach gathering up his notes (perhaps he smiles as he taps the sheaf of paper onto the table) and that's when he tells Niemann he is Jewish. Regardless, Ehrenbach's work provides us with many private conversations between Niemann and Guth. In fact, "Allied Forces Report No. 3042" gives us a surprisingly clear picture of what happened next at Lubizec.

According to Niemann, Guth's idea was put into action that same day. Phone calls were made. New supplies rolled into camp. Planks of wood were hauled off a train. Boxes too. Windows were unloaded along with sacks of nails, shingles, and guttering. It only took a few days to build a fake train station next to the platform, and Guth modeled it after a toy in his son's bedroom. He brought the little model into camp and placed it on his desk. He called in his senior officers and ordered them to build a full scale replica, green roof and all. The men crouched down and examined the tiny station.

Guth looked out his office window. "When the Jews arrive they don't see what they *expect* to see, which is a railway station. Well, we're going to fix that."

A rainfall of hammers echoed around the camp and the air filled up with the smell of freshly cut lumber. Used trolleys for luggage were lined up on the platform. Train schedules to Lublin and Kraków were framed. Travel posters to Berlin, Athens, and Barcelona were placed next to the exit, which led to the massive WELCOME sign. A large clock was placed on a wall and its gigantic hands were set ticking. The guards laughed at how realistic it looked. There were signs for the WAITING ROOM and the TICKET OFFICE. Suitcases were stacked beneath a large sign that read, FOR IMMEDIATE DELIVERY TO JEWISH RESETTLEMENT AREA.

Guth called it "The Last Station" or, sometimes when he was in a more festive mood, "The End of the Line."

Now, whenever a train pulled into Lubizec, people could look at travel posters and train times. They could squint at a clock and imagine other trains coming and going. This wasn't anything to worry about. It was just a junction, just a station. *Yes*, the arrivals could tell themselves with confidence, *we won't be here long. We're going somewhere else. No need to worry. This Lubizec is just a little stop on the journey. We're here to stretch our legs and maybe get something to eat.*

When everyone was off the train, Guth stood on his specially constructed box and cleared his throat.

"Welcome to Lubizec. I am *Obersturmführer* Guth, commandant of this little transit camp. We're very sorry your journey wasn't convenient but we're at war and cannot spare more pleasant accommodation for rail travel. You will be given bread and cups of tea shortly. I give you my word as an SS officer that everything will be better now. Much better. We'll take good care of you here."

Sometimes a person might shout, "Thank you, *Obersturmführer!*"

Guth then announced they would be sent to work in a nearby village, but first they needed to be disinfected with a shower. Men and boys would go first. Women and girls would follow. All females needed their hair cut to reduce the spread of lice.

"You will be treated well," Guth added.

They were taken into the camp at a run and the massive iron gates were shut behind them. After this, the truncheons and whips came out. The separations began.

Guth usually strolled back to his office around this time but occasionally he stayed to watch the Green Squad sort luggage. He paced up and down the ramp and pointed at trash that needed to be hauled away. He nodded at chalk numbers on the side of the cars that weren't scrubbed off properly. He inspected many of the cars himself to make sure that no one was hiding in the darkness and "denying their fate."

It was also around this time that Jasmine wanted to know more about the camp. For what reason, exactly, had she left her home, her family, all her familiar comforts, and traveled to this lonely godforsaken backwater? For what reason, exactly, had her plans and desires been derailed, pushed into the ditch? Arguments boiled up every night about the need to drink seltzer water instead of tap water, and about the strange orange glow on the horizon. What on earth were they doing in Poland and why on earth did they have to stay?

In order to get some peace, Guth did something illegal. Even though it was strictly forbidden to take photographs inside Lubizec (or any other death camp), he took several snaps of the platform, the travel posters, the WELCOME sign, and of luggage being hauled away by blurry-faced prisoners. He also took photos of his office, the SS canteen, and the vegetable garden. He brought these photos home to prove that he ran a transit camp, to prove that he had some desire for a shared life, that he understood her feelings and cared about her curiosities. In spite of his military bluster, he wanted to be a good husband and father. That was important to Guth. He wanted a home life where the outside world could be shut out, especially after what he saw in the trenches of World War I. He could feel the space between him and Jasmine growing, and he took these photos because he could think of no other way to bind her closer. As we shall soon see, however, this only made matters worse.

Guth was so pleased with the effectiveness of "The Last Station" that he wrote a twenty-page report to his superiors about it, and twice a day he stood next to his specially constructed box, waiting to recite his lines. He lit a cigarette and stared down the narrowing tracks. He took several long drags and adjusted his hat. The train blasted its whistle from deep in the woods and a green light was activated that told the conductor to proceed slowly. A great huff of black rose up from the pine trees.

And in this way thousands of people were sent through Lubizec each day. Thousands.

— 6 —

NUMBERS

They came from towns with names like Zakrzówek, Biłgoraj, Szczebrzeszyn, Sokal, and Sambor. Turka, Kolomyya, Włodawa, Zamość, and Sasów. Kielce and Grabow. Kraków and Lublin. Two came from Paris. One came from London. Two hundred and twenty-three from Berlin. It has already been mentioned how they were pushed into cattle cars, how they were stuffed in cheek by jowl, how the doors were pulled shut on greased rails, and how a lock was flipped into place with a clacking thunk. A ladder was placed next to the car and numbers were chalked onto the side to say how many people were sealed inside. 131. 135. 149. 130. 152. The cars were designed to carry twelve cows but the Nazis shoved in entire families and villages. Whole histories were reduced to nothing more than chalk numbers riding down the rails.

Survivors like Chaim Zischer and Dov Damiel offer painfully vivid accounts about what the camp was like from a prisoner's perspective, but for everyone else that rolled into Lubizec, we can only imagine what it was like to huddle on the platform and listen to Guth's speech. Perhaps we can place ourselves on those wooden planks for a moment or two, maybe we can feel our toes inside our shoes—how sweaty and swollen they are—but in the end it's all just guesswork and make-believe on our part. Try as we might, we can't understand the raw fear these people would have felt swimming around inside their chests.

When they were told they were going to be resettled to a work camp in the east, posters were hung up in the ghetto and a truck with loudspeakers crawled down the cobblestone streets. The message? Resettlement would occur in two days and no more than fifty kilograms were allowed. Pack lightly. Bring only your most valuable goods. Extra clothes are not needed. Pack lightly. Bring only your most valuable goods. No more than fifty kilograms. Pack lightly. Bring only your most valuable goods.

When Mina Auerbach heard this she decided to pack a rag doll her grandmother had made from an old blanket. The doll had two buttons for eyes, wide bands of fabric for hair, and she wore a pink dress. Mina was only four but she gathered up her doll and stuffed it into a pillowcase.

Semion Wallach, who was seven, wondered which toys to bring while his mother, Hanel, wrestled between packing a skillet or packing a photo album. There was also her wedding ring to consider. If she wore it, the Nazis would steal it, so maybe she should stitch it into the hem of a dress? Hanel got out a needle and thread. She went to work.

We can only imagine what it was like to look at our things (all that stuff that makes us who we are) and wonder what to leave behind. Fifty kilograms is nothing. Should we take this or this? What about this? And when the SS came with their machine guns and dogs, shooting people in the street and always yelling, yelling, yelling, we can see ourselves jogging towards the train station with the last of our earthly possessions. We might drop something on the ground and realize we can't go back for it because we will be beaten. We watch this valuable trinket skitter away and in that moment we feel as if we are losing everything. Our fingers tighten on our suitcase handle because, if we can only keep the rest of our possessions together, it means not everything is lost. Clothing and candlesticks become symbols of something much larger. Our fifty kilograms feels like a protective talisman because as long as the Nazis don't take everything away from us it means that resettlement—and *life*—waits up ahead.

Although we can imagine this, what must it have been like to stand in a crowded cattle car and feel it judder towards the unknown? We might close our eyes and imagine the muggy heat or the rocking sway as we rumble over points on the tracks, but these are undefined details because, of course, hardly anyone survived. Their stories were snuffed out, erased, and we have so very few eyewitness accounts.

Upon arrival at Lubizec, the doors would have rolled open and people would have looked up at the stinging sunlight, but what must it have been like to hear the guards shouting in German? They have rubber truncheons and their faces are flushed with anger. Flecks of spit fly from their mouths as they scream.

"*Schuhe zusammenbinden! Geld und Dokumente mitnehmen!*"

Abraham Krolikowski came from a small village and he couldn't understand what they were saying so he stroked the bristles of his moustache. Others like Jerzy and Jozek Blatt were at the end of the long platform and they gripped their suitcases. These twin brothers owned a bookstore before the Nazis invaded and they enjoyed heated conversations over pots of mint tea. They adjusted their tortoiseshell glasses and looked around.

"*Schuhe zusammenbinden! Geld und Dokumente mitnehmen!*"

Giesela Wilenberg, who had a mist of freckles on her face, hugged her two daughters. "What are they saying?" she asked in Yiddish. "What's that?"

Someone else, perhaps David Stawczinski, might have thought about translating. He was a music teacher and, even in that moment when fear prickled his throat and his stomach burned for a lump of bread, even then he might have wondered if there was a piano nearby. Perhaps he could tell the Germans he was a musician and he couldn't do hard labor? He opened his mouth to translate, but a woman behind him spoke up instead. The confidence in her voice was surprising.

"They're saying, *Tie your shoes together. Bring your gold and documents with.*"

Shoes were taken off and suitcases were stacked onto wagons. The engine huffed and vented as the conductor peered out of his hatch. Mina Auerbach held on to her rag doll and stroked its thick brown hair.

"Don't be afraid, Miss Doll," she whispered. "I'm here."

"*Schuhe zusammenbinden! Geld und Dokumente mitnehmen!*"

Hanel Wallach instinctively put an arm around her son and nodded to herself that she had made the right decision to bring a skillet instead of a photo album. She curled her toes inside her shoes and realized her mouth was dry. She sucked on her front teeth to make some spit. When she swallowed, she felt the delicate bones in her ears pop. It was such a small thing but it suddenly seemed so grand and important. Her whole life came down to a forgettable moment of daily biology. She swallowed again and listened to her ears pop.

Where is this Lubizec? she wondered. *Where are we?*

Others may have entertained thoughts of escape but what they didn't know—couldn't know—was that farmers were promised two bags of sugar if they caught a prisoner. Escaping from Lubizec would have been like escaping slavery in the Deep South of the United States during the nineteenth century. Where would you go? Who could you trust? All of this was made harder if you didn't speak Polish and, to make matters worse, you entered the camp with your entire family. Would you abandon your child? Your parents? Would you leave everyone you loved as you made a mad and useless dash for the barbed wire? Even if you managed to slip through the fence, where would you go? It was a world of machine guns and forest.

Where is this place? Hanel Wallach wondered again. She shielded her eyes from the sun and squinted into the pine trees.

What these people were thinking is of course a matter of conjecture but we do know that a man named Rabbi Israel Hirszman refused to be afraid. After everyone was marched beneath the huge WELCOME sign, he whispered words of encouragement. He touched people on the shoulder and patted children on the head. While we cannot know what Rabbi Hirszman said to people like Giesela Wilenberg, Hanel Wallach, and David Stawczinski, we do know what happened next.

It began when Guth was lighting a cigarette. As he fiddled with his lighter, turning this way and that to block the wind, the rabbi adjusted his wide-brimmed hat and bent down for a fistful of sand. He took a step forward and yelled out, "You there. German."

Guth looked up, slowly.

"Yes. I'm talking to you, German."

Prisoners never spoke to Guth, especially not after they had been herded into the Rose Garden. They usually acted like a bolt of lightning had gone off because they were jittery, alert, waiting for the thunderclap to come.

Guth lowered his unlit cigarette and looked amused. "Yes?"

The rabbi held up his fist and let the sand fall into the wind.

"Do you see what I am doing, German? Do you see this? One day you will vanish into flying dust but my people will remain." The rabbi threw the remaining gravel onto the ground and pointed at the guards. "Shame on you. Shame on all of you."

A guard immediately marched over to the bearded man and aimed at that spot where the spinal cord meets the skull. In a cracking flash the rabbi's head opened up in a spray of pink mist and bone. He stood for a moment, then crumpled to the ground like a wet rag. His wide-brimmed hat wheeled away towards the barbed-wire fence where it got hung up, briefly, before skittering into the woods.

Blood pumped from the rabbi's head. It stained the sand with grainy dark blobs. The gunshot startled everyone in a way the screaming had not yet done, and the air became charged with shock.

The guard holstered his pistol and turned to the group. He cleared his throat and spoke loudly but without anger.

"Men and women must separate. It's time for your disinfection showers. There must be no lice in this camp. No lice."

Guth went back to lighting his cigarette as screams filled the air.

When Giesela Wilenberg saw this she might have hugged her daughters and looked around at the wooden guard towers. *This is the last of Earth*, she might have thought. Maybe she kissed her daughters and enjoyed the smell of their unwashed hair.

When the separations began, Hanel Wallach refused to give up her son. The deputy commandant, *Oberscharführer* Heinrich Niemann, came towards her with a truncheon the size of a chair leg and he began beating her on the head with it.

"He must go over there," he grunted. "Over there. Over there. Over there."

But Hanel refused to give up her boy. She hunched into a protective loving shell and held her son's head as blow after blow landed on her back. In this moment of ruinous blinding pain when Hanel teetered on the brink of unconsciousness, her son was dragged away. He kicked wildly against the dirt.

"Mama, help! Where are they taking me?"

As Hanel stumbled after him, she was beaten all the harder. Heinrich Niemann's truncheon became a blur of action and, when he was finally finished crushing her head open, he stood up and wiped sweat from his forehead. He panted.

"Whew. These Jews keep me fit."

Maybe Semion Wallach was picked up by some stranger and shielded from the corpse of his mother and maybe he went limp in this stranger's arms as they were quick-marched off to the undressing area.

"I've got you, boy," the man might have cooed. "I'll be your father now. You can trust me."

While we can't know these things, we do know that after the men stripped off their clothes and ran down the Road to Heaven many of them chanted prayers.

Men like our bookselling brothers, Jerzy and Jozek Blatt, would have run across the dirt and looked up at the bright blue sky. It was such a beautiful day, so full of life and potential, but they didn't know where they were going or why the wooden walls on either side were painted brilliant white. It felt weird to run naked. Their scrotums and penises flapped around and this made them feel even more vulnerable. It was hard to run on the sandy dirt and they worried about tripping and being beaten. Men around them were being hit on the head. Rubber truncheons broke arms, and faces were split open with hissing whips. The terror and confusion was absolute.

They rounded a corner and saw a whitewashed building with the Star of David above the door. Something was written in Hebrew. THIS IS THE GATE OF THE LORD. Flowers were on either side of the entrance and this was oddly reassuring. Almost welcoming.

When they got inside the brick building, the floor was covered with bits of sand that had been tracked in by the others. Most of the men had black fluff from their socks stuck beneath their toenails and they stood around panting. Their eyes darted left and right. They looked up and down.

"It's a shower," someone said.

Jozek Blatt looked up to see showerheads hanging from the ceiling. "That's a good sign," he said, pointing.

"Yes. A good sign."

The air became more humid as others pushed in.

"Ugh. It stinks of chlorine."

"Make room. Make room. I'm getting squashed."

"Ouch. Careful."

It could be that David Stawczinski, our imaginary piano teacher, closed his eyes and thought about playing a baby grand in some restaurant. Bits of Rachmaninoff twinkled in his ears and this calmed him. He tried licking his lips but his mouth was dry, and maybe, in these last few minutes of life, he glanced down at his hands. His knuckles and tendons had spent years learning how to tap dance across the stage of a piano, but now they were just curled fists against his chest.

When the metal door slammed shut and the screws were spun home, David's muscles tingled for him to do *something*. But what? He could barely shift his weight from one foot to the other because there were so many men packed in around him. The room was electrified with fear and a low whispering began.

"What's happening?"

"Where are we?"

"Stop pushing."

"We'll be fine."

"Yes, fine."

"They wouldn't kill good workers."

"It wouldn't make sense."

"No sense at all."

"It's just a shower."

"Yes. Just a shower."

An engine was clattering behind the wall and the guards beyond the door began to laugh.

David felt like he was going to hyperventilate and his head swiveled around at each new sound. He tried to swallow but he couldn't. His throat was dry. His palms were sweaty. A wild energy gripped his muscles but he also felt paralyzed, jacketed.

"Will it take long to die?" a little boy asked.

David looked at the steel door and saw a glass peephole. An eye peered in. It looked to the right, the left, it blinked a few times, then disappeared. Someone on the outside shouted, "Time to die!"

"What was that?"

"What'd he say?"

"I couldn't hear."

At first there wasn't much to notice except that the engine had shifted into a higher gear and something overhead made the vents change direction. David, like the other men in that room, looked up and began pushing at his neighbors nervously. Whispering turned into shouting as everyone began to realize why the engine was whining at such high speed and why the door had been screwed shut. The vents blew out something hot, but no one realized how much poison was spilling into the room because carbon monoxide is colorless, odorless, and tasteless.

The room began to sizzle with panic. Survival instincts kicked in and the men lurched against the steel door because it was the only exit. Those at the front were crushed and their rib cages cracked. The whole room floundered with shouting and hollering as men turned into beasts. They clawed and gouged for escape.

David began to feel lightheaded and he watched an old man with white hair begin to convulse. His eyes rolled back into his head while—in the corner of the room, in those places not yet soaked with gas—a young boy tried to climb the wall with his fingernails. He boosted himself up onto the backs of others and roared for help. Several men in the center began to vomit. Those against the door banged on it with their open palms.

"Let us out! Let us out!"

David found his hands doing things that surprised him. He punched and pushed and clawed and ripped. He burned with incandescent rage and wanted revenge against the Nazis for putting him in this caged-animal situation. He held his breath and told himself he'd be fine, that somehow he'd survive, and while he was thinking this an image of his mother floated into his mind. She was in a park, the sun was shining, and she held out her arms. Men jostled against him but David Stawczinski held his breath and focused on the park. He counted to ten. One . . . two . . . three . . .

He'd have to breathe again and he wondered how the gas would feel in his lungs. Would it hurt? Would he cough? He kept on counting.

Six . . . seven . . . eight . . . nine . . .

He made it up to twenty-three before he had to take another breath and when he opened his esophagus to let in the air it felt like he was drowning in a deep river of thistles. A dizziness made him see purple dots. Fireworks went off in his skull and he felt like he was falling off a tall canyon. He closed his eyes but that sinking, tumbling, dropping, oozing feeling remained with him. Men and boys collapsed around him as he continued to hold his breath. He stumbled backwards and began to weep. Another inhale. The room stank of vomit and piss and shit and although he could smell these things he couldn't smell the gas that was killing him.

There was so much he still wanted to do, there was so much he still wanted to see. He felt an overwhelming sense of regret, not that he was dying, but that in thirty-two years his dreams had somehow eluded him. He wanted to perform in Warsaw, Kraków, and Lwów, he wanted to see Paris and walk around the ancient streets of Rome, he wanted to drink wine on the Mediterranean and ride a camel in the Sahara and maybe take an ocean liner across the Atlantic, but in one horrible moment he realized none of it was going to happen. None of it.

He closed his eyes and thought about his mother standing in a park. It was a beautiful cloudless day and he began to count. One . . . two . . . three . . .

His mother was waiting for him. He ran to her.

We can never know what it was like inside that gas chamber. We can only make guesses. We can only hypothesize and speculate. Precisely because we can never know what these victims were thinking or feeling, we bump up against the central paradox of Lubizec itself: Whenever we read eyewitness accounts from former prisoners, we know in the back our minds that at least *this* person survived, at least *this* person made it out, at least *this* story won't be hopeless, and this means our focus necessarily shifts from death to life. The absolute unrelenting horror of the Holocaust is dulled because we know that eyewitness accounts by their very nature are stories of life. But Lubizec was not a place of life. It was a place of clockwork murder and annihilation. To understand it we need to read hundreds of thousands of stories just like David Stawczinski's, and then we need to imagine each of them dying.

Our hearts, though, can only take so much horror.

Because of this, the victims become faceless ghosts that are pushed into gas chambers. We watch the door swing shut and we turn away. It's easier to cope with Lubizec if we do this, but in order to understand the place in any meaningful way we need to know about women like Giesela Wilenberg and we need to imagine her worrying about what the guards will do to her naked daughters. Perhaps she draws them close and tells them everything will be okay. Maybe she wipes their tears away. It could be that she tries to be strong even though inside the secret corridors of her mind she is quaking. She holds their hands and when the steel door booms shut she leans into their ears. As the gas kicks on, she tells her daughters to look into her eyes.

"Look at me. Look at me. Are you listening? I have *loved* being your mother. Do you hear me? I love you. I love you. I love you."

While we cannot know what these people were thinking or feeling we must not allow ourselves to see them as faceless numbers. That's what the Nazis did—they were numbers that needed erasing. All the sunrises they had seen, all the lips they had kissed, all the shoes they had bought, all the tears and underhanded deeds and acts of generosity and presents and toothaches and music and laughter and hugs and stomachaches and blisters and dancing, it all got snuffed out in Lubizec. Imagine 710,000 candles flickering away and then, in one gigantic storm, they are all blown out. There is a sudden intake of breath and then—

One of the more heartbreaking stories about Lubizec occurred on August 27, 1942, and we only know about it thanks to "Allied Forces Report No. 3042." The story would have slipped into oblivion if Captain Joe Ehrenbach hadn't interrogated Heinrich Niemann as well as he did in 1946. The fact that Niemann brought the story up at all suggests how unusual it was, even for Lubizec.

It was raining heavily that day, a real monsoon, and when the afternoon transport arrived everyone was surprised to find 150 boys stuffed into a single car. Apparently an orphanage had been liquidated near Warsaw, and as the rain came down harder and harder, Guth climbed onto his specially made wooden box. He held a black umbrella and spoke into a microphone as the boys cupped their hands to catch what was falling from the heavens. They opened their mouths and stuck out their tongues. Thunder rumbled in the sky and lightning shocked the horizon. The rain came down onto the platform so hard it looked like dancing sparks. One guard said it was like a river had been turned upside down.

"I think I saw Noah building an ark," another guard joked. "It was a huge amount of rain."

The boys weren't listening to Guth so the guards began hitting them with truncheons. A terrible wailing filled up the platform as rain guttered off the cattle cars and, standing in the middle of the boys like a protective willow tree, was a tall man in a hat. When the guards asked who he was the man simply answered, "The director of the orphanage."

Although we don't know this man's name (let us call him Aron Joffe so that at least he has a name), he could have abandoned these boys and taken his chances at Lubizec, he could have said he was by himself and that he was a hard worker, but that's not what he did. Instead, this tall man stood in the middle of 150 terrified boys and did something profoundly good.

"You're all with me," he shouted. "Boys, boys. We'll be shown to our rooms shortly. Hush now. Stop crying. You're all loved."

When order was restored, the guards stepped back under the long wooden awning. Guth stood beneath his umbrella and continued his speech as if nothing had happened. He smoked a cigarette and flicked it against the glossy wet train.

"Welcome to Lubizec," he said, climbing down from his box.

The boys were herded into the Rose Garden, where they clustered around the tall man in a hat. Aron Joffe, as we are calling him, looked around as if sizing up the camp. He nodded as if coming to some kind of horrible realization. Water dripped off the brim of his hat.

"Boys, boys," he said. "Listen. Do I have your full and complete attention? Good. As you've all heard, we need to take a shower. Yes, I know it's raining and . . . yes, we probably don't need a shower but . . . listen to me . . . listen . . . after *that* we'll be given bread and butter and cookies."

Some of them cheered.

"We need to follow the commandant's orders first and then he'll give us a big, beautiful meal." He stressed the last word with a smile. "I'm sure the guards won't hit anyone if we follow their orders. Isn't that right, Herr Commandant? No more hitting?"

Guth usually went back to his office but on that rainy afternoon of sheeting water he stood beneath the hemisphere of his umbrella and nodded. The boys were then marched down a narrow path. They stomped in puddles. They took off their clothes and talked about eating boiled eggs, different kinds of cheeses, apples, and potatoes. The director of the orphanage encouraged them to think of other foods as he took off his waistcoat and unhooked his belt. He folded his trousers and took off his hat as the rain kept on coming down.

"What else will we eat?"

The boys began to shout. Toffee! Pierogi! Matzah ball soup! Pears! Cherries! Lamb! Salmon!

When the director was completely naked he covered up his penis with one hand and kept the list going, as if he were conducting a symphony. "What else? What else?"

The boys, all 150 of them, marched up the Road to Heaven shouting out food they would soon be eating. The guards stood in the pouring rain and didn't raise their clubs. They simply watched the boys file past them into the whitewashed building as if they were on some kind of strange field trip. The director paused when he heard the clattering engine. He covered his mouth and let out a little gasp.

"Oh, my God. You boys are *so* wonderful," he said with tears in his eyes. "Thank you for being so good and beautiful. You're all loved. Do you know that, boys? All of you. That's right. I'm coming too. I'm here, boys. I'm here."

When everyone was inside, the man ran both hands through his wet hair and turned to Guth.

"How can you bring yourself to do this?" He broke down. "They're such good boys. They've done nothing wrong."

Thunder crackled and roiled the sky, but Guth said nothing.

Crying came from inside the brick building and the director wiped his eyes. He took a deep breath, smiled, and stepped in.

"It's okay. I'm here, I'm here."

Guth stood beneath his black umbrella and tried to light another cigarette as rain came down harder and harder, faster and faster. The huge steel door on Chamber #4 slammed shut. A moment passed, then another. The flowers outside the gas chamber quivered as the rain pelted them. There was the sound of a prayer being sung in the gas chamber but when the engine revved into a higher gear the singing turned into screaming. At first it sounded like they were all going down a roller coaster together, but then it turned into absolute terror. It was like a breaking wave of screams. Above it, a man shouted out words of love.

"I'm here, boys! I'm here!"

Hans-Peter Guth looked at the sandy path covered in little footprints. The rain began to fill them in.

More trains would be arriving tomorrow and he needed to send the weekly numbers to Berlin. He walked across camp, opened the door of his office, and leaned his umbrella against the wall. Thunder crackled across the sky, booming and rumbling. It made the windowpanes shake. Guth sat down in front of his typewriter and consulted the train schedules.

They came from towns with names like Zakrzówek, Biłgoraj, Szczebrzeszyn, Sokal, and Sambor. Turka, Kolomyya, Włodawa, Zamość, and Sasów. Kielce and Grabow. Kraków and Lublin. Two came from Paris. One came from London. Two hundred and twenty-three from Berlin.

Hans-Peter Guth rolled in a sheet of paper. He began to type.

```
21.8.1942 - 3,837
22.8.1942 - 3,914
23.8.1942 - 3,966
24.8.1942 - 3,801
25.8.1942 - 3,972
26.8.1942 - 3,999
27.8.1942 - 4,152
```

They were just numbers to him. Just numbers.

— 7 —

TROUBLE AT HOME

On the same day the boys were all murdered, Guth went home early to be with his own children. The rain had slowed and he cantered up the cinder driveway on his horse. He went into the house, where he took off his dripping woolen coat. He hung it on a peg and placed his SS hat, which was sodden with water, onto a section of newspaper. Splats wrinkled the front page. The headline was about the war in the east—the Battle of Stalingrad was underway. Everyone expected an easy victory because the city had been pounded for weeks from the air. A thousand tons of bombs had rained down and there was nothing left but vast fields of rubble and burnt rafters. Resistance should be light. The war would soon be over and Germany would control all of Europe. Victory was inevitable.

Sigi and Karl were surprised to find their father home so early. Rain streaked down the patio door in thick veins of running water as Guth unbuttoned his charcoal-gray uniform and kicked off his jackboots.

"How are my darlings? Give me hugs."

They whined about being bored and about how the rain was keeping them inside. It's not fair, they pouted. There's nothing to do. Even the radio didn't have anything decent on and they were tired of their toys. They wanted some excitement. Some fun.

Guth gave them his full attention. He touched their heads and got down on the carpet to play "tanks and soldiers" with his son. Together they picked up Panzer tanks and crawled towards Stalingrad. Gunfire came from their mouths as they inched towards a shoebox that was supposed to represent the city, and that's when Guth, getting into the spirit of the game, held up a finger as if to pause the war. He got out matchboxes and lined them up around the shoebox.

"There's the enemy. Go get him."

Woompf, woompf, woompf went the mortars. *Boom!*

Guth reached over to the Soviet line and threw the matchboxes high into the air. He pointed at a small opening and yelled, "Get in there. Go, go, go! There's the enemy's weakness."

Karl plowed his tank into the shoebox and threw the remaining matchboxes up towards the ceiling. Hundreds of wooden matchsticks rained down onto the floor and Karl stomped on the shoebox while yelling out a language of explosives.

"Boom, boom, boom!"

He picked up his tank and did a victory lap around the room.

"Down with the Soviet Union! *Sieg Heil. Sieg Heil. Sieg Heil.*"

Guth put his hands on his hips, nodded in satisfaction, and turned to his daughter. She was reading yet another book about Old Shatterhand and the dust jacket showed a grizzled old mountain man pointing at a valley. He held up a rifle and seemed to be rallying the reader towards adventure.

"Good book?" Guth said while tugging on both of Sigi's pigtails.

She batted his hand away.

"Must be good," he smiled.

She nodded towards a wicker basket on the table. "That came for you."

"Who's it from?"

A shrug and she went back to reading.

It was from Guth's superior in Lublin. There was a scrawled note from *Hauptsturmführer* Odilo Globocnik that thanked him for "solving thousands of little problems at Lubizec." The basket held chocolate bars, pickled herring, cherry jam, and a bottle of champagne. A cheap bottle, Guth noticed, but he held it up and admired the deep green.

He sat down in a leather chair and yawned. He ran his fingers through his coppery hair and smiled. "You're lucky to live in such times, children."

He pulled out a silver cigarette case and slouched back with one leg draped over the kneecap of the other. Rain threaded its way down the patio door as he sat in a room full of antique furniture and expensive bone china. Cigarette smoke drifted up to the wooden beams of the reading room, and hanging above the marble fireplace was a painting of Adolf Hitler.

"Lucky indeed," Guth said, closing his eyes.

Sigi looked up. "How come you're home so early?"

He took the next day off work. It was the first time he'd done such a thing since they moved to Poland and he decided that a hike was in order. The Villa overlooked a massive private lake and there was a little island full of trees in the middle that Guth had yet to explore. He said they should load up a wicker basket with ham sandwiches and row across the water to see what mysteries waited for them on the island. Sigi liked the idea and gathered up a pad of paper to map what they found. Karl wanted to bring his compass.

"Good. Be prepared," Guth said.

Jasmine, however, refused to come along. We know from her unpublished diary that their marriage was beginning to strain by late August 1942 and, although they still shared the same bed, they bickered whenever their door was closed. In *The Commandant's Daughter*, Sigi mentions how she heard murmuring deep into the night. A peculiar mood filled up the house but Sigi couldn't pinpoint why her parents were so snippy with each other. She worried it might be her, that *she* had done something wrong, and she tried to be extra nice to the whole family. She cleaned bedrooms even though the Polish girl was hired to do such things. Sigi also cleared away dishes and tidied Karl's room.

On the morning they decided to explore the island, her father was fidgety. Restless. His leg bounced up and down at the breakfast table and this made the coffee in his mug jiggle. Jasmine refused to look up, even though her husband tried again and again to jump-start a conversation.

"Weather looks good today . . ."

"Those sandwiches'll taste good after paddling around in a rowboat . . ."

"We should spend more time together as a family . . ."

"I *said*, we should spend more time together as a family. What do you think, darling?"

She covered a bread roll with cherry jam and bit into it. "Do whatever you want." A quick swallow and she wiped her mouth with her thumb. "But tell the kids. Do it today."

Guth crossed his arms. It was the look of a man who didn't like being bossed around.

"It's one thing to hide it from me but . . ." she trailed off. There was a smile, as sharp as a saber cut, and she stood up. She smoothed her flowery flowing dress and looked at her children, who were eating quietly.

"Have fun with your father," she said, reaching for her purse. Her heels clicked down the hallway and she closed the front door without slamming it. Silence filled the house. The soft effervescent bubbling of seltzer water could be heard in their glasses.

Guth tore off a bit of bread and popped it into his mouth. "So," he finally said. He squinted at the lake. "Should be nice out there today."

We should pause and consider the two different versions of Hans-Peter Guth that are before us in this moment. There is the man who snuffed out entire villages and towns, a man that can only be described as a serial mass murderer, and yet there is this other man, a man who obviously loved his children and enjoyed being a father. We almost want Guth to go home after killing thousands of people and inflict pain upon those he loved because it would make us feel better if he beat his wife, or sexually abused his kids, or drank too much, or whipped his horse, or had an affair with the maid, or sodomized boys. We could write him off as a disgusting human being. But this wasn't how Hans-Peter Guth acted when he stripped off his Nazi uniform. Instead, he went about the business of being a loving father and husband. How could this man go home after watching children die in such horrible ways? How could he separate his two worlds so completely, so thoroughly, so cleanly?

It could be that Guth was in fact a monster at home and that Sigrid's book is an attempt to whitewash history—this is certainly possible—anything is possible—and yet it is unlikely that Sigrid lied about how deeply her father cared about her. What are we supposed to *do* with this information though? What comfort is there in knowing that Guth had the capacity for love but he chose to make a fist of his heart whenever he crossed over the threshold of Lubizec? How are we supposed to reconcile Guth the Commandant versus Guth the Father? For now, that answer must be set aside, but these two different worlds will soon collide in surprising ways.

He stood up and made a shepherding movement towards the patio. "Let's go. Let's go. Let's go. Get your things."

They loaded up the wooden rowboat with a picnic basket full of sandwiches that had been wrapped in wax paper. Guth told Sigi and Karl to put on their life jackets before he muscled the boat out into the water. Sand scratched the hull as he pushed it out into the clear water and then, in one graceful motion, he pulled himself into the boat. It wobbled a bit as he sat down.

"Beautiful day," he said, squinting at the cloudless sky. He reached for the oars.

He wore plaid shorts, a white T-shirt, and he was barefoot. Sigi wasn't used to seeing her father's legs and she pretended not to look at them. He was tanned and toned with muscle. He was attractive. Even Sigi knew this. There was a thick, earthwormy scar on his thigh where he got hung up in some barbed wire during the last war. It happened in a trench somewhere when he was fighting the British. Back in 1917 or 1918. She wasn't sure which. He never talked about it. She studied its long purple shape out of the corner of her eye, how it twitched and relaxed as he rowed across the lake, and it was such a beautiful day.

A train whistled deep in the woods and the sound echoed across the glassy water. The whistle came again and Guth glanced at his wristwatch. There was a nod of approval.

"Is that your train station, Papa?" Karl asked.

He said nothing. He kept on rowing.

Sigi let her hand trail in the water. She liked how her fingers split open the surface and made a soft burbling sound. A fish flapped up and she turned to see spreading ripples from where it had splashed. The water was gray and gentle. Her father pulled on the oars and she watched them dip in and out of the lake, over and over again. They were moving fast and she enjoyed the speed as well as how her body moved in rhythm to the oars. Karl held a compass and yelled out directions.

"South! Southeast!"

Oaks and pines towered up from the island and Guth rowed hard until they slid up onto a sandy, gravely beach. It scraped the bottom of the boat. All around them were pebbles and mud and minnows. The surface of the water was slick, sun dappled, and shimmeringly alive.

"We're here," Karl clapped. "We're here. We're here. We're here."

They pulled the boat up into some weeds and Guth looked around. "Now what?" he asked.

"Indians," Karl said, already pushing into the ferny undergrowth. He picked up a stick and brought it up to his face. He took aim and shouted, "I see three of them! Bang, bang, bang!"

Pine needles were everywhere, along with dragonflies that zipped through shafts of honeyed sunlight. In *The Commandant's Daughter* Sigi writes about her time on the island as something she wanted to safeguard and preserve forever. For the rest of her life she would remember it as a perfect day in the Garden of Eden. Her father was out of his uniform and everything associated with Nazism was far away. There was no war. There was no Hitler. There was no Holocaust. He was simply her father. For Sigi, the island came to represent a type of lost innocence, and as she grew older and had to grapple with what her father had done, she felt that if she could have kept him there forever maybe she could have stopped him from killing all of those innocent people. For her, the island became a symbolic place where her father could still be redeemed.

"Bang!" Karl yelled.

"How many now?" Guth asked.

Karl wiped sweat from his forehead. "Twenty-three. Bang! Twenty-four!"

"Good. Good. Keep this island safe."

Guth put an arm around his daughter as they weaved through trees. It didn't take long to reach the other side of the island, and when they did, they circled back, slowly. Karl shouldered his imaginary rifle and ran ahead, jumping over fallen trees and stopping every now and then to look at a turquoise beetle or some wide mushrooms. When they returned to the rowboat they opened the picnic basket and pulled wax paper off their sandwiches. They bit into apples—crunching down on the juicy hardness—and they stared at the Villa. It looked tiny and fragile. Like a toy. Sunlight flashed off one of the windows as it opened. A train clattered in the wilderness and Guth checked his watch again.

"Trains are fun," Karl said, dropping a fist-sized rock into the water. It sploshed.

When they finished eating, they packed away the wax paper and apple cores. Guth lit a cigarette and leaned against a tree. He looked happy, content. He crossed his legs at the ankles and let out a little groan of happiness.

From somewhere across the lake, a crow began to complain. *Craaaaw-caw.*

"Papa?" Sigi asked.

"Mm-hmm?"

"You're supposed to tell us something."

A pause. "I am?"

"Mom said you had something to tell us."

Guth took a long drag on his cigarette but didn't open his eyes.

"Is it what you two are arguing about?"

He dug a bit of sandwich out of his back molar and flicked it into the water. "Arguing? What do you mean?"

"This morning. Over breakfast. Mom said you're supposed to tell us something."

Another pause. He nodded and opened his eyes. "Okay," he said, sitting up. "Okay. Yes. You should know."

Sigi and Karl leaned in as a dragonfly floated past. Guth studied the far side of the lake and acted as if he were speaking to himself. He told his children they needed to be strong, that Germany was at war, and that certain sacrifices had to be made.

"I'm sorry to say that your grandmother was killed in an air raid. It was a quick death. She wouldn't have felt much."

Sigi and Karl began to shriek but Guth snapped his fingers for them to quiet down.

"People die in war all the time. She was an old woman and she had a full life."

Karl continued to cry but Sigi gathered herself and wiped her eyes. Her bottom lip trembled. "When did it happen?"

"A month ago."

"A *month* ago? But . . . can we go to her funeral?"

Guth stood up and waved his hand as if a mosquito were floating around him. "There wasn't a funeral. Now help me load the boat and we'll—for God's *sake*, Karl—stop your sniveling. Crying won't bring her back. People die all the time but sacrifices need to be made."

He fit the wicker picnic basket into the rowboat and dropped his cigarette into the water. It hissed like a snake.

They rowed home in silence. Karl wept quietly, with his back to Guth, as Sigi stared out at the calm gray lake. She tried not to cry as the wooden oars squeaked against their metal locks. Beads of water ran down the oar shafts and trickled back into the darkness.

Sigi would later say her grandmother's death made the war real in a way that nothing else had up to that point. In her book she wonders how this one death could have taken up so much space in her heart when, just five kilometers from her bedroom, thousands of people were being gassed every day. She goes on to explain that her grandmother died in a firestorm. It happened near the docks of Hamburg on the night of July 26, 1942, when the Royal Air Force set its crosshairs on the submarine pens. Due to bad weather, the bombs drifted badly off target and they blasted into residential property. A thousand homes were immediately engulfed in flame and huge tornadoes of fire lifted up to the clouds. Two days later, a telegram was sent to Guth's office. His mother had been found in an air-raid shelter, unburned but dead. As the firestorm raged overhead, and as oxygen was sucked up to feed the towering flames, she and many others were caught in the vacuum below. Their lungs couldn't inflate and they were slowly asphyxiated—they panted for air until there was none left. When the door to the air-raid shelter was finally opened, everyone inside looked like they were in shock. Their mouths were open as if they were in the process of saying, "No." The shelter had become, in effect, like a gas chamber.

What angered Jasmine was how Guth lied about it. When she first heard about the raid she asked if his mother was okay. "Was her house hit? Have you heard from her?" Guth stared at his red wine and said she was fine, just fine. Four days later Jasmine asked the same question and again he gave the same answer even though he knew—he *knew*—she was dead. Five weeks passed, and when Jasmine finally discovered the truth she was horrified by her husband's indifference.

"Hans. She was your *mother*."

"Lots of mothers have died in this war. Lots. What do you want me to say?"

It wasn't just the icy way in which he talked about her death that angered Jasmine, it was also his evasiveness. Shortly after she first heard about the bombing, she sent a care package to help the old woman with her rationing cards, and Guth knew she was doing this, but still he said nothing. He watched her wrap the package with brown paper and he offered to mail it.

What made Jasmine prickle, what really made her ball up her fists in anger, was how Guth painted fib onto fib, even though she repeatedly asked about his mother.

"Did she get the package? Is she okay?"

He said they talked on the phone and that she was doing well. "She's fine. Just fine."

When Jasmine realized how much he was dancing around the truth, she stewed with rage—this had been an ongoing problem since Berlin—and she demanded that he start telling the truth or there would be consequences. Serious consequences. After all, *she* didn't want to live in Poland.

When the rowboat crunched up onto the sandy shore, Guth and the kids walked up the stone steps. Their bare feet left watery prints on the flagstones. The sliding glass door was open and Jasmine was inside, smoking. She used an ivory holder because it made her feel elegant. Like a movie star. When she saw the stunned looks on her children she opened her arms and gave them a hug. The three of them cried as Guth looked on. He leaned against the wall and crossed his arms.

Jasmine gave her children a few kisses. Lipstick butterflies hung on their cheeks. She smoothed their hair and said, "I'm sorry, my dears. Now . . . give your father and me some privacy. We need to talk about adult things."

Karl went upstairs, dragging his feet against each tread, but Sigi slipped into the front hall and positioned herself next to a mirror. It was large and reflected what was happening in the lounge. A grandfather clock ticked out the seconds. Her parents said nothing for a long time. They looked at the floor and rubbed their faces. The heavy pendulum kept swinging back and forth.

Jasmine adjusted a bra strap and finally said, "Why did you lie?"

He turned to stare at the lake. His reflection looked back at her.

"Did you hear me?"

"State secrets are—"

"I'm not talking about stupid state secrets. I'm talking about your mother. Your *mother*, Hans. She dies five weeks ago and you go around acting like she's still alive. Who does that? It's not normal."

He lit a cigarette. He turned back to her and picked a fleck of tobacco off his lips. "I've been under a lot of pressure lately."

"You said the same thing in Berlin when you were euthanizing those people and it just seems that—"

"Stop. We're not talking about that again."

"I don't care about that. What I *do* care about, Hans, is how you said you were involved in security at a mental hospital and how you never once said anything about putting people out of their misery."

"It was Reich's business."

"No, no, no." She got up and began to pace. "You don't understand. You lied to me about what you did in Berlin and you lied to me about your mother. It just comes so *naturally* to you. That's my problem. How can I believe anything you tell me if you can't even mention the death of your own mother? I didn't come to Poland for this."

Guth opened his mouth as if to say something but she silenced him. She pointed to the front door. "Is that place a transit camp?"

"Jasmine."

"Yes or no? I'm your wife."

He took a pull on his cigarette and held it. When he exhaled, his words were made of smoke. "Don't be like this. I need to come home to a loving wife."

"Yes or no?"

"Stop. Stop right now."

"Because I've heard rumors in this backwater hole-of-a-place and I need to know the truth. For once, can you please just share something with me?" Her voice rose but she calmed herself. She smoothed her dress and cleared her throat. "I deserve that much at least after moving here from Berlin."

"Ah yes, marvelous Berlin. Look, I won't be interrogated like a common criminal."

Jasmine reached into her purse and tossed several black-and-white photos on the table. They skittered to a stop. One was of a fake train station, another of a travel poster to Barcelona, and there was one of the WELCOME sign.

Guth pointed. "See? I've tried to share."

"You also shared rather extravagant lies about your mother. You're good at deceiving people. But I'm not other people. What am I to you?"

He moved to hug her. "Darling . . ."

She backed away. "What are you burning in that place? The sky is stained orange every night. Are you burning bodies?"

"Don't be ridiculous. Jews are filthy creatures. When they arrive into camp, their clothes are teeming with lice. We give them fresh trousers and shirts and then we burn what's left over. We're burning their clothes. Their *clothes*, Jasmine."

"You say that now but how can I believe you? How can I believe anything you say?"

"Jews are filthy."

"I know that. You know that. Everyone knows that. I need to know you're telling me the truth though, especially after I've sacrificed so much by moving out here. I want to know you can trust me and that you need me and that we've got a shared life. A shared life, Hans. These these these killings . . . they're not true, are they?"

He shook his head.

"Because I'll march into the woods if I have to and if I find out you've lied to me again I'll go straight back to Berlin. *With* the kids. I'll pack our bags so fast it'll make your head spin." Her voice was full of sparks and her eyelashes were beaded with tears. "Don't think I won't. I'm sick to death of this."

As Sigi watched her parents in the mirror it felt like she was in a darkened cinema watching a color movie. That wasn't really her mother—it was a beautiful actress—but when the woman in the mirror threatened to move away, something raw and cold bristled in her chest. Would they really leave? For the first time Sigi began to wonder about Lubizec. Really wonder about it. What happened there? Was her father a bad man?

In *The Commandant's Daughter*, Sigi writes about her mother's thought process and how she could view his evasiveness as somehow worse than genocide. In a long chapter devoted to this topic, Sigi comes to the realization that her mother was obviously a terrible anti-Semite but that she also felt her husband was aloof, detached, and totally unwilling to have a shared life based on trust and openness. She was clearly unhappy in Poland, and she must have seen Guth's dancing around the truth as a convenient opening to leave him, but it wasn't necessarily what was happening in Lubizec that got her angry—it was what was happening inside her own home. This is the only way Sigi can explain how, for her mother, lying could be worse than trainloads of people being shoved into gas chambers. Although such thinking is horrible for us to hold in our imaginations, we need to remember that millions of Germans just like the Guths were more interested in what was happening in their own homes than what was happening to the Jews. Morally speaking, we have gone through the looking glass here. Black is white. White is black. Ethics have been rewritten.

"Don't lie to me, Hans. If I find out you've lied again I'm going to leave."

"Don't talk to me like this."

"I'm warning you."

"You're warning *me*? Do you know who I am?" he half shouted. "You're warning *ME*?" His whole body tightened and his mouth twisted into a volcano top. He knocked a chair aside and looked around as if a joke were being played on him. "YOU'RE WARNING *ME*?"

Sigi pushed away from the mirror, suddenly very scared. It was one of few times her father had raised his voice.

A second passed before he closed his eyes, took a deep breath, and spun his wedding ring. Around and around it went, slower and slower, until, finally, at last, he opened his eyes. There was a smile of calm. He said, "I'm sorry. I didn't mean to lose my temper."

Jasmine crossed her arms. She narrowed her eyes.

Guth walked across the carpet and reached for the overturned chair. He righted it and shuffled the photographs into a neat little pile. He tapped them onto the table like a deck of cards.

A train whistled from somewhere deep in the woods and he turned to the noise. He checked his watch and made a face. "I should get to work."

"That's right. Run away. You promised to stay home all day but that must have been a lie too."

He walked around the perimeter of the room so that he wouldn't have to cross her path. He jogged upstairs. A few minutes later he came down in his SS uniform. His jackboots clacked on the wooden floor as he reached for his officer's cap and placed it on his head as if it were a crown. He adjusted his pistol. And then, without saying a word, he patted Sigi on the cheek.

Then *SS Obersturmführer* Hans-Peter Guth marched outside and slammed the door.

— 8 —

THE ROAD TO LUBIZEC

There is of course the physical road the commandant took to Lubizec after his fight with Jasmine, the narrow dirt one that led through the forest to the camp, but there is also the long, twisting, metaphorical one, the one that began when he joined the Party in 1931. He wasn't born a serial mass murderer, but like thousands of men from his generation, he slipped into Nazism almost effortlessly. Guth was tight lipped about his early years but we do know a few things worth mentioning at this point in time.

Sigi would later say in *The Commandant's Daughter* that trying to understand her father was like "looking down a foggy road at night." Even historians would have trouble shining a light into the landscape of his youth but we do know he was born near the shipyards of Hamburg on January 1, 1900. Because of this moment of happenstance his mother often joked that he was as old as the twentieth century itself, and as he grew up so did the dizzyingly fast modern age swirling around him. Wireless telegraphy and the telephone were shrinking the world, cinematography made pictures move on a wall, cars appeared with spluttering petrol engines, homes were lit by electricity, radio antennas pulsed Morse code through the air, Joseph Lister developed antiseptic surgery, J. J. Thompson was probing the structure of the atom, an obscure German named Einstein published something called *The Foundation of the General Theory of Relativity*, and the Wright brothers built a flying machine that actually worked. Ships crossed the Atlantic at the breakneck speed of five days and subways burrowed beneath the streets like gigantic metal worms. The world had never been so full of such dazzling, awe-inspiring technological wonder.

Guth's mother spoiled him with chocolate and took him for long walks around the ritzy part of Hamburg. Trams clattered beside them as she wondered about big American cities like Chicago and New York.

"Oh my angel," she whispered, "isn't life big and pretty?"

His father was a foreman and whenever he came home from the shipyards he stank of creosote and sweat. A black mask of dust was on his father's face, and as he collapsed into a chair he snapped his fingers for a pipe. He never touched alcohol except on New Year's Eve when he allowed himself a few glasses of schnapps. He was deeply religious and made sure his sons (Wilhelm, Karl, Hans-Peter) were educated in the ways of the Roman Catholic Church. Guth's father had strong views on Jews, socialists, and anarchists. As a foreman he was used to barking out orders, so there was no room for disagreement.

Guth became an altar boy. He watched a thurible of incense get waved around the tabernacle and he listened to the old priest murmur Latin. He often wondered how bread and wine could be changed into the body and blood of Christ, because one minute it was food and the next it was something else, something holy. It was like a magic trick. And in these moments Guth wanted to be a priest so that he too might hold such secret power in his hands. He liked the idea of standing in front of a crowd and commanding them to kneel down before almighty God. He also liked the hierarchy of the Catholic Church because everyone knew their place: Priests were at the bottom, then came the bishops, then the archbishops, then the cardinals and then, at very top, was the pope. It felt militaristic and proper. Guth liked being in God's army.

Germany too was caught up in militarism when the Kaiser promised to build a navy that would make the British tremble. The shipyards of Hamburg thundered with noise as rivets were driven into steel and battleships were outfitted with monstrous guns. "They bristle like hedgehogs," the *Hamburger Zeitung* proudly stated in 1912. These ships were launched with bottles of foaming champagne, and as they slowly churned towards the North Atlantic, fireworks boomed overhead. A brass band played. People cheered. Guth forgot about the priesthood as he watched these mighty vessels go out to threaten the world.

He developed broad shoulders and his mother began calling him a "gentleman of the first order." By 1914 he was self-conscious about a mole on his neck (it was the size of a pfennig) and he wore starched collars to hide it. He was meticulous in school and his teachers noticed he always liked things done a certain way. He excelled at math. Did poorly at art. When the Great War began he ached to join his older brothers at the front, but he was only fourteen so he took it upon himself to lift weights. With luck, the war would last.

And last it did.

As Germany slogged through one bloody battle after another, and as the years ticked by in an awful stalemate, Guth finally went down to the recruiting office and lied about his age. It hardly mattered by 1917 though—they would have taken anyone with good eyesight.

He was assigned to the 112th Landwehr Division and was sent to a strangely named place called Passchendaele. He never talked about what he saw in the trenches but history tells us it was awful. Lice, maggots, rats, fleas. Everything was muddy. Trees had been blasted away. Whole towns were reduced to nothing more than skeletonized buildings and, worst of all, bodies rotted in the muddy shell-pocked waste of no-man's-land. The dead were everywhere and Guth got used to seeing hundreds of bodies scattered around him. It was normal to see torn limbs, smashed skulls, and meaty insides that had been pushed outside. When shells exploded they tossed chunks of the dead high into the air—cartwheeling—and when the British ran towards his trench he opened up his machine gun and watched them fall like stalks of wheat. He rattled out so many bullets his machine gun nearly overheated. Killing became routine. It became as normal as eating or sleeping. His brothers and friends were cut down at places like Ypres, Verdun, and the Somme. Death was sprinkled onto everything. He grew numb to it.

When the war finally ended in 1918, he trudged back to Hamburg in old soggy boots and told his mother he was finished with guns forever. He'd never shoot again, not even to hunt partridges in the forest.

But as he stared at his bitten fingernails one night he considered that it wasn't the army's fault Germany lost the war. Not at all. The army would have kept on fighting for months, maybe years, if only the people back home grew a spine and supported them. The newspapers called it an "armistice" but that wasn't the same thing as "surrender." The more he thought about this, the more he bubbled with rage. Guth slapped the kitchen table with an open palm.

"My brothers died for this? For *this*? We were stabbed in the back!"

He enrolled at the University of Hamburg shortly after this because he wanted to reinvent himself. He read books about management and administration. Dressed in a new waistcoat and hat, he thought of himself as a scholar, as an intellectual, as someone on the move. He began to feel he survived the war for some unknown reason and he sat back in a chair each night, imagining an ordered universe. A hierarchy kept things nailed into place, and it was only when order broke down, it was only then that chaos threatened to swallow everything.

He joined the Party in 1931. He liked to tell the story of how he poured himself a tall brandy and sat near the radio. It was a cold October evening and leaves were being plucked from the trees one by one. They skittered down the darkening street. He lit a cigarette, kicked off his dark shoes, and wiggled his toes. A politician was speaking. Someone named Adolf Hitler. As this Hitler spoke, slowly at first, then more loudly, Guth sat up. He nodded at the man's wisdom.

"Yes," he said. "Yes."

The universe clicked into place and two days later he put on a Nazi uniform. He snapped himself back to military attention.

Up to this point, Guth may seem like someone who got caught up in the tide of history but we should never lose sight of the fact that he became the Commandant of Lubizec. No matter how much we try to understand his background or search for clues that might point us towards the mass murderer he became, we must never forget he willingly assumed control of a death camp. True, he suffered during World War I, but he committed breathtaking crimes against humanity in World War II. We may feel a twinge of regret that he joined the Nazi Party, we may even wish he could "re-choose" a new path for himself, but in the end he made sure the trains arrived on time and he personally inspected the gas chambers each morning to make sure they were in perfect working order.

And here is one final thing to consider: Of the 710,000 souls murdered at Lubizec, virtually all of them saw Guth sometime during the last thirty minutes of their lives. This, *this*, is what he will always be remembered for. He was an architect of genocide. He devoted himself to murder. The gates of Lubizec opened wide for him and he saw not horror, but opportunity.

As he stepped across the threshold he adjusted his uniform. Clean, well fed, and straight backed, he passed under the WELCOME sign.

— 9 —

THE ROASTS

We almost get a sense that Guth was relieved to return to Lubizec because no one questioned his authority there. Inside the camp he was a god. He was sovereign. He did whatever he liked. In the Villa he had to follow certain rules and expectations, and after his big fight with Jasmine it's almost as if he decided to jettison the outside world completely and let the camp itself become his new home. This does much to explain not only why he spent increasing amounts of time at Lubizec, but it also helps us to understand why he began sleeping in his office by early September 1942.

"There's just so much to do," he told his wife over the phone.

While it is safe to assume Guth would have carried out his orders with the same enthusiasm even if he had a perfect home life, the fact that he and Jasmine were now snippy with each other should in no way overshadow or somehow explain away his crimes. Even if he had a wonderful marriage, we get a sense that Guth would have willingly dispatched thousands of lives a day. For him, home life had nothing to do with ridding the Third Reich of so-called "useless eaters" (as Jews were sometimes called). Guth threw himself into the camp. He barked out orders and wanted to know why sand hadn't been raked on the Road to Heaven, or why flowers hadn't been changed in front of the gas chamber, or why suitcases were allowed to pile up on the platform.

"Astonishing. Can't I leave this place for twenty-four fucking hours without it going to hell?"

Prisoners took off their caps and scuttled away as he passed. He demanded a tall brandy from one of his junior officers and marched into his office, where he sat down in a grand chair that had been stolen from a nearby castle. He worked at his typewriter while sunlight filtered through the window.

It would be nice to comfort ourselves with the idea that Guth looked up when the shrieking began, but that noise was so much a part of the soundscape of Lubizec that he didn't notice it. It was no more special than car horns in a city or seagulls at a beach. He simply went about his business like a grocery clerk. Goods came in. Ashes came out.

The air in his office was thick with cigarette smoke. A slide rule sat on top of a ledger and he studied a plan for a new drainage ditch. The last transport of the day had been processed and he sat back to rub his eyes. The Roasts would soon be lit and he decided to watch. He called Jasmine and told her he wouldn't be coming home.

"Don't wait up," he said. "The camp needs me."

He emerged from his office with a ledger and a sharpened pencil. His boots sank into the sandy ground. Frogs and crickets began to sing beyond the perimeter of the fence and fireflies appeared as he walked by the vegetable garden and turned left at the SS canteen. Lawn chairs were scattered around the front door. The lights were on and, through the window, he saw men lifting steins of warm beer. A phonograph was playing a song about fighting for the Fatherland.

In black we are dressed.
In blood we are drenched.
Death's head on our caps.
Ja! Ja! Ja!
We stand unshaken!

He walked up the Road to Heaven, passed through the gas chamber, and moved out through an exterior door to Camp II. Silence hung in the air and he took no notice of the prisoners who snapped off their caps as he marched past. To him they were just walking corpses. He wore leather gloves even though the evening was warm and pleasant.

There wasn't a crematorium at Lubizec because it had been decided to burn bodies in an open field just north of camp. After the daily gassings, the dead were dragged over to a wooden table where their mouths were opened with crowbars and their teeth were checked for gold fillings. The corpses, which only an hour before had been living mothers, daughters, wives, husbands, sons, nieces, nephews—all beloved human beings with a rooted place in the universe—were now just carcasses tugged across a field.

They were laid out on a grillwork of truck chassis. Five such chassis were lined up in a pit (old rail lines were later used) and the bodies were stacked head to foot in order to maximize space. Women burned better than men so they were placed at the bottom. And because fat people burned better than skinnier people, large women were placed on the very first row.

"It was like building a campfire," one guard said. "The Roasts were huge. Massive. We used to call them the Bonfires of Hell."

One would think that burning thousands of bodies a night would require a huge number of SS guards but, in fact, only a handful were needed. As with virtually every other aspect of the camp system, the Nazis forced the Jews to do their dirty work: It was prisoners who cleaned up luggage from the platform, it was prisoners who sorted clothing, it was prisoners who pulled bodies from the gas chambers, and it was prisoners who stacked their brothers and sisters into pits. We can only imagine what this was like. Again, language fails us.*

When Guth arrived that evening, the pile was already shockingly high. The whole mass of flesh had been marinated in gasoline. Fitted between the bodies were logs that had been bathed in tar. Fat people, thin people, the old, the young, teenagers, babies—they were all formed into an enormous brick of organic matter.

---

*Aside from a failure of language, there is also the problem of *wanting* to visualize the Roasts. Who wants such images in their head? Burning thousands of bodies a night is too grotesque, too obscene, too off putting. It is an assault on our sense of goodness and decency. Even though the story of the Roasts needs to be in a book like this, we instinctively want to turn away and shield our souls from such things. However, it is important to remember that massive outdoor cremations happened every night at death camps like Bełżec, Sobibór, and Treblinka. It was standard operating procedure. What follows is an accurate portrayal of how thousands of bodies were turned into dust. But how are we to reckon with such things? How?

At Guth's command, the prisoners lowered torches onto the victims' remains.

The flames licked the sky, slowly at first, but as the jumble of heads and arms and torsos began to blacken, odd colors like green and purple, mustard yellow, and gaseous blood shimmered into the night. Pyrolysis. Chemiluminescence. Oxidation. Incandescence. The whole pit began to shake with roaring heat.

Everybody stood back.

There were four such pits at Lubizec and they were each built at a slight angle so that, as the bodies burned, a steady stream of human fat might leak into the lowest corner. When it looked like the fire might need more fuel, the prisoners were ordered to scoop up this liquid fat with a smelting ladle and toss it back into the fire. The Roasts often burned deep into the morning but Guth tried to avoid this because the smudgy black smoke made the new arrivals nervous.

When Dov Damiel was interviewed about this in 1977, he said it was nightmare work. Demonic. They had to drag corpses over to the blazing pyre and it was common to see bodies move and twitch as muscles began to contort. When he mentions this in the interview, he stares at the floor and clears his throat.

"The dead, they look like they were rising back to life. Sometimes their mouths begin to open and . . . and the sexual organs of men . . . their penises they grow bigger as blood superheats inside their members. At the top of the pile, the bodies they sometimes sit up as they curl into the fires. It was horrible. Horrible. I will never forget the Roasts. Ever."

The SS watched all of this with great amusement. They pointed at bodies that were twisting in strange ways and they drank vodka, or port, or whatever else they could lay their hands on, and Guth allowed this to happen because it made the "necessary work" easier. Laughter filled the air as the guards got drunk and fired guns into the blazing hellfire mass of human flesh. Livers, stomachs, diaphragms, windpipes, kidneys, elbows, gallstones, bunions, tongues, ovaries, fingers, wombs, eyes, pinky toes, bellybuttons, and hearts, it all went up in flame. Little bits of the universe perished and we are still trying to understand what this means even today.

Guth stood a few paces back and took notes, which was easy to do because the fire was so intense, so bright. Shadows danced around and sparks floated up until they mingled with the stars.

The smoke was dark, like used motor oil, and granular ash swirled around everyone. Guth took off his cap and wiped sweat from his brow as the landscape baked in invisible waves of heat. The stars blurred as if underwater and a horrible crackling filled up the night as teeth exploded like popcorn. The sky became an ugly burnt copper and still the bodies continued to glow.

"If you closed your eyes," Dov Damiel said, "it sounded like rain, like heavy rain falling on a street."

In the interview there is a long pause. The camera pans in on Damiel's face.

"After the first day I worked the Roasts, I had trouble eating. I kept looking at my hands, these hands, and thinking about the dead I touched. Sometimes, sometimes I am eating an apple or pear today and I think of the dead. I see them as if it happened an hour ago. My hands, they have touched such horrible things."

Another pause. The camera comes in closer still.

"At the Roasts it was impossible to take a breath and not also take in the atoms of the dead. Their ash and smoke went down my throat. They filled up my lungs and made me cough. They coated my tongue. I would spit, and I could taste them. How can human beings do such things to each other? I ask you. Where was God on these nights?"

Among the SS that night was Heinrich Niemann, that giant of a man who beat Hanel Wallach for refusing to give up her son. He had already drained one bottle of vodka and he was on the prowl for more. His speech was slurred and he stumbled around as more bodies were dragged over to the fire. One new prisoner, someone who hadn't yet gotten used to the casual brutality of Lubizec, moved slowly, too slowly. He held the corpse of a woman. He carried her body as if he were a groom ready to bring her across the threshold of a new life. Her body was slack in his arms, but he kept kissing her shaved head. It was his wife. They had been separated in the Rose Garden a few hours earlier and now, at the edge of the Roasts, he finally found her again. He stumbled forward with tears streaming down his face.

"Oh my honeybee. My honeybee," he said. The man walked up to the guards and began to sob. "How can you do this to her?"

"I'll show you," Niemann said, and he pushed the man into the fire.

A shriek lifted up as the man scrambled over the body of his wife. His clothes became a wick and he screeched and screeched as he pulled himself out of the pit. He ran like a torch towards the woods. The grass began to catch on fire and that's when the SS got nervous because he might burn down the whole field. One of the guards aimed his pistol but missed because he was too drunk. There was another shot, but still the prisoner was screeching out in agony. A final shot hit home and the flaming body dropped. It stopped moving.

Guth wrote something down in his ledger. The flames licked higher and higher as he nodded to the remaining bodies.

"Faster," he said. "Faster."

The moon swung in its tethered orbit across the sky and still the Roasts continued to burn.

The four pits at Lubizec were rotated so that one of them was always in use. After one pile of beloved flesh was torched, the remains were allowed to cool until, like an old campfire with wisps of smoke coming off it, the ashy leftovers could be sifted. Prisoners scooped bucketfuls of debris and dumped them into giant sieves in order to find bones that needed extra attention. Guth wanted only ash left over—no bones. He was very clear about this. It was for this reason the prisoners used steel mallets to hammer down bits of skull, ribs, and femurs. Pelvis bones had to be pounded down because they were so dense. The prisoners used an anvil and they pulverized the remains until there was nothing left but dust. Occasionally they found a diamond that had been swallowed by a victim in the wild hope it might remain hidden in their stomach, but such things were always found during the sifting process. In this way, nothing was allowed to escape Lubizec. Nothing.

When the ash was so fine it looked like it had been tipped out of a cigarette tray, only then was it carted away in a dump truck. The powder was scattered into a pond. Thousands upon thousands of lives were reduced to nothing more than dust flittering down through water. Whole generations coated the rocks at the bottom. Algae turned gray because there was so much ash, but this too was about to change, especially when Guth realized the cremains could be used as fertilizer. He sold ash to local farmers (not telling them what it was) and he invested the money back into the camp itself. He got potbelly stoves because winter was on its way and he didn't want his guards to get cold. He also bought them a movie projector and a ping-pong table.

Dov Damiel, Chaim Zischer, and the other prisoners watched all of this in numb horror and vowed to tell the world about it somehow, someday. What they couldn't have known is that their lives were about to take a strange new turn.

Things at Lubizec were finally about to change.

10

OLD SHATTERHAND

In Jasmine's unpublished diary, she writes about Berlin before the war and how the shops were always packed with people, how cafés on Unter den Linden stayed open until sunrise, and how everyone strolled around the parks at dusk. Cigarettes and pipes flared to life in the growing darkness. She enjoyed watching blue sparks fly off the trolley cars and she especially enjoyed shopping with friends and ending up at some wild party in the back of a restaurant. True, she didn't miss hearing gunshots in the middle of the night, nor did she miss covering the phone with a heavy blanket when it wasn't in use; there were rumors buzzing around of men planting devices in phones and, because of this, you had to be careful about what you said in your own home. Of course *she* never said a bad word about the Party, but it was still alarming to think that another ear might be listening into your conversation. And whenever the SA had yet another parade down the street, you had to stop and give the Hitler salute or risk being beaten.

These however were just tiny annoyances and Jasmine was mostly delighted with "the New Germany," as she called it. She liked how blackened swastikas marched down the street in huge banners of red and she also liked how her country—*her* country—was becoming a world power once again. She particularly enjoyed the 1936 Olympics and how the city was buffed clean for tourists who came from Europe, America, and Asia. It was nice to have them in Berlin but, since they weren't exactly German, it was equally nice to watch them leave.*

---

*Of the 1936 Olympics in Berlin, Jasmine writes in her diary that the "American black, Jesse Owens, stole 4 gold medals from us in the 100 meters, 200 meters, long jump, and 4x100 meter relay. It's unfair. You might as well have deer or gazelle on your team."

She believed Hitler was a great man and agreed with his policies about the Jews ("pests can't live in our house," she found herself saying at a party), although she couldn't understand why some women went absolutely mad for Hitler. She saw delirious young women scoop up dirt he had recently walked upon and she saw them place it with trembling hands into metal containers. They kissed it as if it were a holy object. They cried. They wept. One woman pulled out clumps of her hair she was so ecstatic. He was a great man, yes, but it seemed a bit odd, a bit too much really, to treat him like a prophet or a demigod. The Führer was just a man—a man with wonderful ideas about Germany's future to be sure, but a man nonetheless.

Jasmine met Guth at a raucous, wild, over-the-top party on Unter den Linden and she was immediately drawn to his good looks and his SS uniform. She also liked how he couldn't say where he worked. There was an air of mystery about him.

"What do you do?" she asked while sipping a martini.

"Reich's business."

"*What*, though?"

A slow smile. "Reich's business."

They kept on talking until he kissed her wrist and placed his SS hat on her head. They went someplace even louder and then, after that, a place where champagne flowed and someone banged out bright tunes on a piano. There was an enormous swastika cake made out of marzipan and it was circled by huge wet strawberries, the largest ones Jasmine had ever seen. Trumpets blared out and women danced around with long strings of pearls. They talked until the sun came up and then stepped over people who had crashed out on the dance floor. They grabbed a bottle of champagne and moved out into the pale morning light. They held hands and walked along the river, where she wore his SS hat at a jaunty angle. She liked feeling his eyes on her when she looked away.

When Guth was sent to Poland, it felt like they had been banished to some hinterland because there were no parties, no piano bars, and no new restaurants to discover. Lubizec was a tiny village in a dense forest of nothingness. It was like living on a lost continent. Oh sure, there were a few lakes to paddle around but it was dull and boring. Humdrum. Tedious. Try as she might, she just couldn't understand why her husband had been exiled to such a dead place. What had he done wrong? Why was he running a transit camp for Jews?

These are just some of the questions in Jasmine's diary. She clearly enjoyed having a large home on a private lake, and she also enjoyed having a servant jump whenever she rang a little brass fingerbell, but in reading her choppy handwriting, it becomes clear that she was losing patience with both Guth's evasiveness and her new station in life. She missed Berlin and her extended family. She missed the hustle-bustle. She also had a problem with state secrets driving a wedge between them and she wanted to discover the truth about Lubizec because, if she could just find out what was really going on, maybe she could use it as an excuse to go home.

"This is the last straw," she envisioned herself saying. "I'm going back to Berlin."

As the days ticked by, ideas boiled in her head. Did he really love her? Was he capable of sharing his life with her? Maybe he was having an affair? He sure didn't seem very interested in her sexually any more.

Although there are many reasons why she might have decided to find out about Lubizec once and for all, what we can say with absolute certainty is this: What she does on September 8, 1942, is both unexpected and startling. It will change her family.

It began when she woke up and reached beneath the duvet for her husband. He wasn't there (again) and his side of the bed was cold (again). As she dressed in front of the large bay window, turning this way and that to admire her reflection, she looked at the lake and found herself thinking about the camp. It was out there somewhere, like a dark magnet, and her eyes searched the treetops, wondering about it. The sky was hazy.

She put on an old pair of hiking boots and moved down the grand wooden staircase, where she reached for a hunting cap. She twisted her bronze hair into a bun, went into the dining room, and began rummaging around in a drawer.

Karl was busy playing with a tin model of Hitler. He placed the Führer in a shoe and pretended to drive him towards a frontline of matchboxes. Sigi was reading another book about Old Shatterhand, but when she saw her mother in a man's cap and weeding through drawers for something, she used her finger as a bookmark and looked up.

"Here they are," Jasmine announced to herself. She slid a pair of opera glasses into a leather satchel and turned to the maid, who, at that moment, happened to be bringing in an armful of logs.

Jasmine's voice was stern and businesslike. "Watch the children for me, Malina. I'll be gone for a few hours."

Sigi put down her book. "Can I come?"

Jasmine kept speaking to the maid. "Don't forget to clean the windows and get those apples cored."

The country girl let the logs tumble into an iron grate. Bits of bark fell on the carpet and she bent down to sweep them up.

"Can I come?" Sigi asked again.

"No," Jasmine said, without looking at her. The air curdled as she moved down the dark hallway and slammed the front door. A string of decorative bells jiggled into silence.

Sigi touched an eyelet on her hiking boot. Why was her mother dressed so strangely and how come she needed opera glasses? What would Old Shatterhand do if he saw such a thing?

Without thinking about it, Sigi tied her laces and slipped out the front door so quietly the bells hardly jiggled. At the far end of the cinder driveway, her mother was pushing into the woods.

Sigi followed. She ran on her tiptoes like an Indian scout.

Sunlight got caught in a cathedral of branches. It was murky and Jasmine threaded her way through the trunks, stopping now and then to look at a compass. Her feet stepped around pinecones and large stones. She knew roughly where the camp was supposed to be and she decided to circle around to the north. It was dangerous to approach Lubizec and she was reminded of this when she saw a large wooden sign nailed to a tree. It had a skull on it along with the words, DANGER! REICH ZONE OF INTEREST. TRESPASSERS WILL BE <u>SHOT</u>! The angry eyesockets of the skull made Jasmine look around.

She thought about turning around but what purpose would that serve? She would only be back where she started, and if she told her husband she was coming to see the camp, he'd only try to stop her. No, it was best to approach the camp and pull out her opera glasses. She'd get close enough for a quick peek and then run home. If it was a transit camp she could put the matter to rest, but if it wasn't a transit camp—if it was something else—well—she'd cross that bridge when she came to it.

Jasmine studied the skull for a long moment and wondered if the guards would really shoot her. There were so many trees around it seemed impossible that a bullet could hit her from a long distance, but it was still an ugly thought. It made her shudder. What would it be like to have metal come through your chest?

She looked at her hiking boots and rolled a pinecone beneath her toe.

A robin sang from somewhere overhead and, in that moment of gentle peace, she stepped over an invisible line. She put one foot in front of the other and moved beyond the wooden sign. It felt like she was crossing a border.

It was strange to look at the ground for twigs that might snap beneath her weight, and it was stranger still to wonder if her sternum was in the crosshairs of a riflescope, but she took off her cap and let down her long curly hair. It tumbled over her shoulders. Cobwebs would get caught in the strands but surely they wouldn't shoot a woman, especially not a good German woman with bronze hair and blue eyes. They'd see that in a riflescope surely.

Jasmine kept walking. Slowly. Carefully. Watchfully.

When she slapped a mosquito, the sound seemed too loud, too noisy, but she didn't like the idea of a bloodsucking needle sinking into her skin.

"My God," she whispered. "I left Berlin for this?"

The little compass needle bobbled in her hand as she walked to the northwest. A terrible smell clawed at the back of her throat—it was campfire and something else—bacon fat—rancid butter—burnt fish. She covered her mouth and kept on moving through matted leaves and twigs. Shafts of sunlight pierced the air and the wind whooshed overhead, making the branches creak. There was another sign, one that had the twin lightning bolts of the SS. It read, in white paint, RETREAT OR DIE.

An engine was running up ahead. It sounded like someone was using a gigantic typewriter. It revved into a higher gear and a whiff of gasoline floated on the wind.

She stepped closer. It felt like she was on a tightrope. Gently, gently. One step, another step. Easy now.

She saw a wall of barbed wire and every hundred meters or so there was a guard tower. Each one stood on four legs and the guards had machine guns slung over their shoulders as if they were backpacks. Each tower had searchlight. A sharp terror made Jasmine's muscles coil into hyperawareness and every atom in her body felt like it was being pulled away from the camp, like some kind of magnetism tugged at her to run away, but slowly, very slowly, she crouched down and lay behind a tree. The wind rocked the leaves overhead and the engine—wherever it was—continued to thrum. Cicadas were screaming up ahead.

She reached into her satchel and noticed that her hands were shaking. The ground was cold against her chest and she brought the opera glasses up to her face.

So there it is, she almost said out loud.

Everything was in a jerky circle of vision in her hands and she saw that the guards faced in, towards the camp, as if they were busy watching the inmates. They seemed more concerned with what happened inside Lubizec than what happened outside it. Maybe if they heard something in the woods, they'd assume it was a deer or a falling branch? Jasmine couldn't be sure, but beyond the silvery threads of barbed wire, she noticed what looked like men running around in ratty shirts and trousers. Each of them dragged something slender and rubbery behind them. It was hard to see what they were tugging through the grass but each of them moved quickly and they dashed back to a large wooden shed in an endless circle of work.

She lowered the glasses.

Jasmine breathed heavily and thought about running away, but if she did that now she wouldn't be any wiser about what lay beyond the barbed wire. Was it a transit camp or a prison?

She brought the glasses back up to her eyes and studied the guards. They still had their backs to her.

Good, she thought. *Good*.

Barbed wire had been coiled around the ancient trees and the entire perimeter of the camp was made up of living trunks rather than posts that had been pounded into the ground. It must have been her husband's idea. It had his hallmark because it was so practical, so handy. Why put in huge wooden posts when barbed wire can just be wrapped around existing trees?

She also noticed a sign, and what it said made her blood turn cold.
DANGER MINEFIELD.

She looked at the ground beneath her rib cage and wondered if explosives were hidden in the earth. Was she lying on something right now? If she stood up, what would happen?

She searched for signs of digging—little mounds of dirt or disturbed pine needles—anything—because if she rolled over or stood up or coughed, maybe something a few centimeters down in the earth would click and this would send wet pieces of her body flying up into the trees.

As she thought about these unpleasant things and carried on a mental conversation with herself about how stupid she was, one of the guards began yelling. He was in a dark uniform and he ran across the field with a rubber truncheon. He began beating one of the prisoners and the man let out a terrible scream. The rod became a blur as he beat the man harder and harder. Spouts of red flew into the air. The other prisoners kept on dragging their loads but Jasmine still couldn't tell what they were pulling. Sandbags maybe?

She looked at the face of the guard through her opera glasses and recognized him as Heinrich Niemann. He came to the Villa one evening for dinner and made crude jokes all night long. He swilled two bottles of red wine and stuffed massive forkfuls of sausage and potato into his mouth. She made the mistake of wearing a low-cut dress that evening and whenever she bent over for anything he stared at her breasts.

"He's a good soldier," Guth later said.

And now this good soldier was cleaning his rubber truncheon with the hat of the man he had just beaten. He stopped to light a cigarette and looked out at the trees. Jasmine froze. She didn't drop the opera glasses or make any sudden movements because she didn't want to draw his attention. Niemann blew smoke out of his nose, dragonlike. From somewhere inside the camp a pistol went off. There was another shot. Niemann twirled his shoulder as if he were working out a kink or a sore muscle and he strolled away, blowing plumes of smoke into the air.

Jasmine sighed with relief and turned to the other prisoners. What on earth were they tugging across the grass? It looked like—

She lowered her opera glasses and felt something icy crawl up her spine. Slowly, almost against her will, she brought the glasses back up to her face.

The bodies were naked, many of them were bruised, and the women didn't have any hair. She didn't understand any of it. She squinted at what she thought was a huge pile of wood and let her eyes refocus. It was—arms, legs, heads, feet—it was a compressed jigsaw puzzle of flesh. A truck appeared from around the corner and, as it bumped over the uneven ground, sheets of ash flickered down. The wind caught this fine powder and it drifted away.

Her heart filled up with magma when she thought about her husband coming home with his fabricated stories about this place being a transit camp. She didn't know what was happening in Lubizec but she knew this much: He had lied once again.

Jasmine became a capped geyser of heat and she wanted to run away from the camp as fast as she could, not because she was disgusted by a truckload of human ash or the sight of prisoners being beaten, but because she was furious with her husband. Before we address this monumental failure of empathy, it needs to be said that something happened in that moment which made Jasmine wide eyed with terror. There was a loud crack behind her and she turned towards the noise.

Was it a guard? A falling branch?

Her eyes moved back and forth. She didn't see anything. And then Sigi stepped out from behind a birch tree and tiptoed forward as if she were in an adventure story. She carried a stick and looked around as if she were hunting bears. Jasmine wanted to run to her daughter but she glanced at the guard towers. She also thought about that sign, the one that read, DANGER MINEFIELD. She stood up, slowly. She waved an arm, which caught Sigi's attention, and the girl in hiking boots stopped walking.

Time became a syrup that Jasmine had to wade through as she crept for her daughter. She expected a bullet to flash through the air at any moment or maybe there would be a tremendous eruption of dirt and her daughter would be blasted up into the trees. It crossed her mind that if they were spotted by the guards, maybe she could raise her arms and say that she was Guth's wife. Could she yell such a thing before they started shooting with their machine guns?

When she finally reached Sigi they tiptoed through the dense trees, and when they were far enough away from the camp, they broke into a mad run. Their legs pumped hard and they gulped in air. Jasmine pulled Sigi up a muddy hill and they slid down the other side. Leaves got stuck in their hair. Burrs attached to their trousers. They jumped over small rocks and scratched their arms on thorny bushes. They ran and ran and ran until they reached a golden wheatfield. Only then did they stop.

They bent over and grabbed their kneecaps. They panted. The sun felt good on their skin as they wheezed in air.

The fear inside Jasmine crystallized into anger and she slapped her daughter across the face. Hard. "That was *stupid* to follow me."

Sigi nodded, surprised that she had been hit. She rubbed her cheek and backed away.

They began walking down a dirt road and the sound of their boots fell into a steady rhythm. Dust floated up from their heels. They examined the nicks and cuts on their forearms.

When they reached a little vegetable market, Jasmine added, "You've been reading too many of those damn adventure novels."

Sigi nodded.

"Do you have any idea how dangerous that was?"

"*You* went."

Jasmine stopped walking. "I'm the adult here and I had my reasons." She pointed a finger at her daughter. "Don't go near that place again. You hear me?"

There was a nod and they continued down the sun-drenched dirt road towards home. It was a beautiful afternoon, the farmers were in the fields, and soon Jasmine and Sigi turned up the long cinder driveway for their house. Lilac bushes lined the way and a bee hummed through the air, its wings moving so fast it looked like a bead of water was boiling on its back.

Jasmine patted her trousers and realized—"Damn it"—she'd dropped the opera glasses and her hat somewhere.

"What's wrong?"

Jasmine's voice was soft. "Nothing. Everything's fine now. I'm, I'm sorry I slapped you. That was wrong of me."

They went inside and called out to Malina, the maid, for some blueberry juice. Sigi kicked off her hiking boots and walked down the hallway, dragging her fingertips against the oak walls as she went. The patio door was open and a breeze lifted the curtains. They billowed like sails.

Sigi flopped into a chair and reached for *Old Shatterhand*. She tugged out a leather bookmark that was embossed with the word, *Jungmädelbund*. Seeing it, Jasmine remembered how much Sigi enjoyed her meetings back in Berlin. The "Young Girls League" met twice a week and it was associated with the Hitler Youth. They wore long black dresses, white shirts, and they had kerchiefs with an enamel swastika pin. Most of the girls had pigtails and they went on long hikes in the woods. They sang songs. It made Jasmine miss

Berlin all the more. She strolled over to the bookcase and pulled out a souvenir program for the 1936 Olympic Games.

Mother and daughter sat like that for a few minutes, each absorbed in a world they would rather live in.

Jasmine looked at the book in her daughter's hands. Old Shatterhand wore a bearskin robe and stood on a plateau that over-looked a thickly treed valley. In the distance, smoke threaded its way up to the sky. Old Shatterhand seemed to be saying to the reader, *Let's go into the woods. Let's explore.*

"Listen to me," Jasmine said. "I don't want you going near that camp again. In fact, I don't want you leaving this house without asking me."

Sigi rolled her eyes but when she saw the look on her mother's face, she nodded.

Malina came in with two glasses of blueberry juice but Jasmine waved off her glass and went to the drinks cabinet instead. She poured herself a three-fingered brandy and sat near the fireplace. Her mind wandered back to Berlin. She thought about the blue sparks flying off trolley cars, and busy cafés, and cute shops full of interesting people. There was so much to do, so much to see.

She looked down at her wedding ring. It suddenly felt heavy and tight.

11

WHILE OTHERS STEP INTO THE DARKNESS

Guth didn't come home that night even though Jasmine waited up and looked through old photos of happier times. The moon was a pale coin in the sky as she sipped brandy and seltzer water. She wasn't drunk, but she was mellow. The kids had been tucked into bed ages ago and Jasmine sat in a frilly pink nightgown carrying on an imaginary conversation with her husband. She used words like *marriage* and *trust* and *together*. At no time did she gaze out the window and look at a sky stained dark orange with fire. It had become so commonplace that she merely lit some lavender candles out of habit and went back to her photos.

"Transit camp," she grunted.

She slapped the album shut and stared at her painted toenails. *Now what?* she wondered.

Malina was already preparing a breakfast of fruit and yoghurt when Jasmine came downstairs the next morning. The stove needed a good cleaning and she ordered the young woman to scrub it "until it shined like a mirror." Jasmine then went into the front hallway for the telephone. Her shoes clicked on the wooden floor as she picked up the black receiver. The cord was twisted. She dialed her husband's number and heard the phone ring once, twice, three times.

"Guth here."

She had been practicing the speech all morning and the words just poured out like a faucet. Her voice was clear and she nodded at the end of each sentence.

"Listen to what I am about to say, Hans. I am going to drive to your camp. I will be there in five minutes. I would appreciate it if your guards did not shoot me. I will honk the horn as I approach." She took a sharp breath and enjoyed taking the power back. She added, almost as an afterthought, "I'll be there soon. We need to talk."

She hung up before he could answer.

Jasmine pinned a red hat to her hair and shut the door, gently. The phone rang from inside the house but she marched across the cinder driveway and got into her Mercedes. She adjusted the rear-view mirror and watched a plume of blue exhaust lift up. The steering wheel felt good in her hands (it gave her power and direction) and when she pressed on the gas pedal, tiny stones pinged off the undercarriage.

She drove past the village church and the old ladies selling their vegetables. Horses clopped through town and groups of men waited at the train station in huddled black forms. Swastikas dripped down the front of a library and she climbed a low hill towards the camp. A wooden sign announced she was entering a REICH ZONE OF INTEREST but there were no guards on duty and the little dirt road bumped along through a haze of honeyed light. The morning sun stumbled through the trees.

She didn't slow down and she didn't care if the shocks were damaged on the chassis. It felt good to hit potholes at full speed and to feel the ruts grab ahold of the steering wheel. The car bounced along, enormous clouds of dust lifted up behind her, and when a corner came she took it sharply—it gave her a thrill to feel the back end slide out—but she righted the car just in time and began practicing the second part of her speech. Murmured words came to her as she glanced at herself in the rearview mirror.

There was something up ahead and she took her foot off the gas. "What's this?"

It was another Mercedes parked sideways in the road, forcing her to stop. Her husband was leaning against the front fender and smoking a cigarette as if he had all the time in the world. Two tiny swastika flags were on the chrome headlamps and the whole car was buffed to a high black shine. When her tires finally stopped rolling, he flicked his cigarette on the dirt road and came towards her with open arms.

"Darling," he said.

He wore a silver wristwatch that she'd never seen before and his hair was cut much shorter than usual. Although there were bags under his eyes he looked alert and awake. When he kissed her on the cheek she could smell coffee on his breath.

"What a nice surprise," he added. "Sorry I've been so busy at work."

He lit yet another cigarette and seemed like an actor playing a part. There was something uncanny about him because he was her husband and yet, at the same time, he wasn't quite the man she married. Being this close to the camp made him somehow different, somehow changed. Metamorphosed. He glided on power and spoke to her like a king speaking to his court.

"While it's good to see you darling, turn that car of yours around and go home," he said shooing her away. "You can't be here. We've talked about this."

Two gunshots came from the woods. She glanced at the noise but Guth never took his eyes off her.

"Darling. Did you hear me?"

She kept looking into the trees.

"Jasmine."

The sound of her name brought her back to the dirt road and she felt pebbly stones beneath her heels. She took a step forward and let the memorized lines of her speech roll off her tongue.

"You lied to me again, Hans. That's no transit camp. You're burning people in there."

"No. We're burning *Jews* in there."

"You need to—"

"My dear, this place doesn't officially exist. Do you understand what I'm saying? You don't get to drive up for a visit and you definitely do *not* get to ask me about it. What happens here can never be known to the outside world. And that . . . includes . . .

you." His eyes narrowed to slits. He stared at her and then added, with a smile, "Now get into your car and drive home. This place is beyond you."

We want Jasmine to be outraged that her husband is killing people on an industrialized scale, but instead she is angry that Guth is totally disinterested in the two of them being a married couple. She wants a shared life but he is distant, aloof, and slippery. While she may have qualms about "burning people" in Lubizec and perhaps she is a little nervous about how the place has changed him, her anti-Semitism blots out any possibility that a monstrous crime is being committed. We should note that it isn't the killing that bothers her—it's the burning of corpses. How the corpses came into existence hasn't crossed her mind yet. This is why she can say, "You're burning people in there" and not, "You're *killing* people in there." It is an alarming gap in her thinking.

We only know about this conversation because of her unpublished diary. In it, her words are choppy and full of exclamation points. She is angry that Guth didn't mention his mother's death in the air raid sooner, and we also learn about her frustration that she is "marooned in terrible Poland!!!"

At no time does she wonder about the thousands of people murdered at Lubizec, and this makes reading Jasmine's diary obscene. She outlines her confrontation with Guth in great detail, yet we know little about what happened in Lubizec during this same period of time. Put another way, we have a very clear picture of September 8 and 9, 1942, but it focuses exclusively on a rocky marriage. Of the estimated 6,200 souls that were murdered during this same forty-eight-hour period of time, we have nothing. It is a blank. While thousands of others stepped into the darkness, Guth and Jasmine quarreled, and it is this quarrel that takes up space when we consider September 8 and 9 in the history of the camp. This is the banality of genocide: that everyday life is allowed to go on and murder becomes just background scenery.

As Jasmine states in her diary, she stared at Guth for "a long hard time on that road until he blurred into double vision."

Her husband eventually turned away and reached for something in the backseat of his car.

"Presents for the kids," he said, pulling out a child's suitcase. He came over and placed it on the hood of her car. The latches sprang open and he pulled out a toy airplane, a dented gold bracelet, and a camera.

"Where'd you get this stuff?"

Guth shrugged as if to say, *It dropped into my lap.* He leaned in to kiss her but she stepped back.

"We really need to talk, Hans."

"No. *You* need to go home," he said pleasantly, while walking back to his car. He paused and snapped his fingers. "By the way, my men walked the perimeter of the camp last night searching for . . . oh, I don't know . . . anything suspicious. They found these."

He tossed a pair of opera glasses to her and she caught them, clumsily.

"They look like yours."

"No. They aren't."

"They also found this." He held up a hunting cap. "It's strange, but it looks just like mine. How did it get in the forest next to your opera glasses, I wonder?"

"I have no idea."

He dropped his cigarette and scrunched it beneath his boot. He looked up and smiled. "Now who's lying, Jasmine? Look, be a good wife and go home. Stay away. This place is beyond you."

A train huffed in the distance and a curl of smoke lifted up from the trees.

"I have to go," he said, walking around the snout of his car. His shadow stretched across the chrome headlights.

"I'm leaving. For Berlin," she blurted out. "I'm taking the kids with me."

Something caught his eye and he pulled out a pure white hand-kerchief. He spat on it and began rubbing. Jasmine watched this and realized he was buffing bird shit off one of the car windows. He rubbed and rubbed. He spat and continued erasing the little spot that annoyed him. The train blasted its whistle and the engine grunted to life. Guth didn't notice the jet of black soot rising up into the sky, nor did he see birds wheeling away in a peppery sprinkle. His whole body was focused on his Mercedes. He kept rubbing and rubbing.

"Berlin. I mean it," Jasmine yelled over the approaching train. "We're leaving tonight."

The train came closer. The engine gathered speed. Fifteen wooden cars were pulled behind, and each one of them had arms sticking out of barb-wired openings. A face floated up in one of the windows and sank away. There were screams for help, screams for water and, as these 1,700 souls traveled down a final kilometer of greased rail, husband and wife said nothing more to each other. They got into their cars and turned in opposite directions. Huge clouds of dust were left in their wakes.

A minute later, the forest was silent again. The circling birds settled back onto the trees. Dust settled back onto the road.

It was as if nothing had happened. Nothing at all.

— 12 —

ZURICH

Jasmine took her children and drove up to Lublin the next morning, where they caught a train to Warsaw and then, from there, an express to Berlin. When Guth found out about it, he calmly told her to return home, immediately. She refused and said that if he wanted to talk about the matter further she'd be at her parents' house in the district of Charlottenburg. They came from good money and they had a huge stockpile of tinned food, jam, sugar, and flour. She wasn't going anywhere. She was hunkering down with people that she loved.

When she hung up, Guth stood beside his desk and stared out the window. A breeze kicked up some leaves and they skittered away in a small tornado of wind. He replaced the telephone in its holder and snapped wrinkles out of his uniform. He had other problems to deal with. Rather large problems, as it turned out.

The machinery of the camp moved along with unstoppable terror and the killing took on a rushed, frantic schedule all its own. It didn't matter if it was blazing hot or if a thunderstorm crackled overhead—the timetable of murder never changed and Guth had gotten used to it. He liked how predictable everything was. It made him feel calm. Soon a week passed without his family, then two weeks, then three, and he adapted to life without them. He let Lubizec absorb him so completely that he began to sit in his office thinking up new ways to streamline the slaughter and make everything more cost effective. Even though Guth was a skilled bureaucrat who snuffed out innocent life, and even though he was responsible for implementing the Final Solution with no moral qualms whatsoever, his superiors in Lublin and Berlin began to ask questions about his leadership. It had nothing to do with the gas chambers or the number of Jews he was killing—not at all—not that. It had to do with a small area of camp we have not talked about yet.

"Zurich" was located in Camp I and it was made up of eight long, wooden barracks surrounded by barbed wire. On each door were painted signs that either read *Bekleidungslager* or *Effektenlager*, but no one ever used these labels. Each barrack was stuffed with items stolen from the transports and it all needed to be sorted and tallied before being sent on to Berlin. One barrack held nothing but folded trousers and jackets. Another held nothing but shoes, thousands and thousands of shoes. It was possible to walk into one barrack and see piles of jewelry as tall as a desk, as well as barrels full of wedding rings. There was an enormous pile of glasses in one barrack because, if someone entered Lubizec with poor eyesight, they were, as a rule, immediately sent to the gas chambers. It made no sense to have prisoners bumbling around in the rain if they couldn't see properly, and the guards quickly realized that hitting a prisoner on the head often resulted in eyewear flying off and breaking anyway. Why save someone with poor eyesight when they were only going to be a burden later on? It was therefore decided that no Jew with glasses would ever be saved at Lubizec. As a result of this camp law, there were now so many glasses that Guth had them stored in a barrack until he could figure out what to do with them all. There were also thousands of wallets, purses, and photographs. The guards called this area of camp Zurich because it was like walking into a Swiss bank. Anything you could possibly want was there: clothes, booze, hats, watches, gold, silverware, money, diamonds. It was a place of unlimited wealth.*

Thanks to Chaim Zischer's book, *The Hell of Lubizec*, we know a surprising amount about this area of camp, as well as many of the guards. Names like Rudolf Oberhauser, Christian Schwartz, Sebastian Schemise, Gustav Wagner, and Heinrich Niemann have

---

* Other death camps had similar such stockpiles. These heartbreaking warehouses become inevitable when you murder thousands of people a day (final possessions have to be stored somewhere). Auschwitz, of course, was the largest and most infamous. The huge barracks there were called "Canada." They were the size of several football fields.

become synonymous with the brutality of the place. Zischer's role as a dentist (that is, a prisoner who extracted gold teeth from the dead) meant that he was under the command of *Unterscharführer* Peter Franz, who was called "Birdie" because he had the odd habit of saying, "I've got you now, birdie," before shooting a prisoner in the head. He ordered them to lie on the ground with their faces turned away and then he pointed his pistol at that little spot above the ear. Before he fired he always said that phrase, "I've got you now, birdie." It had become such a scripted line that other guards would often ask him, "How many today?" Birdie would hold up three fingers or maybe seven to show his tally.

"He was short," Zischer says in his book. "His eyes were hard green marbles and you didn't want his attention for too long because you might hear that dreaded phrase, 'I've got you now, birdie.' Then it was off to the Roasts with you."

Things that made Birdie angry ranged from stealing, to yawning, to slapping mosquitoes, to having your tummy rumble, to needing the toilet, to hiccupping, to passing wind, to wearing a watch. Any one of these infractions could make him bring out his pistol and then a prisoner would hear that phrase, "I've got you now, birdie."

Peter Franz was directly responsible for the murder of hundreds of prisoners. Maybe thousands. He was also in charge of Zurich and it was his job to make sure everything was sorted, labeled, weighed, boxed, catalogued, tracked, and placed onto railcars. Faceless men in the halls of Berlin seemed to think the amount of gold and money had gone down at Lubizec even though the number of transports had gone up. They wanted to know why profits had declined when traffic into the camp had become so brisk.

A stern letter was written telling Guth that his guards were under investigation and that special attention would be given to Peter Franz. It was made known that an SS judge was on his way to Lubizec. A review was going to be carried out but the letter also stated that "under no circumstances should the resettlement of the Jews slow or stop. The primary function of your camp must continue while the secondary, more economical function, is under scrutiny."

Guth was furious.

After yet another transport of human beings had been turned into a truckload of ash, he ordered his men into the Rose Garden and snapped them to attention. This was designed to knock them off balance because this was where the Jews were ordered to separate; it was a place where husbands and wives were torn apart, it was place of shrieking violence. Above all else, it was a place where the SS were in total control but, now, Guth made them stand there, uneasy and scrutinized.

Dov Damiel was stunned to see his tormentors fixed at such attention. He worked all the harder because forty guards were watching his every move.

"It was terrifying," he later said. "Guth lined them up in the Rose Garden and I had never seen such a thing. It was like he was reminding them who was the chief bully at Lubizec. He was saying, 'This is my camp.' He was saying that everyone, Jew and gentile alike, was under his fist. No one was allowed to disobey him."

Guth paced. He said nothing at first but then he started shouting.

"I mean really shouting," Dov Damiel said in a 1977 interview. "We had never heard him shout before. No one had. His whole face, it becomes a purple beet, and then this killer, he holds up a single finger and that's when the shouting really begins. No matter where you stood in camp you could hear this raging. I thought he was going to pull out his pistol and shoot a guard. I really did."

Guth stood in front of his uniformed men like a thunderhead. He paced and said this was no way for the SS to act and that stealing from Zurich must stop immediately. He said he wouldn't have his camp taken away from him because he had worked too goddamn hard to become commandant and he'd be damned if someone took away his camp, *his* camp. Any guard caught stealing was a "miserable fucking thief" and he would be sent to the Russian front.

"You assholes better shape up! I expect you to be as hard as Krupp steel!"

Dov Damiel and Chaim Zischer also worried about an SS judge nosing around the camp because they wondered if all the prisoners would be shot beforehand. It would be easier for the guards to shoot them with machine guns and then repopulate the camp with fresh prisoners who had never seen the stealing firsthand. Why take any chances? Liquidate everyone. Purge and start over. Wipe the slate clean.

Zischer was certain he would die. "Why keep me alive when I had personally seen Birdie steal suitcases of gold? Suitcases, I tell you. Huge leather suitcases that took two hands to carry."

As for Guth, his anger cooled like cracking lava. He adjusted his peaked hat with both hands and there was a long ragged sigh as if he were dealing with stupid children.

He lit a cigarette, walked across the sandy ground for his office, and yelled out one final command.

"Birdie. My office. Now."

— 13 —

THE VISIT

It was early October and he threaded his way through the woods because it centered him. It calmed him. Leaves fluttered down in slow flipping twists of burnt color and he enjoyed the side-to-side motion of his horse moving through the cold light. It was peaceful, like a painting. Occasionally he stood up in his stirrups and took in a lungful of fresh air. Every now and then he ducked to avoid a branch while, all around him, leaves swam down in dark, beautiful colors. When he arrived at Lubizec he hopped off and led his horse to a little stable. Puddles of water were everywhere—they reflected the sky above. Guth handed the reins to a prisoner and made his way to the office.

There was much to do with an SS judge coming to investigate the camp and he spent most of his time following Birdie around with a clipboard. They spent many hours sifting through silverware and weddings rings, and during one of these long sessions of cataloguing and counting, he reminded Birdie that everything in the barracks belonged to the Third Reich. They stopped before a pile of enamel pots and Guth nudged one with his foot. It rolled and wobbled to a stop.

"If you need things for the black market, take these. No one's going to miss a few pots. As for gold and silver though . . . well, that's off limits. Understand?"

Birdie nodded.

"Good. Good."

We might wonder why Guth covered for Birdie at all. Why protect him? Why not send him packing for the Battle of Stalingrad that was raging in Russia? These are excellent questions and although we cannot answer them with historical documents, we can certainly hypothesize why Guth chose to shield Birdie in the first place. After all, it would have been far easier to step aside and point the finger of blame at him, but that's not what Guth did. Instead, he used his power to protect this guard, which is rather telling, if not downright intriguing. Why do such a thing?

Guth was a perfectionist, so it could be that he didn't want others to see any flaws in his camp, and to admit that one of his own henchmen was skimming off the top would mean he didn't have total control over his deathdom. It might have been better to cover such things up rather than to lose face. We should also remember that Birdie was very good at what he did. He was ruthless and murderous—he kept Lubizec ticking along smoothly—and for Guth this would have been paramount. For all of his bluster about sending his guards to Russia if they misbehaved (a rich word in its own right: "misbehave"), there isn't a single report of this ever happening. Perhaps Guth remembered his own horrors in the trenches of World War I and he thought he was sparing his men? Although it is perverse and very uncomfortable for us to think about, it could be that Guth thought a death camp was a better assignment than frontline service. He may have felt he was doing his men a favor by keeping them away from enemy fire. Or maybe he didn't want to train new guards. Or maybe he just liked the amusing stories Birdie told in the canteen.

We can't know the depths of Guth's mind, but it is odd, indeed, that he protected Birdie rather than turn him over to the authorities. This, unfortunately, is one of the many unsolved mysteries of Lubizec. We want easy answers, but the more we dig into the past, the more we are forced to stand back in mute horror and confusion.

Our attention is more rightfully placed on those who were murdered though. Who were they? Where did they come from? What were their stories? What would their grandchildren and great-grandchildren have accomplished in the twenty-first century? These are more painful questions to consider (and we will get to them at the close of this book), but, for now, we will focus on the upcoming investigation by that judge.

"So," Guth said, pulling out a cigarette.

He stood in Zurich and watched prisoners run in and out with suitcases full of clothes. When the flame of his lighter was brought up to his lips, his pupils shrank. He puffed once, twice, and blew smoke up to the rafters.

"Let's count the money again, Birdie. Show me the books."

Guth usually left camp at dusk and clopped down the dirt road into twilight. Stars came out and he had the Villa to himself. He ate little. He wrote to Jasmine, begging her to return, and while this could be seen as a lovesick husband pining for his wife, he must have been aware that having his family in Poland was a good deal safer than having them in Berlin, which was being bombed by the Allies on a regular basis.

We also know he wrote a letter to his immediate superior, Odilo "Globus" Globocnik. Guth writes in his usual clipped professionalism about running the camp and he closes the letter with an offhanded gesture, but it is clearly the main reason he wrote the letter in the first place. Just before his signature he says, "We have known each other for many years, Globus. I can assure you an SS judge does not need to visit my camp. Peter Franz is a good man. Very decent. His integrity is beyond reproach. He has run the warehouses in a first rate manner. He has my <u>full support</u>." Guth underlined this last part himself.

SS Hauptsturmführer Odilo Globocnik responded with a terse letter. He said his hands were tied and that an SS judge would be arriving sometime in the next forty-eight hours.

Although we cannot know what Guth was thinking during this period of waiting, we do know he slept in his own bed at the Villa and that the sheets were made of fine Egyptian cotton. The duvet was padded with goose down. He may have listened to the house settling around him. The creaking of beams. Wind against the roof. The flutter of a curtain. It seems reasonable to assume he was worried about the investigation, but maybe he slept just fine. Maybe he dozed off and didn't think about the investigation any more than he thought about killing thousands of human beings.

Maybe he began to snore. Softly.

His name was Erich Bolender and he was much younger than Guth expected. He was tall, he wore the black uniform of a high-ranking SS officer, and his hair was so blond it almost looked bleached white. He got out of his chauffeured Mercedes with a sloppy "Heil Hitler" that suggested he was used to being the most important man in any given space. The young buttery sheen of his skin was at odds with his crossed eyebrows, which made him look perpetually furious. He took off his leather gloves, tugging at each finger carefully, and passed them to his chauffeur. He studied the camp and spent several seconds watching prisoners haul suitcases from one end to another. He covered his nose.

"What's that stench?"

Guth stepped forward and saluted the young man who was, somehow, his superior. They walked through the Rose Garden, turned left, and when they passed the canteen Bolender paused. He nodded at the raked sandy ground and commented on the flower-pots that dotted the camp.

"Very nice."

"Thank you. I thought we'd have a drink before seeing the ware-houses," Guth said, opening the door to his office. "Cognac perhaps?"

The young man held up a hand. "Not for me. I don't drink."

Guth looked confused but went around his wide desk and sat down. He pushed aside a pile of paperwork and smiled. "Welcome to Lubizec."

We know what happened next because Guth's second in command, Heinrich Niemann, the same man who was interrogated for "Allied Forces Report No. 3042," was in the corner taking notes. Guth wanted a witness during this meeting so he asked his deputy to take notes about what was said. According to Niemann, Guth showed no signs of worry and he smiled frequently. He even leaned back in his chair and laced his fingers behind his head. The potbelly stove was lit and this filled the office with the pleasant odor of burning applewood. A clock ticked on the wall and Bolender watched the brass pendulum swing back and forth. It caught the sunlight.

"A smoke perhaps?" Guth said, offering his silver cigarette case.

Bolender hesitated for a moment but reached for one. He tapped it against the desk a few times and leaned in to the lighter when it was offered. The men sat back, not quite relaxed in each other's company. They puffed away, tapping ash into a gigantic tray.

"Let's understand each other from the beginning," Bolender said, looking at the tip of his burning cigarette. "I'm here to find out if anything was stolen from . . . Zurich? That's what you call the warehouse here? I expect your full cooperation in this matter, Guth. And if I find anything out of order, or if I find you've hidden something from me, well then, things will get very nasty for you."

"My camp is at your disposal."

The young man spread his arms like a benevolent king. "Then we'll get along just fine. Maybe I could get some coffee before you show me around?"

Guth looked at Niemann, who in turn stood up and left the office. He hustled across the sandy ground and went into the canteen, where he went about the business of making a pot of coffee. The cupboards were packed full of bags of sugar, pickles, pots of jam, evaporated milk, jars of honey, and huge cans of tomato sauce. Near the door was an enormous wooden bin full of potatoes and turnips.

The standard issue coffee from the army tasted vaguely of burnt acorns, and no matter how long the water steeped in the pot it never got dark. It remained the color of dishwater. However, next to this large bag of swastikaed coffee was a smaller one, one from the black market. Niemann couldn't decide which beans to use—high quality, which would taste better, or standard issue, which wouldn't raise any questions—so he mixed them together. Half came from the government and half came from the black market. It was a strange thing to worry about but Niemann let the decision rumble around in his mind as the water boiled.*

When he returned to the office with a steaming pot and three

---

*During his interrogation in 1946 for "Allied Forces Report No. 3042," Niemann was asked if he put as much thought into killing Jews as he did in choosing coffee beans. He said "No" and acted like the question was absurd.

cups hooked through his meaty fingers, the men were busy talking about Berlin. The mood was sunny.

"So you've actually spent time with the man himself?" Guth asked.

Bolender recrossed his legs. There was a look that said he enjoyed telling this story, and when he reached for his coffee, he nodded with great seriousness. "Oh yes, I've met him many times."

He took a sip and made a face before putting the coffee back on the desk. He gave it a little push and went on to talk about the first time he met Hitler. It was at the Reich Chancellery and he was wearing a business suit.

"When he's not in uniform the Führer looks like a schoolteacher or a hat salesman. There's nothing particularly special about him. He's very softspoken until something sets him off, and then Hitler can drill holes into the air with his eyes. His eyes are . . . utterly piercing. I've never seen anything like them and they're very hypnotic. It's almost like he's holding on to your soul."

Guth offered another cigarette.

The young SS judge reached across and continued speaking. "His mustache isn't as dark as you'd expect either. The films and photographs make it appear darker than it really is. It's more of a light brown in real life. You know he doesn't drink, don't you?"

"So I've heard."

"He's also a vegetarian. Won't touch meat if his life depended on it."

"That's the rumor."

Bolender tapped the desk. "No. That's the truth." He looked around as if he were about to share a secret. "Any guesses what his favorite movie is?"

Guth shrugged.

"Go on. Have a guess."

"I haven't the faintest idea."

"*King Kong*. The Führer loves it. He can't get enough of that hairy ape smashing New York to pieces. Plus he's got these little fruit candies he likes to suck on. They're made especially for him and they've got little swastikas stamped onto them. They're not bad. A bit tart for my taste but I recommend the cherry if, that is, you ever get a chance to meet him."

Guth studied the wood patterns on his desk. He nodded at some inner thought before saying, "Germany is lucky to have him."

"We are indeed. He's transforming Europe right before our very eyes. I mean, the man conquered France in a couple of weeks and that's something we failed to do in four *years* of fighting in the last war. We're a world power again, Guth. Even the Americans are trembling at the thought of dealing with our armies." A short pause and then, "Mark my words. National Socialism is the future of Europe. Russia will soon be for us what India is to the British—unlimited colonial wealth beyond imagining. We're the future of the world, Guth. We Germans."

The clock on the wall struck twice. The gears clicked forward and, almost immediately after, there were two quick blasts from a train whistle. It pierced the air.

Guth stubbed out his cigarette and stood up. "That's the afternoon transport."

Bolender got up. He flicked ash off his sleeve, snapped the front of his uniform tight, and followed Guth outside. As they walked across the Rose Garden he lowered his voice and leaned in close.

"It's my first time in . . . in a camp like this. What's the liquidation process like?"

Guth kept walking. He ordered his guards to take up their positions beside the travel posters for Berlin, Athens, and Barcelona. A plume of obsidian smoke lifted up on the horizon and a train rolled closer and closer. Bolender gave the train a Hitler salute as it screeched to an earsplitting stop. The other guards did no such thing and they looked at him with controlled smiles and sideways glances. Muffled shouts for help could be heard from within the locked cattle cars. The engine ticked and huffed as Guth climbed onto his wooden box. A breeze picked up.

He waited for a moment before shouting out a single word: "Begin."

The locks were swung open in blurring arcs of clanking steel. People flowed out of the cattle cars like a great stream of water finding a new riverbed and the guards began shouting for them to line up. Children cried. Families huddled in tight clusters. Suitcases were tossed out of carriages, hitting some people in the head. The stench of stale diarrhea, sweat, and death swirled into the air. The new arrivals squinted at their surroundings, sunblind. There was a mass of faces, hats, shawls, and Star of David armbands.

"Where are we, Mama?"

Guth held a microphone and cleared his throat. "Welcome to Lubizec." The words echoed down the platform. "Welcome. My name is *Obersturmführer* Guth, commandant of this transit camp. We are sorry your journey wasn't at all convenient but we're at war and cannot spare more pleasant accommodation for your rail travel. You will be given bread and cups of tea shortly. I give you my word as an SS officer that everything will be better now. Leave your suitcases behind. Everything will be returned to you shortly."

When he lowered the microphone, the guards took out their rubber truncheons and began shouting for them to move. "Faster. Faster."

As the victims moved off in a river, bodies were pulled out of the transport and dumped onto the platform with sickening thuds. It started with the last car. Five bodies were tossed out like rag dolls, then two came from the carriage in front of that, seven were tossed from the next carriage, and so on, until, at last, the living had trooped beneath the massive WELCOME sign and the dead were left behind. There were so many of them—their limbs akimbo, their mouths and eyes open—that it was possible to walk down the platform by stepping only on suitcases, legs, and arms.

Guth motioned for Bolender to follow. The two men walked beneath the WELCOME sign and it was Guth who personally closed the iron gates.

Deep-throated and full-lunged screaming was taking place in the Rose Garden. Prayers were mumbled, love was declared, and during all of this terrible noise something odd and unaccountable happened. It hushed the entire camp and made everyone stop what they were doing. A huge cloud of butterflies appeared out of nowhere.

There were hundreds of them and they fluttered and danced drunkenly through the air. A few landed on the SS and opened their wings like little flowered books. Children held out their hands. A young girl laughed as two got caught in her hair. Everything stopped as if peace had been sprinkled onto the camp. Even the SS guards smiled at the butterflies.

And then, just as mysteriously as this orange cloud of silent wings appeared, it lifted over the barbed-wire fence and disappeared into the woods.

A long moment passed.

Then another.

The guards shook themselves awake and went back to separating the Jews. They pulled families apart, but the sticky lingering of last-second hugs slowed everything down. If seen from above, this separating process might look like a cell dividing or like dough being ripped apart. The men were marched off and the women were forced to stay behind.

"That was really quite beautiful," Bolender said.

"What was?"

"The butterflies."

Guth nodded. "Yes. Beautiful. I've never seen anything quite like that before. My kids would've liked it, especially my daughter." He shook his head as if to clear away an unwanted memory. "Shall we see Zurich now?"

Bolender held up a hand. "No. I think I'd like to see the entire operation . . . from beginning to end."

"It's brutal."

"I can handle brutal."

"As you like. This way."

They walked beneath a giant swastika flag that was limp in the windless air and then turned into a courtyard full of naked men. Two white walls acted as a funnel, and when the guards saw Guth appear they began hitting the men down the Road to Heaven all the harder. Rubber truncheons came down on skulls and backs. Purple bruises blossomed open on skin.

"Run, you rags. Run!"

Legs and penises and torsos stampeded down the path. Some of the older men soiled themselves and streams of shit ran down the inside of their legs.

"Faster."

When the last of them had thundered by, Guth and Bolender strolled up the Road to Heaven with their hands behind their backs. Blood and shit peppered the sand. Footprints were everywhere and the white walls were sprayed with dark flecks of bodily fluid. A tooth was in the sand.

Bolender pointed at the Hebrew inscription above the door of the gas chamber.

"What's that say?"

Guth scratched the tip of his nose and smiled. "This is the Gate of the Lord. That was Birdie's idea. He's a good soldier, our Birdie. Very decent."

Bolender pointed at the flowerpots. "These are such a nice touch."

They stood outside the brick building and watched the guards push the last remaining men into a chamber. They used rake handles to squeeze them all in. The steel door boomed shut and the guards spun the winged screws. A muffled shouting could be heard and that's when one of the guards, Rudolf Oberhauser, knocked on the door with a single knuckle. He put his mouth to the eyehole and shouted cheerfully, "Time to die." He yelled it a few more times. "Time to die. Time to die. Time to die."

The victims slapped the walls.

Guth nudged the young man who was his superior. "Follow me."

They stepped outside and moved towards a running engine. It was bolted to a concrete platform and, beside it, was a massive steel tank. A webbing of vents connected the engine to the building and Guth had to shout above the tremendous noise.

"These two guards are the only ones allowed around the engine. Prisoners can't be here."

"What?"

"I said prisoners can't be here. Acts of sabotage."

Bolender nodded. "How long does it take?" he shouted.

"Twenty minutes. Sometimes thirty."

"What?"

"Twenty minutes." Guth held up two fingers.

They watched the machine clatter away before they went back into the building. Instead of the sound of pistons riding up and down in fiery metal chambers, they now heard screams. Horrible screams. Throaty screams. Deathly screams. There were cries for help and wild bangs on the door.

Rudolf Oberhauser smoked a cigarette as if he were waiting for a bus. Every now and then he leaned into the peephole to see what was happening. He stretched. He yawned.

As they waited for the inevitable silence, the doors on either end of the building were propped open, which allowed wind to whistle through the corridor and make everyone's shirts flap. It was cool and refreshing. Oberhauser's cigarette smoke was snatched from his mouth and carried away into the bright light of day.

Meanwhile the metal door kept banging and vibrating. Fists sounded like hammers.

The screams were loud, terrible, and panicky.

Bolender looked pale. "Is it always like this?" he asked.

No one answered. Prisoners in ratty suits waited with leather straps and hooks. Some of them had stretchers. One or two had pliers.

When the door was finally opened, the entire first row slumped out. Their lips were blue from carbon monoxide poisoning and their eyes had rolled back into their skulls, which made them look like they were glancing heavenward. The living began tugging at the dead. Streaks of blood were everywhere and some of the victims had lost their fingernails as they tried to climb the walls. The bodies were wet with sweat and blood and vomit. An ear lay on the floor. The living took away the first corpses that had tumbled out and they began to pull at those immediately beyond the door to make a path deeper into the chamber.

When Bolender saw this he began to choke and rushed outside

to throw up. A stream of chunky vomit poured from his mouth—it spattered his boots—and a long thread of clear snot hung from his nose. He threw up again.

Guth was emotionless. "Get him a bottle of seltzer water. We still have the women and children to do."

Erich Bolender spent the rest of the day in front of enormous piles of jewelry. Birdie showed him around Zurich and they went into one musty barracks after another, but as these two men looked at typewritten charts full of numbers, Bolender wasn't very talkative. He said little when they came to a table full of wedding rings. He said nothing at all when they stood before sacks of human hair. The burlap bulged out like giant tumors and they were all stamped with the inky words, REICH PROPERTY.

When Chaim Zischer delivered a bucket of gold teeth, Bolender watched them tumble out into a little heap of enameled bone.

"The sound of teeth clacking together isn't something you're likely to forget," Zischer later said.

Birdie asked the young judge if he wanted to see anything else.

Bolender shook his head.

"How about the Roasts? We sometimes find diamonds in the ash. We have these huge sieves to make sure nothing gets by us. It's worth seeing, and of course we send everything back to Berlin because it's the— . . . sir? Do you want to see the Roasts?"

Bolender shook his head again, this time more slowly.

"Maybe some dinner then? The food's not bad here." Birdie began to laugh. "We sometimes call it Café Lubizec."

The sun was beginning to go down when they walked back to Camp I. A chill was in the air and the wood-burning stoves were already blazing when they stepped into the canteen. The air inside was warm and pleasant. Guth was there. Niemann too. Others were hunched over chessboards or writing letters home. A phonograph was playing and the record wobbled slightly as it spun in a slow, lazy, black circle. Smoke wisped up from cigarettes and pipes. Every kind of comfort was available. Meats and cheeses. Steins of beer.

Chocolate. Loaves of bread. Raspberries. Champagne. The guards were in various stages of drunkenness because their so-called work was finished for the day. The next train wouldn't arrive until morning so they lifted their glasses. Many of them had large forearms from all the beatings they had carried out. A few rotated their shoulders and winced in pain as if they were nursing some kind of sporting injury. They laughed and told stories. Many of them ate herring with black bread, downing it all with mugs of warm beer.

Someone gave Bolender a tall crystal glass of whiskey. The man who had come to pass judgment on Lubizec stared at it for a long moment. It was cut to resemble a pineapple and he gave the glass a slow turn in the candlelight.

When the thick molten amber touched his lips he drank it back in one quick pull. He gave a sour shudder and replaced the glass on the table.

"I'm going to bed," he announced.

He left early the next morning and his car drove away through falling leaves. He filed his report a few days later from Berlin and, in the warped sensibilities of the Nazi justice system, he found no evidence of crime.

EVIDENCE

Today I will be a prophet once more. If international finance and Jewry inside and outside Europe should succeed in plunging the nations once more into a world war, the result will not be the Bolshevization of the world and the triumph of Jewry, but the annihilation of the Jewish race in Europe.

—Adolf Hitler, Reichstag, Berlin
January 30, 1939

I herewith commission you to carry out all preparations with regard to organization, the material side and financial viewpoints, for a solution of the Jewish Question in these territories in Europe which are under German influence.

—Hermann Göring, Reich Marshall,
letter to Reinhard Heydrich,
July 31, 1941

As an old National Socialist, I must state that if the Jewish clan were to survive the war in Europe, while we sacrificed our best blood in the defense of Europe, then this war would only represent a partial success. With respect to the Jews, therefore, I will only operate on the assumption that they will disappear. [...] We must exterminate the Jews wherever we find them.

—Hans Frank, Governor-General of the General
Government (occupied Poland),
addressing senior officials in Kraków,
December 16, 1941

A judgment is being visited upon the Jews that, while barbaric, is fully deserved by them. The prophecy, which the Führer made about them for having brought on a new world war, is beginning to come true in a most terrible manner. One must not be sentimental in these matters. If we did not fight the Jews, they would destroy us. [...] Fortunately, a whole series of possibilities presents itself for us in wartime that would be denied to us in peacetime.

— Josef Goebbels, Reich Minster of Propaganda, diary entry, March 27, 1942

Members of the SS must apply one principle unreservedly: be honest, decent, loyal and true to those of your own blood. And to no one else. The fate of the Russians and Czechs is completely inconsequential to me. We shall tap the good German blood which is among those peoples, we shall obtain it by stealing children, if necessary, and we shall bring them up in Germany. Whether other peoples flourish or die of hunger interests me for only one reason: we need them as slaves for our culture. We Germans, who are the only people on earth who treat animals decently, shall also display this trait when dealing with human animals.

I would like to be frank with you about another serious issue. I am referring to the evacuations of the Jews—the liquidation of the Jewish people—it's one of those things people talk about casually. "The Jews will be exterminated," every Party member says. "It's in our program: elimination of the Jews. Fine. Let's go ahead and do it. A small matter." But then they turn up, these 80 million honest Germans, each with a respectable Jew, and they say, "All the others are pigs but this here is a fine Jew."

But none of them has witnessed or endured it.

Most of you know what a pile of 100 corpses looks like or what a pile of 500 or 1,000 corpses looks like. I believe having gone through this and, at the same time, maintained our decency, has hardened us. Moreover, it is an unnamed chapter which shall remain forever unspoken about in our history.

—Heinrich Himmler, Reichsführer of the SS
Poznań, Poland, October 4, 1943

Large Metal Sign at Lubizec:

WELCOME

In order to avoid sickness you must present your clothing and all belongings for disinfection. Gold, money (including <u>ALL</u> foreign currency), jewelry, and photographs should be given over for deposit. Cleanliness and truthfulness in this transit camp is everyone's business!

Example of Train Schedule:

From: Reich Railways, Department 33
P Kr 9021, (December 15, 1942), Lublin – Lubizec

Destination	Arrival/Departure
Lublin	09:37
Żabia Wola	10:02/10:28
Osowa	11:56/12:57
Bychawa	15:31/21:13
Kraśnik	23:31/09:47
Aleksandrówka	10:52/06:45
Lubizec	08:00/(08:42)

Train Composition: 1 engine, 15 cars

Camp Dimensions: Lubizec:

A large upturned rectangle measuring 275 meters on the northern and southern boundaries with the eastern and western boundaries measuring 600 meters; the camp was bisected across the middle with a fence camouflaged by tree branches, thus separating Camp I and Camp II. Barbed-wire fencing (non-electrified) surrounded the entire grounds as did a "moat" of anti-personnel landmines commandeered from the defeated Polish army.

Four watchtowers, one at each corner of the camp, and two additional towers in the middle of the eastern and western boundaries respectively. Each tower had one guard armed with an MG 34 air-cooled 7.92 mm machine gun as well as a Sauer 38H semi-automatic pistol. Searchlights affixed to the towers were turned on at dusk. A seventh tower was in the middle of the camp and it overlooked the so-called *Himmelstraße* (Road to Heaven). The central tower had two guards armed with MG 34s. A radio played folk music from a loudspeaker.

Gas chambers were located in Camp II. It was the only brick building in Lubizec and it had four chambers that held 250 to 300 victims each. Carbon monoxide from a captured Soviet tank engine was installed on a concrete pad; fumes were fed into these chambers by way of steel piping. The more tightly packed in the victims, the more lethal the fumes. A generator attached to the engine supplied electricity to the entire camp.

Four burning pits were located on the northern end of Camp II. They measured 10 meters by 50 meters by 2 meters. Ash was sold to farmers as fertilizer.

Camp Personnel of Importance: Lubizec:

SS Unterscharführer Gustav Wagner
SS Unterscharführer Michael Hustek
SS Unterscharführer Kurt Hackenhold
SS Unterscharführer Christian Schwartz
SS Unterscharführer Sebastian Schemise
SS Unterscharführer Rudolf Oberhauser
SS Unterscharführer Peter "Birdie" Franz
SS Oberscharführer Heinrich Niemann
SS Obersturmführer Hans-Peter Guth (commandant after
   May 1942)

To: *SS Hauptsturmführer* Odilo Globocnik
From: *SS Obersturmführer* Hans-Peter Guth
Date: 28 November 1942

Dear Globus,
I write today in the hope of bringing a new matter to
light about the special treatment rooms in Camp II of
Lubizec. After a shipment arrives it can be processed
at a fair rate of speed. It has come to my attention that
further refinement of methods can yet be accomplished.
I recommend all facilities have a lightbulb placed in the
middle because when the doors are screwed shut and
sudden darkness fills the facility this brings about panic.
If a light were to remain on during the processing, the
noise might be lessened.
    Might I also recommend that all future facilities have
larger drains installed in the floor? After processing,
waste materials make cleanup a challenge and therefore
a problem of time management. A larger drain and more
powerful hoses will allow for faster cleaning. This means
faster turnaround and an increase in production.

I look forward to having a meal with you in Lublin when we meet again.

Heil Hitler!

Hans-Peter Guth

Plunder:

suitcases, purses, knives, scissors, watches, pencils, razors, hats, underwear, scarves, earrings, enamel pots, dice, belts, combs, necklaces, slide rulers, bracelets, wallets, lipstick, toothbrushes, raincoats, pendants, bibs, diapers, mallets, diplomas, kiddush cups, wedding announcements, cufflinks, ties, crutches, newspaper clippings, screwdrivers, tweezers, herbs, chess sets, apples, cigarettes, gin, antlers, drapes, pliers, boiled eggs, shtreimels, typewriters, tape measures, yarmulkes, stamps, monocles, evaporated milk, nylons, diaries, mezuzahs, coal, perfume, onions, fingernail clippers, records, shoehorns, prams, brassieres, marmalade, aspirin, sweaters, teacups, pacifiers, wooden toys, tefillins, identity cards, French francs, Polish zlotys, U.S. dollars, British pounds, Russian rubles, potatoes, flashlights, suspenders, sewing kits, jars of dirt, whiskey, diamonds, chocolate, fountain pens, copper wire, stale bread, syringes, fishing poles, salami, bologna, mascara, hammers, blotting paper, compasses, Star of David armbands, powder puffs, ice bags, tobacco boxes, cameras, hairpins, artist brushes, aprons, needles, mirrors, alarm clocks, bandages, sardines, house keys, vials of poison (used), thimbles, birth certificates, gloves, candles, skillets, violins, pillows, blankets, yarn, coins, flour, ink, canes, soap, seeds, pearls, oboes, turnips, corsets, socks, rings, marbles, pipes, rakes, furs, books, vests, maps, kettles, oats, dentures, dolls, photo albums, sugar, and love letters.

Number of eyeglasses: approx. 323,500
Artificial limbs: approx. 14,500 wooden legs and 57,000 leg braces
Total weight of clothes gathered at Lubizec: 8,875 tons
Total weight of hair gathered at Lubizec: unknown

Death count: 710,000 (estimated)
Survivors: 43

PART II

— 15 —

GAS AND BURN

Chaim Zischer was one of the forty-three survivors. As a young boy growing up in Lublin he was unusually smart and enjoyed reading the Talmud. There was serious talk of him going to the Academy of Sages, and perhaps grander things waited for him in the future. He enjoyed strolling in the parks just south of town and he often leaned against an oak tree to admire the rise of the horizon or the green veins of a leaf. "Contemplative" was how his mother liked to describe him. He liked that word because it sounded grown-up and he imagined himself becoming a great thinker, perhaps becoming someone who lived in an empire of ideas and maybe, just maybe, people would come to him one day for advice. Maybe they would call him "wise."

He met Nela when he was seventeen. It happened in a bakery when they were both reaching for the same *pączki*. It was a large crispy doughnut with raspberry filling and when their hands nearly touched beneath the glass they both laughed. He said it was hers, and she said it was his, and then they both reached for it again, which made them laugh even harder. She had bright hazelnut eyes and her smile filled up the whole bakery—it was like July sunshine. In the end he said "I'll buy you the *pączki*" and she said "Let's share it on a bench outside Maharam's Synagogue." So they walked down the jostling street and talked about the weather and how much they liked that particular bakery and of course within five minutes they found out they knew many of the same people.

"How strange we've never met before," she said, coming to a green iron bench.

Chaim opened the wax paper and tore the gooey *pączki* in half. He offered the larger chunk to Nela and watched her lean forward to bite it carefully. She covered her mouth with one hand and let out a little groan of happiness.

"Oh. So good. Oh, my goodness."

A raspberry seed was stuck in her front teeth and this made Chaim laugh all the harder. The day was bright and warm and generous and it was so *good* to be alive, he thought.

An oboe played down the street and crowds bustled in a mighty flood of noise. The rush and burble of voices sounded like a river flowing over a rocky bed but he saw only her, he heard only her.

They were married a year later and he couldn't believe she was standing under the wedding canopy with him, which acted as a symbol of the new house they were going to build together. She was in a modest white dress and there were so many people circled around them it felt like they were being crushed. Everyone was smiling and they kept on saying how it was an excellent match. And when he stomped on a wineglass wrapped in a linen towel everyone erupted into cheers. *Mazel tov! Mazel tov!* There was dancing and dancing and more dancing. Wine too. There was plenty of wine. And of course there was raspberry *pączki* for everyone.

A son was born sixteen months later and this pleased Zischer to the bone. He couldn't have been happier. His boy, Jakob, came into the world on a cloudless winter night and Chaim paced the cobblestones below, smoking a pipe. He glanced up at the moon and wondered what was going on behind the locked door of the nursery. There was an awful lot of panting and screaming and grunting so he stayed outside with his father and his brothers. They talked about local politics as they walked up and down the snowy street, but his gaze kept creeping back to the candlelit window. The gas lamps around him flared like jailed ghosts. Snowflakes fluttered down.

When he was finally allowed inside, he took the steps two at a time. His son had bits of dried blood matted to his hair but Chaim didn't care about this. He brought his son to his chest and kissed his pink new forehead. He silently asked God to give his son a long and healthy life. "May only goodness and beauty touch this child. May the world be gentle to him."

When Chaim first heard about Nazism he thought it was a poison that rotted the mind and turned decent people into wolves. He also thought Germany would come to her senses and turn away from Adolf Hitler. The man was a crackpot. He was an evangelist of hate. Surely the Germans could see this?

Yes, he predicted, cooler heads would prevail. Just be patient. This Hitler has bitten the apple of power but people will soon turn away from him.

But when Poland was invaded in 1939, he knew Nazism was more than a passing political fad. It was something new and terrible. Tanks were soon chewing through wheatfields. They rumbled over low stone walls and swatted young trees to the ground. He watched columns of black-helmeted SS march into Lublin on September 18. They filed through Krakowska Gate and down the little cobblestone hill toward the castle. Their boots echoed off the medieval buildings in a terrifying stamping unison and he watched them march across the brick bridge into the castle where, an hour later, the flag of Poland was yanked down and a giant swastika was unfurled. It hung in the sky like a gash, and that's when he knew his world was lost—that's when he knew things would be different forever.

Posters were glued to shop fronts that ordered all Jews into a ghetto and this was followed by beatings, the closure of all twelve synagogues, and endless demands for money. Medical equipment was taken out of the Jewish hospital on Lubartowska Street and hardly a syringe or stethoscope was left behind to treat its hundreds of patients. Even the beds were stripped away. Many of the windows were broken out of spite.

Other things began to happen. If a German was strolling down the sidewalk it now meant everyone else had to walk in the gutter. Zischer saw a young boy—no more than ten or eleven years old—who didn't get off the sidewalk quickly enough. A German officer pulled out his pistol, pushed the boy against the wall, and shot him. It was as fast as a car accident. One minute the boy was walking along and the next he was dead. It was shocking, yes, but what really haunted Zischer was the sound of it. There was a loud *krumpf* as the bullet cracked into the boy's skull, like a melon being split open. Zischer stumbled away when he saw this and he went home to hold Jakob close to his chest. How could he protect his child from such wild beasts? The Germans were not men. They were animals dressed as soldiers. He kissed his son's forehead and tried not to think about that sound, that splitting.

They lived in the ghetto for two years and he became resourceful at smuggling in bread and tinned goods from someone on the outside. Snow fell. The seasons changed. Random shootings and beatings continued to happen. The old were shot against brick walls. Children that had been newly orphaned begged in the street and people went around selling whatever they thought would make money—toffee, books, boiled eggs, candles, matches, Star of David armbands. One man walked around with a huge tray of sliced bread. It was covered with barbed wire to keep thieves from snatching a slice and running around a corner. Another sold milk by the glass. But there was never enough food in the ghetto. Stomachs rumbled and it became popular to talk about extravagant meals no one could possibly afford. Men and women dropped dead of hunger and people walked past their bodies, no longer horrified by the sight of death.

Somehow life carried on and underground theatres popped up. Music was played in backrooms and it was easy to delude yourself that everything was still normal. You could sip coffee at a table and talk with your friends as if you hadn't a care in the world. The Star of David armbands became so commonplace that no one gave them a second thought and there were even times when Zischer walked around the ghetto, lost in a world of his own fanciful making. He imagined strolling the countryside and having a picnic. He twisted and turned down the streets with this pleasant image in his head when a wall suddenly appeared in front of him. Whenever this happened, he remembered that little boy being shot. The horrid realities of the ghetto immediately came rushing back and he stuffed his hands in his pockets, telling himself it would all be okay in the end.

Such moments of mental freedom happened to everyone in the ghetto but they were always interrupted by a brick wall, or a dead body, or the sight of a Nazi strutting imperiously down the street, and in these horrible reawakenings to Hitler's World, everything felt so much worse. Zischer ran up the steps to his small apartment and held his wife. They rocked their son and listened to the distant rattle of machine guns.

"We'll be fine," Nela said. "I don't know how but we *will*." She nodded, as if placing a period onto the sentence with her chin.

And then one morning, when the sun was hardly up, Zischer and his family were rounded up on Furmańska Street along with hundreds of others. The sky was an ugly sulfurous yellow when they were marched away under heavy guard. Guns crackled in the streets as motorcycles with sidecars revved around corners. Dogs snapped and barked. Near the sooty rail yards the air stank of coal and iron. Some of the men rocked back and forth, praying to God.

The journey to Lubizec lasted two days, and when they finally arrived he watched the commandant stand on a wooden box. It was raining slightly. There were travel posters on the walls. And then—

He had no words for what happened next.

One minute he had his arm around his wife and the next he was plucked from a running group of men because he looked strong and healthy. Of the 1,400 people that arrived into camp with him, he was the only survivor. He was the only one to be spared, and it happened when a guard ordered him to unpack suitcases while, one hundred meters away, his mother, father, brothers, grandparents, aunts, uncles, cousins, nieces, nephews, friends, his wife and his son, they were all shoved into the unknown. His whole world was snuffed out—Nela, Jakob—everyone—and it happened so fast. It only took thirty minutes to wipe out everything he knew and loved. Only thirty minutes.

Zischer was so stunned by the overwhelming scope of this crime that he kept looking around, waiting for the universe to stop it, but the rain kept falling down, and the wickedness was allowed to continue. Days passed, then weeks, and still the trains kept on coming. Clothes were dumped into ever higher piles of fabric and still the universe did nothing to stop the murders. He watched it all. It was like being handcuffed to devastation.

Sometimes it didn't seem possible that Nela was really dead. Maybe he imagined it all? Maybe she was somewhere back in Lublin with Jakob and it was all just a bad dream? But there were other times, especially when he saw the Roasts being lit at night or when he saw a toddler with black hair, then he knew that her ashes, and the ashes of his boy, were scattered somewhere in the fields.

As Zischer makes painfully clear in his memoir, the first three days at Lubizec were the worst, and if we are to understand what happened next in the history of the camp, we first need to understand what it meant to be a prisoner. Zischer's account is generally considered to be the best and he says it was possible to look at new prisoners and tell if they would last more than twenty-four hours at Lubizec.

"It became a sixth sense to us," he said during one interview. "There was a vacancy in their eyes. They looked right through you."

He goes on to explain how one such prisoner, a Hasidic Jew from some remote corner of Poland, had been plucked from a new transport. His forelocks and beard were snipped by the guards and he was told that his entire family (indeed, his whole village) had been gassed. He was then forced to carry their bodies to the Roasts. It was nearly midnight before this man was whipped back to Barrack 14. He took a bunk near Zischer and began to wail. He rocked back and forth, reciting the Kaddish in great broken sobs. The other prisoners told him to shut up before the SS came in to beat them silly, but this man kept on weeping and rocking.

He shouted out, "May his great name grow exalted and sanctified in the world he created as he willed."

Another prisoner—a man with sharp features and a huge Adam's apple—was slapping mosquitoes when he heard this. He threw a shoe at him.

"Why are you reciting the Kaddish, idiot? Look around. Does it look like God lives in this place?"

The weeping man paused for a moment. His eyes were bloodshot and full of tears.

The prisoner who threw the shoe continued slapping mosquitoes. He held up something between his fingertips.

"Do you see this? This is what we are in Lubizec. Bugs. Pests. Something to be thrown into the fire. Now stop your weeping and your prayers. We all need sleep."

"Hey," someone laughed a few bunks down. "Do you know why God isn't in Lubizec?"

It was an old joke, so another voice called out the answer. "God isn't in Lubizec because he ran up the Road to Heaven."

The new prisoner stared at the dirt floor. His voice was weak. "They made me touch the dead. I carried my own daughter to a gigantic fire. My own daughter." He began to murmur again. "May his great name grow exalted and sanctified in the world he created as he willed."

"Shut up," another prisoner shouted. "There'll be more trains tomorrow and we need our rest."

"More trains?"

"Plenty more. They're killing all the Jews of Poland in this place. Now go to sleep."

The new prisoner hugged his knees. He continued rocking back and forth. A searchlight roved across the barrack window and this cast eerie shadows on the floor. When it moved away, the shattered man began to sing a new prayer. The other prisoners did not interrupt him.

> Remember the promise You made to Your servant
> for it has given me hope,
> even as I am humiliated by those who mock You.
> From the teaching of Your Torah I have not strayed.
> From the teaching of Your Torah I have not strayed.

And then this man who witnessed the destruction of his family, and his village, and his entire way of life, fell into a deep silence. Sometime during the night, he hanged himself with a belt.

Zischer quickly realized that Lubizec could be boiled down to one simple and undeniable truth: the day was for killing, the night was for burning. The guards called it "Gas and Burn." It was as reliable as gravity. It was fixed, permanent, and habitual.

The day started at 0600 hours when folk music blared out from the central tower and a single guard came into the barracks with a rubber hose. He beat it against the wooden bunk beds and yelled out, "*Antreten zum Appell. Antreten!*" (Fall in for roll call. Fall in!)

He walked across the dirt floor and smacked his hose against the bunks.

"*Antreten! Antreten!*"

The prisoners spilled out of their barracks and assembled in the Rose Garden where other guards walked the perimeter and smoked cigarettes. Many of them yawned. Some munched on bread or they held steaming cups of coffee. A jaunty tuba sounded from the central loudspeaker and it conjured up images of a beer hall. It made Chaim Zischer think of lederhosen, long tables, and mustardy, greasy bratwurst. Sometimes he could almost taste the fatty seasoned beef juice running down his chin.

"*Antreten! Antreten!*"

The polka music blasted out as three hundred prisoners ran into the sandy parade ground. When they were all standing at attention and panting heavily, the guards ordered a small group of them to collect the buckets of shit and piss that acted as toilets. They also brought out the dead. No one was allowed to move or speak as the ragged limp corpses were dragged by their legs and heaved into a wooden cart. Many bodies had a belt around their neck because they had decided to hang themselves from the low rafters inside the barracks.[*]

---

[*]One of the least talked about aspects of Lubizec is the high suicide rate. Even if a prisoner survived the first hour of arrival into the camp, there was a good chance he would take his own life before the month was out. This was true for all of the Operation Reinhard death camps, and we can only guess how many prisoners committed suicide under such dire circumstances, but the number must be in the thousands.

Zischer stood at attention with his hands on the seams of his trousers. He always tried to be in the center of the parade ground because it meant being farther away from the guards. Men on the edges were often hit, but being in the middle offered some degree of protection.

Zischer stood there—ramrod straight, cap off, chest out—and he watched leaves skitter across the parade ground. They blew in from under the fence, they flipped and tumbled and danced across the sandy ground, and they slipped away beneath the opposite fence. They were free. Bewilderingly free. A rooster sang out in some nearby field. Surely, Zischer thought, that farmer could hear the folk music, the gunshots, and the screaming. Who was this man that lived so close to a portal of death and was able to turn away from it? How did he get on with his day? Zischer hated this Polish farmer living so close to the camp. It was a pure hatred, more pure even than what he felt for the Nazis, because this Pole was a fellow countryman and he was doing absolutely nothing to help. Zischer hated this man down to the marrow in his bones.

Breakfast was served at a long wooden table held together by rusty nails and they had to file past "Quickly! Quickly!" in order to get their rations. They got a crust of rye bread, some thin oatmeal, and a cup of coffee that tasted suspiciously like dishwater. The metal ladle clicked and clacked against an enormous soup pot as the prisoners filed past, one by one. Coffee was slopped into cups while the guards yelled, "*Schneller. Schneller.*" Still the ladle clicked at a furious pace.

"*Schneller. Schneller.*"

Through Zischer we gain a deeper appreciation of what it might have been like to be a prisoner at Lubizec. All of the official documents, train schedules, and interrogative army interviews with camp guards offer us strong historical information but we would be wise to remember that these are Nazi sources. Zischer describes what it was like to watch people run down the Road to Heaven with truncheons and whips flailing at their naked bodies. He witnessed the sandy path covered in blood and diarrhea. He watched one group of prisoners rake the sand while another group furiously applied white paint to the walls.

"They did this to cover up the spatter," Zischer said in 1985. "The whole thing was magic. One minute you see people and the next you see corpses. It was hocus-pocus."

Thanks to Zischer we know about moments in camp that would have vanished into time and never been known about by anyone. We know, for example, that the guards liked to see how many people they could cram into a single chamber. We also know the steel doors were lined with green felt in order to keep the poison from leaking out. We know that Rudolf Oberhauser yelled out the phrase "Time to die" shortly before the carbon monoxide was pumped in. The inflection in his voice was always the same, almost like a song he liked to sing at a beer hall. "Time to *diiieeee*."

Zischer mentions, in stark clinical terms, how the gas chamber had to be mopped out after each use because the floor was smeared with blood, feces, and urine. A fresh coat of paint was applied to the walls to hide the awfulness of what had just been done. To struggle for air, even for a few moments, as some of us have done for one reason or another, is terrifying enough, but most of the victims at Lubizec beat the walls for twenty minutes as they searched for breathable air. It would have been an excruciating and very long death. Most people today probably imagine these victims smelling the gas and coughing a few times before they blacked out, but this wasn't the case. We would like to think of them falling asleep, as if their heads were falling onto a large pillow, but the reality was far more terrifying and far more slow. Twenty minutes is a long time, especially if you know you're dying.

In his job as a "dentist," extracting gold teeth and metal bridgework from the freshly dead, Zischer used a crowbar to open each mouth and then, with pliers, he wrestled out anything of value. It was hard and exhausting work. Horrifying too, because sometimes gas escaped from the lungs and this made it seem like the corpse was waking up.

A bucket of water was next to him and he tossed in tooth after tooth.

Sometimes he stared at the dented bucket near his feet. Bits of gum floated on the surface and, as he watched a large thread of pink spin in a slow lazy circle, Zischer promised himself he would survive. He had been smart in school and he was known for his excellent memory. If he survived (and he didn't know how on earth this would be possible), he would talk about those prisoners known as the *Bahnhofkommando* who opened the cattle car doors, removed the dead, and hosed out the train. He would talk about the *Transportkommando* who hauled suitcases and steamer trunks into Zurich. He would talk about the *Goldjuden*, those men who sorted watches and currency into huge piles of wealth. He would talk about the barbers who cut women's hair and also about prisoners who had to go around camp with baby prams picking up garbage. He would talk about the *Tarnungskommando* who painted the wooden walls on the Road to Heaven in order to hide any traces of blood. He would talk about the *Sonderkommando* who pulled the dead from the gas chambers and hauled them to the Roasts. He would talk about how prisoners were tied to benches, how their buttocks were exposed, and how twenty-five lashes were meted out for stealing clothes or running too slowly or peeing when you weren't supposed to pee. He would talk about pistols being lowered against skulls and how the guards were always killing, killing, killing, killing, killing, and killing. It was as normal to them as breathing. It was automatic. Reflexive. All of the guards at Lubizec were sadists. And he would take extra time—he nodded at this—he would take extra time to talk about the commandant of this place, how hard and flinty the man's face was, how he went about his job with the ease of a butcher. Chaim Zischer promised himself he would survive and talk about these things. He would defy the Nazis by living. Yes. He would do this.

As he stared into the bucket of teeth, he continued to watch a pink thread spin in a circle.

He reached into the mouth of a pregnant woman. He couldn't be sure but it seemed that her child was still alive inside the warm globe of her womb. With a crunch and a twist, one of her molars came loose and he flicked it into the bloody water.

Her body was dragged away, flopping, and he reached for a new mouth.

"Yes," he whispered. He would survive. "Somehow."

Months passed. Snow fluttered down and he shivered as he continued to drop tooth after tooth into the bucket. A rim of ice had to be chipped away and he couldn't feel the metal pliers in his fist anymore. The sun was going down and the world of Lubizec was stained a gloomy blue. Searchlights winked on like giant beasts opening up their eyes. The loudspeaker crackled.

"*Achtung, achtung. Antreten zum Appell. Jetzt antreten.*"

Zischer tightened a scarf around his neck and ran with the other prisoners through hard snow until he reached the Rose Garden. He stood at attention and realized his feet were numb. Some of the men in Barack 14 had frostbite so bad their toes had turned black and their nails had come off. Because of this, he made sure to wear three pairs of socks even though it was dangerous to do so. The guards would shoot him on the spot if they found "Reich property" being used in such a frivolous way, but Zischer believed the guards had better things to do than look at prisoners' feet.

Snow confettied down in fat beautiful flakes. They seemed the size of cotton balls and they landed on bare heads all around him. Everyone stood at attention with their caps off and he continued to watch these perfect flakes.

"*Antreten. Antreten.*"

Snow floated through searchlights as Guth appeared in front of them. He wore a heavy coat.

"This man," he shouted while pointing to a prisoner. "This man was caught stealing Reich property. He will be whipped and you will watch."

The naked prisoner was tied to a sawhorse and one of the guards—Birdie—stood over him with a whip that was made out of hippopotamus hide. Birdie spread his boots to anchor himself in the snow. One of the spotlights glided over and lit everything up like a macabre stage show.

This was a common sight, one that happened several times a week, and a hard shell had grown over Zischer's heart long ago because of it.

The crack of leather splitting open skin filled the night, but still the snow kept falling down in magnificent flakes. Nothing would stop the whipping now. The man would get his twenty-five lashes and that would be that. The earth would continue to spin, the stars would continue to shine, and the trains would continue to come.

At lash number eight the man begged for it to stop. He was delirious with pain and yelled out, "Please! Please, no more! I beg you."

Birdie paused for a drink of vodka. Then he said, very calmly, "We'll have to start over now. Count them off for me."

The whip came down.

". . ."

"What was that? I couldn't hear you. Shout it out."

Again the whip came down.

"One!"

"Good."

"Two!"

"What comes next?"

"—ree."

Zischer shuffled his feet to get the blood circulating and he looked at the dark horizon. The moon was plump. He wanted it blotted out because it felt obscene. Nothing associated with love and romance should be allowed to shine above the gas chambers and fire pits. No moon should be allowed to float dreamily across the warm embers of his people. It was profane and disgusting and vile. He hated the moon. He wanted to rip it out of the sky and smother it.

The prisoner tied to the sawhorse passed out but still the whip kept coming down as if it were a snake rearing back and lunging forward. On and on it went, crack after crack, until, at last, Birdie was finally winded. He panted. He wiped his forehead. The naked man was untied from the sawhorse and he slumped to the ground like a fleshy rag. Zischer doubted the man would live. Birdie had a nasty habit of aiming for the same spot on the spinal cord, as if he were trying to sever it.

Guth stepped forward once again. The searchlight followed him as he paced back and forth. "Cold or no cold, you Jews will wear *one* coat in this camp. *One.* This isn't a holiday resort."

Zischer wondered for the millionth time about climbing over the barbed-wire fence and sprinting into the woods. He glanced at the central tower and saw guards with their machine guns. They stomped their feet for warmth and, when they did this, snow fluttered down from their little platform high above. Beyond them, in a field, a thousand corpses would soon light up the night. Heat would come to Lubizec at last.

Zischer knew he needed to escape. But how?

— 16 —

PASSOVER

When asked why there was so much cruelty at Lubizec, one of the guards, in an interview that was secretly taped by a journalist in 1971, said it was necessary to keep things in order. He explained that without the whippings and the beatings, chaos would have swallowed the camp.

This type of justification is not only difficult to hear but it also sidesteps the real reason why the guards were so brutal: People were humiliated, degraded, and tortured because the guards needed to reinforce their own warped belief system. Put another way, they wouldn't have been able to kill if they thought the prisoners were human beings, and this meant cruelty existed in the camp precisely *because* the guards needed to convince themselves they weren't killing people at all, but subhuman creatures unworthy of life.

It was also a question of power. It was much easier to feel like a true member of the master race if you were able to kill anyone you wanted to. The guards only had to pull out their guns and shoot. There would be no court trial. No jail time. There would be no ramifications whatsoever. The guards could do whatever they wanted and whenever a body dropped in front of them—falling to the ground, lifeless—it reminded them who was in charge. They held the power of life over death and this made them feel like little gods strutting around the camp.

Like any other environment though, Lubizec also had its share of petty rivalries. If one guard saved a prisoner or showed an iota of favoritism, another guard might beat that prisoner all the harder. If one guard relied on a prisoner to sort clothing, another guard might shoot that prisoner just so Guard #1 would have to find a replacement. These small rivalries among the SS had very real consequences on living breathing human beings and this meant the prisoners were always trying to read the guards in order to understand the political landscape of the camp. Which guards were friends? Which guards were enemies? If I am allowed to visit the latrine while Guard #1 is on duty, what will Guard #3 do about this later on?

The guards, however, mostly acted in unison and they took their blood oath to the SS very seriously. They delighted in acts of group brutality because it fortified their own beliefs while simultaneously reminding them they were members of an elite squad. As every German citizen knew from the newsreels and newspapers, not everyone could join the SS—only the best men with the best blood were accepted. The guards at Lubizec wanted to prove their place within the SS, and this often meant they became wild agents of destruction.

One story highlights this in a particularly awful way. It happened sometime in the winter of 1942 when a group of women were beaten down the Road to Heaven. It was -30°C and the wind was howling. Tendrils of snow snaked through the air and it was hard to see more than a few meters. When the women arrived at the gas chamber, the door was shut, and the guards watched them, naked and shivering. They laughed at the women and watched them stand storklike first on one foot, then the other.

"Please let us in."

"We'll f-f-freeze to death out here."

They covered their chests and leaned into each other for warmth. Jets of hot breath escaped from their mouths as they danced around, but still the guards wouldn't let them in.

They stood outside for thirty minutes as the men smoked cigarettes and talked about potbelly stoves. One of the guards, Rudolf Oberhauser, opened the gas chamber door and shut it quickly.

"Whew. It's *hot* in there. Like a sauna."

The other guards laughed as these women rubbed their goose-pimpled flesh. Their jaws chattered as they danced around.

"Please let us in."

They tucked their fingers into their armpits and hunched into little balls.

"P-p-please."

When the door was finally opened, the women pushed into the brick building as a funnel of flesh. The engine was started and thirty minutes later their bodies were tossed into a snowbank. Later that night, as their flesh burned and popped, the guards joked about how these women were warm at last.

"The bitches aren't complaining now, are they?" Oberhauser laughed.

Cruelty took on many forms at Lubizec: People had to wait in the freezing cold, women were groped, glasses were stomped on, arms were broken with truncheons, and victims had to sing as they ran down the Road to Heaven. We also know that if a prisoner was hit in the face and a large purple bruise appeared, that prisoner was shot because the guards didn't want incoming victims to see such wounds. If the new arrivals on the platform saw black eyes or split lips it might frighten them, so we have these heartbreaking stories of prisoners trying to cover their bruised faces. Sometimes a prisoner was deliberately hit on the cheek with a pistol just so they would know, absolutely and definitively, that they would be shot within twenty-four hours. Protecting one's face at Lubizec became more important than eating or sleeping.

"A bruise on your cheek was cured by a bullet to the head," Chaim Zischer later said.

We want these guards to have a moral awakening, but no such awakening can happen within the confines of Lubizec. What do the words *mercy*, *compassion*, and *kindness* mean in a place so far beyond the boundaries of civilization? True, the Nazis did not invent anti-Semitism, nor did they invent laws that forbade Jews to become full members of a society, but they took these historical weapons of hate and pushed them in new and terrible directions. This is how we find naked women huddled outside a gas chamber in subzero weather while the guards are wrapped in warm trench coats. This is why they can laugh and mock. For if they couldn't laugh and mock, they never would have been able to kill. Laughter was the first step towards killing.

Although Chaim Zischer became numb to the physical and psychological cruelties of Lubizec, even he wasn't prepared for what happened one night in January 1943. It would rank as one of the strangest evenings he experienced in camp, and it began when Commandant Guth opened the wooden door to their barrack and clicked on his flashlight.

"Get up," Heinrich Niemann yelled. "Get up, you pieces of shit." He banged a rubber hose against the bunks and carried an oil lamp. A large dirty bubble of light followed him as he moved deeper into the barrack. Shadows stretched across the walls.

"Up, up, up," sang Birdie.

Zischer slept near the entrance because he wanted to be the first one into the Rose Garden each morning (it meant he could stand in the middle of the parade ground and avoid being hit), but on that particular night, when he heard the door open, he jumped down from the top bunk with his shoes already on and he almost ran into Guth. The commandant pointed his flashlight at Zischer and this made him shield his eyes. He expected to be hit on the cheek, but the man in a heavy leather trench coat just stood there.

What's going on? Zischer thought. *What time is it?*

Other prisoners stood beside their bunks, equally confused. Dark shadows were pushed away by Heinrich Niemann's oil lamp as he walked back to the entrance. The bulk of his stomach pushed prisoners out of the way.

"Get up, little chickens. Get up."

There was no electricity or heat in the barracks so the prisoners stood in the cold dark. Flashlights moved over squinting faces and the rubber hose continued to whomp against the triple-layered bunk beds.

Is this the end? Zischer wondered.

A murmur of panic charged the darkness. Eyes darted left and right. Muscles tensed.

"Listen up!" Birdie shouted, pushing someone out of his way. "Your commandant has a message for you."

The wind howled and a clapboard on the roof began to vibrate.

It banged and slapped against the rafters. There was a dark orange glow on the northern end of the camp. *The Roasts*, thought Zischer. He hadn't thought about it when he went to bed, but with the guards shoving men out of the way he wondered if his body would be on fire in the next few minutes. *Was this it?* He exhaled, and the precious heat from inside his body clouded the air.

Guth stepped away from the door and a cone of flashlight followed him as if he were on a stage. He carried a large canvas sack. He had gone several days without shaving and, when he spoke, it was obvious he had been drinking.

"We have . . . a new guard at Lubizec," he slurred. He sucked on his lower lip and held out his arm. "Come here Sebas . . . S*ebastian*. Come here." Guth rocked on his heels and steadied himself against a wooden post. "Say hello."

Because it was so dark no one noticed the man in the shadows of the entrance. The new guard stepped into the light and adjusted his peaked SS cap. The death's head emblem gleamed and his uniform was neatly pressed, freshly ironed. He didn't appear drunk.

Heinrich Niemann pushed his oil lamp forward. "Tell them what you said."

"Yeah," Birdie echoed. "Tell them what's going to happen."

The new guard's name was Sebastian Schemise and he enjoyed telling people he was fated to join the SS thanks to his initials: S. S. He was originally from Munich and he believed that Hitler was a great man, a savior of Germany, a modern-day Caesar in charge of a mighty army. Schemise was as thin as an umbrella and he took great pleasure in killing. In any other society he would have been labeled a psychopath and locked up, but thanks to the fog of war he was able to float up the ranks of the SS almost effortlessly. He thrived on cruelty and it was often noted how calm he was, especially when he was beating someone. As far as anyone could tell, his heart rate never went up. He hit and shot and punched—all without appearing to be angry or out of control. It made him terrifying because he seemed to have no feelings whatsoever. Even the other guards would later comment on how ruthless he was.

Schemise cleared his throat. "Good evening, gentlemen. I'm delighted to be a part of this camp and I look forward to killing some of you soon. I hope you don't take it personally."

"Good humor. I *like* this kid," Niemann said.

"Hear, hear," Birdie added. He lifted a silver flask and took a swig.

Guth reentered the bleached cone of the flashlight. He tried to put one arm around Schemise but stumbled. It was the first time anyone had seen Guth so out of character, so loose, so informal, and the prisoners looked at each other with worry.

And then, as if realizing how chummy he was getting, Guth straightened himself. He blinked a few times. He said slowly and with great care, "We were talking with Sebas . . . tian here. He is interested in your Jew life. What was it you said? Back in the canteen?"

"That we should study the Jews before they're gone. They're a dying breed. They'll be extinct soon."

Guth pointed. "That's it. Yes."

"Tell them about the meal," Birdie laughed.

Schemise pulled out a cigarette. A flame danced on the lighter as he brought it up to his lips. One puff, two puffs. He snapped it shut and looked serious.

"Everyone knows the Jews will be gone in Europe by 1950, so if we want to see their customs and rituals we need to do it now. In a few years such things will be just a memory. A myth. A rumor." A pause as he looked around. "You won't even find anything about Jew life in museums or libraries, but *we* can tell our grandchildren we saw their way of life once. Imagine seeing the last Neanderthal around a campfire? How did he act before dying off forever? What language did he speak before *Homo sapiens* raised a club over his head?"

"I like this kid," Niemann beamed.

"Hear, hear," added Birdie, taking another swig.

"So," Guth interrupted. "We want to see your Jew rituals and how you celebrate—what's the damn thing called again, Schemise?"

"Pesach. The Passover Seder."

"Yes. *That*."

Guth went over to the canvas sack he brought into Barrack 14 and started pulling out a loaf of bread, a lamb chop, some hard-boiled eggs, and a bottle of wine. He tossed everything onto the dirt floor and pointed at six men. He made a gun of his finger and picked them out randomly by pretending to shoot them.

"You, you, you, you . . . you . . . and you."

The meal would take place on the floor because there were no tables or chairs. Chaim Zischer was next to Guth so he was chosen. Dov Damiel was also chosen when Guth's finger was pointed at him. Four other men joined them on icy dirt and they sat cross-legged. The flashlights and oil lamps swam in like gigantic underwater eyes and this made the darkness seem much worse. Zischer felt like he was at the bottom of the ocean, like he was drowning, and even though he was wombed in light, it felt like darkness was crushing in on him.

He closed his eyes and told himself to breathe.

When he opened his eyes he began to gather up the bread and the brown wilting lettuce. The shells of the boiled eggs were warm in his hands—the yolks would taste good and he had to restrain himself from devouring them on the spot.

Guth pulled out his silver cigarette case. "You use unleavened bread for this thing? This dinner? We don't have such bread at Lubizec. Wheat will have to do."

The hot breath of the prisoners floated up in the light. *So this is it*, Zischer thought. *This is how I'm going to die.*

Sebastian Schemise uncorked the wine bottle and passed it to a prisoner.

"Fascinating," he said with wide eyes. He kneeled down and spoke as if they were children. "Now pretend we're not here. Do the Seder like you normally would. You may begin whenever you're ready."

Zischer looked at how the green wine bottle cast an odd shadow on the floor. The bread had burnt seeds on top and there were little pebbles stuck to the lamb chop. *A Seder?* he thought. *In this place?* Not for the first time, he wondered how the Nazis could kill them without understanding anything at all about a religious way of life that went back millennia. The Germans destroyed without even bothering to learn the basics of what they hated. It made no sense. What was the wellspring of their hatred?

In a moment of unbelievable stupidity, he spoke directly to Guth. Prisoners never did such a thing but the words tumbled out of his mouth before his brain could catch them. The sentence hung in the air like a poisonous cloud.

Guth was surprised. "Did you speak?"

Zischer had to say the sentence again or risk being beaten. He looked at the floor. "Herr Commandant, with respect, Passover isn't until April."

Guth took a long drag on his cigarette. The orange tip glowed bright and he held the smoke inside his body for a moment. He leaned forward and his leather trench coat sounded like a door creaking open. He said, "Celebrate it now. You won't be here in April."

"Yes, make it count," Schemise beamed. "This might be the last Seder celebrated in Poland, ever."

Dust floated in the illuminated air and it was so quiet Zischer could hear himself breathe through his nose. His lower intestines gurgled and his heart rocked gently inside his chest. The delicate machinery of his body was still alive, still working, and he closed his eyes to notice it all.

Passover was meant to commemorate not only the bondage of his people in Egypt thousands of years ago, but it was also a reminder of how death passed over his ancestors. It was about hope and survival. Above all else, it was about the exodus of his people from slavery into freedom.

He looked down at his calloused, dirty hands. Dried blood was beneath his fingernails and he couldn't believe these same hands once sat at a dinner table in Lublin. His whole family was there and they dipped vegetables into saltwater. They ate matzah, bitter herbs, sweet paste made from fruits, and of course there was wine. The words of another life floated into his ears and offered him comfort. *Haggadah. Maror. Charoset. Karpas.* At a very young age he asked the Four Questions and his grandfather, who had a scraggily beard, explained to all the children gathered around the table why this night was different from all other nights. The Seder was about family and connection. It was about remembrance and the past. It was about rebirth and hope.

Zischer focused on the dried blood beneath his fingernails and wanted to weep. Everyone who sat around the Seder tables of his past were now gone. Their ashes had been scattered like chaff to the wind and he was the only one left. He looked up at the glowing ember of Guth's cigarette and in that moment the man seemed like a demon who kept fire chained to the leash of his cigarette. Each night this demon-man strolled through the forest and stained the night with blood.

This was much worse than bondage and slavery, Zischer thought. Much worse.

He glanced at the green wine bottle and the lamb chop. What would happen when the mock Seder was over? Would they be shot?

It reminded him yet again that being in Lubizec was like living in those seconds before a car crash. You can see it coming but you're powerless to stop it. Your nerves tingle, your body is a coiled spring, your muscles lock, but you can't do anything because the physics of the rushing world are beyond you.

"BEGIN!" Schemise shouted. He pulled out his pistol and nudged it against the head closest to him. "Begin. We are tired of waiting."

The man with a cocked gun against his ear was Moshe Taube. Zischer and the others didn't know much about him because he hadn't yet earned the right of their interest. He was a new face, a new arrival, and if he survived a few more nights without hanging himself or getting shot by Birdie they might show him a few tricks. For the time being, he was just another shadow waiting to be pulled into the Roasts. What Zischer and the others didn't know—couldn't know—was that Moshe would soon be holding their lives in the palm of his hands.

Schemise pushed the barrel into Moshe's temple and this prompted the man to reach for the wine. He began to murmur the words of blessing.

"Is he speaking in Jew?" Niemann shouted. "Is that Jew?" He lifted his oil lamp and cast dirty light onto the prayer. "I can't hear."

Schemise stood up and crossed his arms. "Louder. Louder."

Moshe Taube paused for a moment, blinked, and nodded as if coming to some kind of inner decision. He raised the bottle of wine as if offering a toast and he intoned the ancient tongue of his people. He spoke with a Ukrainian accent and seemed fearless. *"Ma nish-ta-naw ha-lai-law ha-zeh mee-kawl ha-lay-los?"*

The other men on the floor immediately knew this wasn't the proper order of the Seder but they stuffed bread into their mouths and peeled boiled eggs. They were hungry and they didn't know what else to do.

As for the newcomer, Moshe Taube, he asked the first of the Four Questions again: *"Ma nish-ta-naw ha-lai-law ha-zeh mee-kawl ha-lay-los?"*

The other men passed the wine amongst themselves. They left ghostly fingerprints on the bottle, and after each of them took a long swallow, they repeated the phrase. It was a small act of rebellion and it filled them with strength.

When it was Zischer's turn to drink he glanced at the chiseled face of Sebastian Schemise and wondered if this German knew what they were doing.

The prisoners continued saying that single phrase—"Why is this night different from all other nights?"—as they tore off chunks of bread and peeled speckled shells away from boiled eggs. It didn't represent a Seder in any way and this made Zischer feel like he wasn't dishonoring his past. The six men continued stuffing food into their mouths because they were hungry, scared, and confused. They chewed and swallowed. They murmured that single line of Hebrew as the bottle was passed from hand to hand. Zischer bit into an egg and felt yolk on his tongue. It was the first time he had eaten an egg in years. It felt magical. Alive.

Birdie clapped as if he were watching a play. "Great show."

"Yes," Schemise said. "What comes next?"

The new prisoner, Moshe, looked angry for a moment—he was clearly tired of being mocked and ridiculed—and then he did something dangerous. He got onto his knees as the words of his ancestors continued flowing over his tongue and, while he recited the prayer for the dead, he stood up awkwardly in a pool of dusty light.

His voice grew stronger, more defiant.

A flashlight caught his hair and it surrounded him like a halo. He sang his lament and, when he finished, the guards clapped. They hooted and stamped their feet. Many of the prisoners in Barrack 14 had tears running down their cheeks and someone at the back broke down entirely.

Guth stayed in the shadows. The orange asterisk of his cigarette burned and faded.

When quiet returned to the barrack he dropped his cigarette onto the floor and twisted it beneath his boot.

"You see?" he said, lurching back into the light. "We don't treat you so badly in Lubizec. Where else could you enjoy a Passover? Hmm?"

He pointed at the eggshells on the floor. "This is a *family* meal, yes?" He blinked a few times as if trying to focus. He twirled his wedding ring and was on the verge of tears. "I haven't seen my wife and kids for . . . six months. Six lousy *months*." He puckered his lips and let out an extravagant whistle. "I keep telling them to return, but they stay in Berlin. Fucking Berlin."

He unbuttoned his trench coat and fished around for something. He stumbled and almost tripped over but he pulled out his wallet. He held it up like a prize and passed a photo to Schemise.

"My wife and kids."

The new guard held it to the light. "Very nice, sir. Very nice indeed. A good-looking family."

It is worth pausing here and mentioning that when Chaim Zischer was asked about this incident for a television documentary, he sparkled with rage. He leaned into the reporter's microphone as his face flushed with anger. He almost spat out the words.

"Should I feel sorry for this man, this murderer, this killer of cities? No, I tell you. My family was *dead*, my son was *dead*, my wife was *dead*, my parents were *dead*, my brothers were *dead*, and he's telling us how much he misses his family? Oh, please. There is a big difference between missing your family and having your family gone missing. I have no sympathy for Guth. Did he care about my family? No. No, he did not. He put them in an ashfield."

Zischer then mentions that during the mock Seder he thought about the biblical exodus out of Egypt and he realized that Guth was a modern-day Pharaoh. The man stood before his slaves, dripping with gold and arrogance, and he walked around as if he were immortal, as if the universe had no power over him. Zischer thought about the ten plagues that freed his people from Egypt and he imagined each of them coming to Lubizec: the water changing to blood, the infestations of frogs, and lice, and flies, livestock dying off, horrible boils appearing on the master race, hail smashing into buildings, locusts devouring every green leaf as far as the eye could see, the three days of total darkness, and then, finally, death to every first-born son.

So where was God now? Where were the plagues to save his people? They didn't need to be large plagues. God could change the chemistry of gunpowder so that bullets could no longer be fired, or he could break railroad ties, or he could bring tornadoes swirling down from the heavens to destroy the gas chambers. Anything would do. God didn't need to send frogs or locusts. He could just stop the killing. That's all he needed to do.

And as he looked at the Seder before him, Chaim Zischer decided that when his time came to stand before the Lord and explain his life, he would turn the tables on the Almighty. Instead of explaining his life, he would demand that God explain *his* decisions, and that he would pass judgment on what God had done in 1942. Where were you when my wife and son were destroyed? Where were you when hate ruled the world?

"Beautiful, sir," Schemise said again. He returned the photo with a click of his heels and a little bow. The noise startled Guth and he looked around as if realizing where he was. His face soured and he pointed to a few prisoners.

"Shoot him. Shoot him. And . . . him." He turned on his heel and pushed outside. Snow came swirling in as he trudged into the darkness. The wind howled.

Schemise motioned for the condemned prisoners to come outside while Niemann and Birdie pushed their way to the door. They removed the wine bottle and dragged the light with them. Darkness swallowed the building. No one spoke. No one moved.

There was the sound of a padlock clicking into place and then boots squeaking away on fresh snow. A minute later a pistol cracked into the night three times and the wind picked up. The loose clapboard on the roof began to slap again. It sounded like a machine gun opening up.

All of the prisoners climbed back into their bunks except for the men involved in the mock Seder—they continued to sit on the floor. Chaim Zischer and Dov Damiel were surprised they hadn't been shot and they realized that, in a way, death had indeed passed them over. But for how long?

The six prisoners whispered among themselves.

"Did you hear what Guth said? We'll be dead by April."

"We need to escape."

"Yes, but how?"

"We could dig a tunnel."

"Don't be stupid. The ground's frozen."

There was a pause.

"Even if we escaped, where would we go?"

"Warsaw. We could go to Warsaw."

"Or Kraków."

Another pause.

"We'd have to liquidate the guards."

"And Guth. I'd shoot him personally."

"I've got you now, Birdie."

A searchlight passed over the window and a shaft of white knifed in, momentarily blinding them. Purple dots and squiggly things floated in Zischer's field of vision and then, just as quickly as it happened, inky blackness was poured back onto the barracks.

Zischer let his eyes adjust. The murk took on new forms and he saw things come into focus. Everything seemed clear.

Someone whispered, "I have an idea."

— 17 —

WHAT HAPPENED IN THE ROSE GARDEN

We know that some ninety thousand people died in Lubizec during December 1942 and that roughly the same number perished in January 1943. Towns like Słodowa, Barnow, Belz, and Pawłów vanished from the face of the earth. Synagogues stood empty as whole villages were drained of families. The number of human beings funneling into the camp forced the gas chambers to work almost nonstop during the day and the Roasts were in constant use at night. Two new pits were dug and the heat was so intense it melted huge areas of snow. An oily fountainhead of burnt flesh and boiling marrow blotted out the stars.

To make matters worse, the sun set at 4:15 in the afternoon and this meant the searchlights clicked on as the transports continued to roll in. Snow floated through massive cones of light and everyone jumped out of the cattle cars, frozen and eager for warmth. Thousands were marched off to their deaths with the promise that heat—glorious heat—waited for them up ahead. The guards said there were heavy coats, hats, scarves, and boots for the first people inside the showers.

"Quickly," they yelled while gripping their whips. "It's all waiting up ahead for you."

Chalk numbers were no longer scrawled onto the side of the wagons because no one bothered to count how many people were stuffed inside anymore. The train manifest from the station of departure was now considered "good enough" for such bookkeeping purposes. There was no need to count the prisoners when they arrived into Lubizec because, as everyone now knew, once the train was set into motion it was virtually impossible to escape. If *x* number of Jews departed from such-and-such a place, it was all but guaranteed the same number of Jews would roll into Lubizec. Whether they were alive or dead hardly mattered to the Nazis. The body count wouldn't have changed and that was the main thing.

Guth spent more time in his office trying to figure out how to solve new problems like clearing snow off the rails and what to do with the ash now that the farmers could no longer use it for their fields.*

He had a pile of applewood stacked beside his potbelly stove and he kept it well stoked. Sometimes he twirled his wedding ring as he looked out his office window. Frost clung to the edges. A framed picture of his family was on the desk and he grew tense whenever he heard about more air raids over Berlin. It was during this period of frenzied slaughter that his relationship with Jasmine, which had been icy for many months, was finally beginning to thaw. She mentions in her unpublished diary that she "had decided to forgive Hans for all his little deceptions" and that perhaps she was being "too hard on him since he's under so much beastly pressure."

This "beastly pressure" of course involved the murder of thousands of innocent people, but Jasmine still didn't see any fundamental problem with her husband's job. She mentions in her diary how much she wanted her family back together again, and she also mentions that Guth began to worry that he wasn't around for his children. He missed being a father. And so, at the end of February 1943, the Guth family talked seriously about living under the same roof again. Phone calls were made. Telegrams were sent. Large presents were mailed via *Reichspost*.

Inside Lubizec, however, the world was all snow and midnight. Chaim Zischer and Dov Damiel found themselves in a blur of arriving trains, naked bodies, and death. They had no stove in their barracks, and as they shivered in the dark, they tried not to think

---

* One solution: use it on the footpaths to keep people from slipping. The same thing was done at Auschwitz-Birkenau.

about their lost families because this only resulted in crippling depression. Thinking about life before Lubizec fogged the mind, it weakened you, and it did absolutely no good whatsoever. Only the *now* mattered in Lubizec because the past had been snuffed out and the future was always in doubt. Who knew when a pistol might be leveled against the back of your head? Who knew when you might hear that terrible phrase, "I've got you now, birdie"? You could be whipped to death at any time. No, it was better to live in the present. There was only the *now* because anything on either side of that now didn't exist.

Nevertheless, talk of escape fluttered through the barracks and a core of prisoners huddled together in their bunk beds. Zischer and Damiel were spooned together as they murmured about cutting the barbed-wire fence. Also squashed into their narrow wooden bunk was a former Polish military officer named Avrom Petranker. As far as the Nazis were concerned, Petranker was doubly dangerous because he fought against them in the invasion of 1939 and he also had Jewish blood in his veins. Next to Petranker was David Grinbaum. Tall and lean, Grinbaum had a moon-cratered face because he nearly died of smallpox when he was a child. Moshe Taube, who took part in the mock Seder, was also wedged into the bunk. They whispered to each other as the searchlight floated across the window like an unholy eye. Weird shadows were dragged across the walls and, as the wind howled over the roof, the five men whispered about escape. Slowly, as the searchlight passed back and forth, a plan began to hatch.

"All empires die."

"Yes. This is true."

"Guth is like a golem for the Nazis. He is a mindless follower. A dumb monster. He can be destroyed."

Other prisoners were asked about escape and the idea made everyone itch with hope. As they went about the business of hosing out the gas chambers or stacking warm bodies into the pits, a strange idea began to take root in their heads: Maybe they would live to bear witness about what was happening in Lubizec?

These men had names like Jechiel, Aryeh, Josef, and Scmuel. Omet, Ravid, Joshua, Levi, Kazimierz, and Malachi. No one bothered with last names and, unlike Auschwitz, where a number was tattooed onto everyone's arm, in Lubizec there were no such numbers. The guards referred to the prisoners as "rags" or "pieces of shit." They did this because they saw no need to learn their names. Why bother? In a few months a fresh batch of prisoners would take their places. These prisoners were just shapes that dragged bodies from the gas chambers and yet, as much as the guards wanted these prisoners to be faceless and anonymous, the very opposite was true. The prisoners were all individuals. Some had freckles. Others had crooked teeth. Some were tall. Others short. One had bitten fingernails while another had a scar. One was bald. Another had pimples. One needed to trim the hair that sprouted out of his nose and another had large workmanly knuckles. Many of the prisoners had ghostly pink indents on their fingers where a wedding ring once sat. Such a thing proved that they were beloved, once. Most were married, once. Further back, they had all been rocked to sleep, once. At some point in time, the hot words of love had been whispered into their ears, and once, long ago, in what seemed like another life, they had all been the center of someone else's universe. They were the sun. They were the stars and light. They were the molecules of God himself.

These men with names like Chaim, Dov, Avrom, David, Moshe, Jechiel, Aryeh, Josef, Kazimierz, Scmuel, Omet, Ravid, Joshua, Levi, and Malachi, these men who had once been cradled by loving mothers, these men who wondered what the world might be like when they grew up, these men looked at each other and decided to escape. It was dangerous but they agreed it was better than the oiled mouth of a gun being pressed into their foreheads. If they stayed in Lubizec, it was only a matter of time before they were tossed onto the Roasts.

But to go against what was expected—there at least was something, something to try. Even failure would bring a scrap of success.

The escape would take place after breakfast because they wanted their stomachs full of rye bread. Once they finished eating, that's when they would turn on the guards. Guns would be taken away from the SS and they would shoot their way to the garage where they would hijack one of the "ash trucks". They would then crash through the front gate and drive out towards freedom.

One of the prisoners, Josef Bau, used to drive buses before the Nazis declared that Jews could no longer run public transportation. Bau would be protected by the others as they ran in groups of three to the garage. The guards in the watchtowers would fire their machine guns—that couldn't be stopped or avoided—but Avrom Petranker, the former Polish military officer, told his fellow prisoners to aim at a specific tower and, in this way, covering fire might allow a few men to reach the garage. No one expected to live. They all hoped to live of course, but it seemed more likely they would be gunned down. It was better than doing nothing, though.

"The world needs to know we *did* something," Moshe Taube said. "Let's die for a reason at least."

On the morning of the escape, Chaim Zischer woke up early with a knot of fear in his stomach. He had been startled awake by a terrible nightmare of gunfire and he couldn't fall back to sleep. He wondered how long it might take to die from a bullet wound. Thirty seconds? A minute? His eyes grew heavy and he dreamed about drowning in a lake of blood.

Sometime later, the wooden door of Barrack 14 was thrown open and Birdie yelled, "*Antreten! Antreten!*"

The rubber hose smacked against the bunks.

"Get up, you pieces of shit. Up, up, up!"

Again the hose whistled down.

The world was dim in the bluedawn sunrise and Zischer jumped down from his bunk. His muscles were stiff and he watched clouds of breath leak from everyone's mouths. It reminded him vaguely of horses in a stable. They sprinted outside and Zischer pushed himself to the center of the group in order to keep away from the truncheons and whips. Folk music blared out from the central guard tower as the soft thunder of shoes filled the air. All three hundred prisoners formed up in the Rose Garden, and when they were called to attention, they snapped off their hats in one fluid motion. Zischer's toes were cold and he wiggled them inside his shoes. Soon, he told himself. Soon. In twenty minutes he would be either free or dead.

He smelled the crisp air. Wind flapped against his trouser legs.

Up ahead, Heinrich Niemann paced back and forth. He nearly slipped on a patch of ice but righted himself just in time before falling down.

"You rags need to be taught a lesson!" he yelled at the top of his voice. "Look behind you."

A low whispering filled the cold as the prisoners turned around. There, in the blue murk of morning, were three bodies tangled up in the barbed-wire fencing. They hung like fish in a net. One of them was so badly shot, most of his head was missing from the eyes up. Zischer thought about his own body pumping blood and how the liquid gears beneath his rib cage were going about the silent business of life. His veins were full of blood. His nerves sparkled with electricity. His cells were knitting new cells. His lungs grew big, then small, then big again. He was regenerating into a new person every second, and he wanted this to continue for years to come.

He studied a birch tree in the distance and wondered what it would be like to walk through a world without barbed wire always in front of him. It had been so long, but now the sun was coming up in a ball of orange, and he saw himself walking far beyond the perimeter of the camp. What would it be like to be free again?

"Eyes front!" Niemann shouted.

The prisoners faced the barracks in a rumble of noise. Their long shadows stretched across the trampled snow.

"Those sons of bitches thought they could escape," Niemann said, pacing again. He held up a finger and laughed. "They thought they could cheat destiny. Stupid."

Zischer realized the nightmare he had last night—the one with gunfire—wasn't a dream at all. It must have been real machine guns shattering the night. Bullets really had zipped through flesh and bone. That's what he heard. That's what woke him. That's what made his eyes pop open.

"We're the masters of life and death around here. We decide when you Jews will die. And so, my lovely rags, get on your stomachs."

They all lay down quickly because it would be dangerous not to. The snow was cold against Zischer's cheek and he felt a frozen mound of sand press into his chest. He caught the eye of the man next to him. It was Josef Bau, who was supposed to drive the getaway truck.

What's going on? they asked each other without words.

Fear washed over Zischer and adrenaline fireworked in his muscles when he heard the first shot. There was a pause, then another shot. The sound echoed into the trees. He wanted to lift his head to find out what—*crack*—was going on but if he jumped up now he would be shot for sure. But if he lay still, maybe, yes maybe, he would—*crack*—survive whatever was happening.

On the horizon, a few stars were still out. The sun was the color of a cantaloupe and he found himself thinking about the last time he ate a slice of melon. *Their seeds are so slippery. So these are the things you think about before you die? Cantaloupe seeds?*

The BBC interviewed Chaim Zischer about this massacre in the snow, and he speaks bluntly about what it was like to lie on the ground as a guard walked up and down, randomly shooting first this prisoner, then that prisoner.

"It was Birdie. He lowered his pistol at one head and *crack*, he took a long drag on his cigarette before moving on to the next person. He passed through us like an angel of death. One hand was used for the gun, the other to smoke. First kill with the right, then smoke with the left. His mouth and his pistol were both smoking that morning."

Zischer also mentions how Rudolf Oberhauser and Sebastian Schemise patrolled the perimeter of the camp with machine guns and stomped their feet for warmth. Folk music blared out from the central guard tower and Birdie hummed along to the tubas. He went about killing as though he were a carpenter driving nails into wood.

Crack.

Crack.

Crack.

Each body jumped slightly as a bullet slammed into its skull. Expanding shock waves liquefied memories and whole universes went black as shell casings pinged onto the frozen ground. Blood splashed and pumped onto the snow. The shootings continued and there were so many prisoners murdered that morning that Birdie had to pull out several clips of new bullets. When one ran out, he pulled out a fresh clip and slapped it in with the butt of his palm.

Slowly, randomly, terribly, he moved towards Zischer. The sun was nearly up and a rooster from somewhere nearby called into the morning. Birdie stepped closer and closer. Zischer concentrated on a snowflake not far from his cheek.

So this is the last thing I'll see, he thought. *This snowflake. This useless beautiful thing.*

It sparkled like a diamond and it was so individual, so unique. Birdie's black boots scrunched next to Zischer's head. The man's boot was gigantic and spattered with blood. *So this is how I'm going to die.* He held his breath and imagined a clean room full of light and love. He saw his mother's face. She was folding linen and humming a tune.

Something warm hit Zischer's face. A ringing filled his ears and he fluttered his eyes open.

An unbelievable amount of blood pumped out of Josef Bau's head. It looked like ruby motor oil and Zischer wanted to push himself away from the growing pool, but he lay there with his cheek flat against the numbing snow. The hole was the size of a silver coin and he couldn't look away because that hole could have been in his head. Bau was alive three seconds ago, his lungs inflating and deflating, his heart valves fluttering, but now he was gone. A whole world was once living in Josef Bau's head but now it was leaking all over the ground. Nothing could stop it now. A widening pool of childhood memories and learning and love and thousands of meals and loose baby teeth and learning to tie shoelaces and running after balls and dreaming and walks in the forest and playing with a dog and getting chicken pox and picking bark off a tree and writing a poem and a first kiss and running with friends and watching sunlight come through a window and dancing and drinking wine and laughing—it was all spilling out of Josef Bau. Part of the universe was dying. A tiny corner of it was being drained of light.

Birdie moved down the line, firing here, firing there, creating new holes, draining memory, blackening the universe, killing the future, and his pistol needed to be reloaded every now and again. He continued on, humming.

We should pause to consider that one man and one gun created all of this devastation. Birdie pointed, squeezed, and the gun spoke, bullet after bullet. It was just a standard issue collection of oiled metal parts, gunpowdery chemistry, flint and spark, velocity and unstoppable physics. Yet the gun itself becomes unique at this point and it should be in a museum somewhere under glass, its hammer locked shut—muzzled—so that we can gaze upon it safely and consider how it was used. We know what became of this man who killed these prisoners, but what became of this gun, this Sauer 38H semi-automatic pistol? It was only slightly larger than a fist and it punched out death. Maybe it's hanging in a collector's case in Los Angeles or Dublin or Moscow right now. The fingerprints on its trigger would have been wiped away by time long ago. The collector who owns it probably isn't aware of its history. It's just a thing. It's just something from World War II. It's just a gun.

"It could have been me," Zischer told the BBC. "Bau was shot but it could have been me if Birdie moved a bit differently or if he decided to aim his pistol to the right instead of the left. When I think about this for too long, I feel like a corpse on vacation. Why did I survive when so many others did not? Why was I saved?"

On and on the killings went, rhythmic and terrible, until Birdie flicked his cigarette onto a freshly dead body and complained about his hand cramping up. He holstered his weapon and massaged his palm.

"Ouch," he laughed. "That hurts."

Somewhere in the distance, a rooster called out into the pale morning light. It sounded like laughter. Like cosmic laughter.

Of the three hundred prisoners that ran into the Rose Garden on February 21, 1943, nearly half of them were shot. An exact figure can never be known but these random executions, these sluggish killings, they haunted Chaim Zischer for the rest of his life and he often woke up screaming as the shadow of Birdie crept closer and closer.

"Why does this stay with me?" he asked the BBC. "Thousands of people were killed at Lubizec every day. But when I think about this I feel like an old jug cracking apart."

Maybe it was the helplessness of lying on the snow, or maybe it was the haphazard way Birdie moved the pistol first here, then there, but one thing is certain: When it was all over, the escape plan was in tatters.

Heinrich Niemann made a megaphone of his hands and yelled out, "If you're alive, stand up. Move it, move it. Quickly. There's no breakfast this morning for you filthy fucking Jews. Move it."

The living hauled away the dead. It took twenty minutes of grunting but all of the bodies were eventually dumped into a wooden cart. Their clothes were stripped off and they were stacked onto the Roasts where they, like everyone else that filed into Lubizec, were doused with gasoline. These men who once dreamed of escape had names like David, Jechiel, Aryeh, Josef, Kazimierz, Scmuel, Omet, Ravid, Joshua, Levi, and Malachi. They were little bits of the universe, and now they were gone.

"When I saw these men stacked up and ready for the flame," Zischer told the BBC, "I thought about hanging myself. I did. Really, I did." In the video his chin starts to quiver and he waves his hand. "Turn off your camera."

While the bodies were being cleared away, the door to Guth's office swung open. He walked across the crunchy snow with a letter in his hands. It flapped in the breeze.

"They're coming home," he said triumphantly. "Jasmine and the kids, they're coming home next week." He grinned from ear to ear.

"I'll need some champagne and caviar. And oh!" He snapped his fingers a few times. "I'll need some of that chocolate. The thick bars. From Belgium. Remember? Can you organize that for me, Schemise? I need to get home and do a few things."

Prisoners continued to haul away bodies. They shoveled red snow into wheelbarrows.

"By the way, what was all the shooting about?"

Birdie stiffened. "Discipline. We had to crack a few eggs."

Guth nodded, then went back to talking about cakes, and balloons, and bottles of wine, and a nice big ham—one that was thickly marbled with fat. He and the other guards strolled away towards the gas chambers. They laughed and pushed each other playfully, like boys at a bright carnival.

No one, not even Guth, could have guessed that within two short weeks Lubizec would be in flames. And it would happen in a way that surprised everyone.

— 18 —

BEFORE THE STORM

Guth drove to Lublin to pick up his family. Although we don't know what he was thinking at the time, we do know that two massive swastika flags flapped above the cream-colored train station and that Guth stood on Platform 2. He wore his leather trench coat as heavy snow fluttered down onto the tracks. It covered grease and dirt and spent cigarette butts. It prettied up the world and made everything look unsoiled. Huge flakes stuck to him as a whistle pierced the horizon. A yellow ball of light slowly emerged from the cottony distance, and he straightened the visor of his SS hat as the train chugged closer and closer. Railcars clattered and squealed to a stop as he looked for his family. He stood in front of the first-class section amid signs that said GERMANS ONLY.

The reunion was full of hugs. Guth crouched down and gathered Sigi and Karl into his arms. He kissed them lavishly before standing up and embracing his wife. He kissed her twice on both of her cheeks. The four of them stood in a little circle and talked excitedly over one another about their long journey. A porter grabbed their luggage and they all walked to a black Mercedes in a GERMANS ONLY parking area, one that was right in front of the station. Guth drove his family to a café near Adolf Hitler Plaza where they got sandwiches and bottled blueberry juice for the road. Because it was such a long drive back to Lubizec—at least two hours—Guth brought along some books and toys for his children. As they drove over the frozen road, husband and wife held hands. Her fingernails were painted red; his were clipped short. They both wore their wedding rings. The windshield wipers squeaked back and forth as snow continued to fall and, before them, the road unspooled in a long white ribbon.

Guth hired two more servants to make life at the Villa easier for his wife: A new maid was brought in to tidy up the place and a handyman was added to shovel snow from the driveway as well as keep the furnace stoked with coal. It was dark when they pulled through the front gate, and the headlamps of the car cast beams onto the Spanish-style house. The front door opened and the servants came out to greet the family. Luggage was taken off the back of the car and everyone rushed inside where they laughed about the cold and stomped snow off their boots. Scented candles were lit, while in the blazing fireplace, logs crackled and spat sparks.

Many decades later, when Sigi was an old woman looking back on the topography of her life, she said this was a glorious moment and that it was one of her favorite memories. She kept touching her father's arm to prove that he wasn't a dream, and when she hugged him, his Iron Cross pressed into her cheek. She fingered the silver lightning bolts of the SS on his lapel and noticed the smell of cologne. It was a woodsy vanilla citrus and she pressed herself into him to sniff it deeply. The fabric of his uniform was soft against her face.

"My little baroness," he said, cupping her head. "It's good to have you home."

Sigi devotes a whole chapter of *The Commandant's Daughter* to this reunion, and it is very difficult to read, not just because she writes with such effervescent joy about seeing her father again, but also because there is no mention of the death camp at all. Even though a kingdom of murder was only a few kilometers away, she never mentions it. It's like the place never existed. When she was eleven-years old she might not have thought much about Lubizec during this welcome home party (she was, after all, a young girl absorbed in her own little universe), but as an adult Sigi makes absolutely no reference to the camp during this long chapter of homecoming. This is a problem. A rather large problem. It's as if Sigi has blocked it out because she didn't want to see her father as a man who turned people into ash. She writes instead about how good it was to see him, and we read about giggles, sweetened orange juice, honey-cured ham, and how Guth pulled out a long string of pearls for his wife. These pearls almost certainly came from the cluttered warehouses of Zurich, but Sigi never makes this connection. Instead, she talks about how nice it was to see her father lean over and snap these pearls around her mother's neck.

"It was beautiful," Sigi writes. "They were rare blue pearls and there was a silver clasp on the back that was just exquisite. My mother wore it every day after this and she often stroked it with her fingers when she was deep in thought."

In other parts of her book, Sigi does examine her father's role in the industrialized genocide of the Holocaust, but in this particular chapter, she is mute, tight lipped, in obvious denial. While we should be critical of this oversight, it does reflect the general mood that settled over the Guth household by early 1943. That is to say, it had been decided that no more questions would be asked about Lubizec and that the family would carry on as if the place wasn't a place at all. The camp became negative space. It became a void in the woods. It was unknown and unknowable. As far as the family was concerned, Guth went to work each morning and he returned home each night smelling vaguely of campfire. Whatever happened in between was off limits for discussion.

"It was just so wonderful to be home," Sigi glows in her autobiography. "I loved the grand wooden staircase and the huge marble fireplace where I could read my books in peace. I loved that old home. I was very happy, very happy indeed."

As the weeks passed, the family settled into a familiar routine. Tutors drove down from Lublin to teach Sigi and Karl such subjects as German literature, German history, geography, mathematics, and race theory. On Sundays they had piano lessons. Sometimes a snowstorm kept them indoors, but whenever it was nice outside, they went sledding down a nearby hill. Other times they went ice skating on their private lake. German bombers often cut long gashes of white across the cold blue sky and their desynchronized engines sounded frightening. *Whur-a . . . whur-a . . . whur-a.* They sounded like a plague of insects droning towards Russia. A few hours later they returned. *Whur-a . . . whur-a . . . whur-a.* There were always fewer of them on the return journey. Some of them had streaks of inky smoke trailing from their engines. Once, the children saw a bomber break apart in flight and fall like a meteor.

It would be good to pause at this point and consider the war raging beyond the rail tracks of Lubizec. The Nazis invaded Russia on June 22, 1941, and it remains one of the largest military invasions in the history of warfare. The army, however, was unable to take Moscow before winter and they suffered enormous causalities. Men were cut to pieces as the snow howled around them. Another attempt at smashing the Soviet Union occurred a year later during the Battle of Stalingrad (August 1942 to February 1943) and this too was a crippling disaster. At least five hundred thousand Germans were killed and the Soviets suffered causalities in excess of one million men. It was the bloodiest battle of the twentieth century, and it was quite possibly the bloodiest military engagement in all of world history. Stalingrad was a meat grinder. Men were chewed up and spat out. The ground was littered with their frozen contorted bodies, and daily newspapers had trouble printing the obituaries for so many men. By March 1943, it was obvious to most Germans they were losing the "war in the east."

And yet, although the Nazi Empire was losing ground and finding its status as a master race challenged, it still channeled precious resources towards the destruction of the Jews. Trains kept on rolling towards the death camps even though they were badly needed for the war. Troops were also used to round up the ghettos when they too could have been sent to the front line. Gasoline, which was always in short supply, was reserved for the death camps. All of this makes no sense from a military perspective, but we need to remember that, for the Nazis, they may have been losing one war but they were determined to win the "race war" against the Jews. It was one thing to lose ground to the Soviets but it was another matter entirely to wipe the Jews off the map of Europe. As far as Adolf Hitler was concerned, the first war could be lost, but not the second.

And so, each morning Guth buttoned up his greatcoat and adjusted his peaked officer's hat in the mirror. He left at seven and returned at nine in the evening. Sometimes he came home for lunch and helped his children with math homework. They used a slide rule to figure out addition and subtraction. He was especially gifted at division. Trains whistled in the pine trees and, at night, a dull orange glow warmed the sky above the camp. Flecks of soot mixed with falling snow but no one asked what it was. And still the trains kept on coming.

Although Guth was busy oiling the machinery of destruction, he usually took Sundays off. He rested. He slept in. And it was during a glorious afternoon in early March, when spring was waking up from hibernation and they were snowshoeing in the woods as a family, that he talked about going to Barcelona.

"I'd like to see the place. We should take a holiday," Guth said, passing a shiny metal thermos to his wife.

"But why Spain?"

He opened up his arms and looked around. "Because there's no *snow* there, my dear. We can go swimming in the Mediterranean and eat seafood until we burst." He puffed himself up and waddled over to Karl. "Crab cakes. I want to eat crab cakes until I'm the size of a zeppelin. Give me some of your crabby cakes."

Although we can't be sure why Guth was drawn to Barcelona, it seems reasonable to assume he became interested in the city because he saw a travel poster for it several times a day. As train after train rolled into Lubizec, he saw fake advertisements for trips to Berlin, Athens, and Barcelona. This travel poster almost certainly made him want to crack open shellfish and walk the tangled medieval lanes of a grand city. Maybe he studied this poster for Barcelona and imagined himself sitting under the sun, his shirt off, his eyes closed.

Next to him is a tall drink with a little umbrella in it. He dozes, his conscience unhaunted.*

"I'd love to see the place," he said, taking back the thermos. He stuffed it into his backpack and looked up at the leaden sky. "Let's go someplace warm."

Jasmine was full of excitement. "Why wait? Let's go on a family holiday now. We could stay in a hotel and go shopping in Kraków."

Guth scrunched away on snowshoes. He took long strides and glanced back. "Good idea. I haven't had a vacation since we came to this place so I'll ask for a seventy-two-hour pass. What do you kids think? Should we go to Kraków?"

They cheered and talked about loading up the car.

Back in the death camp, the prisoners were also making plans. They huddled in the dark and whispered about timing, and ammunition, and gasoline.

---

* Our own sense of justice makes us shudder at this image, and the more we think about it the more obscene it becomes. For other disturbing views of Nazi murderers at rest, see the photos in *"The Good Old Days": The Holocaust as Seen by Its Perpetrators and Bystanders* (1988) as well as Karl Höcker's photo album of how he relaxed at Auschwitz-Birkenau. These photos, all taken in 1944, are currently housed at the United States Holocaust Memorial Museum. Labeled as *Auschwitz Through the Lens of the SS*, there are photos of Nazi guards eating blueberries, playing the accordion, and drinking glasses of foamy beer at a resort called Solahütte, not far from the gas chambers. It is chilling to see how relaxed they are. How at ease.

19

THE END OF THIS WORLD BEGINS NOW

Clouds rolled overhead as prisoners ran into the Rose Garden. *Achtung*, a guard shouted, and they took off their smelly hats in one fluid motion. Eight suicides were dragged out of the barracks and their bodies were swung into a wooden cart. The iron springs creaked with each thump. The belts they hanged themselves with were still around their necks, and from the central guard tower happy polka music played out. The sun warmed the air as a sworl of blue appeared on the horizon. It felt warm. Pleasant. The prisoners lined up for their daily ration of bread and lard. Crows cawed from the barbed-wire fence.

Zischer looked around and realized storks would soon be flying back from Africa. Spring was on its way. Life was returning to Poland.

We know from various reports that March 15, 1943, was unseasonably warm, and in the days leading up to the escape attempt the temperature averaged a balmy 15°C (60°F). Huge banks of snow were melting and the Rose Garden became a soupy mixture of water, sand, and gray snow. Boots sank into the sloppy mess and it was very difficult to walk, let alone run. Socks had to be wrung out. All of Lubizec trickled with brown water, and every now and then, huge sheets of snow slid off the barrack roofs—they woomped to the ground. After enduring subzero weather for so long, it must have been almost tropical for the prisoners to experience such heat again. Jackets were unbuttoned and they did away with their scarves. They no longer needed to blow into their hands or worry about frostbite. They stopped dreaming about fireplaces and hot-water bottles. They turned their faces to the sun.

The executions in the Rose Garden seemed like a hundred years ago because so much killing had happened since then. Life (or in this case, death) had moved on. Chaim Zischer and Dov Damiel had to remind themselves it wasn't that long ago they were forced to lie on the ground and listen to bullets crack into skulls. At night, some of the men in Barrack 14 whispered about what they'd like to do to Birdie. It was a powerful elixir, talking about such things— it filled their muscles with magic and their faces glowed whenever they imagined him kneeling on the wet ground.

"I've got you now, Birdie."

Then they pulled the imaginary trigger. He was resurrected through fantasy and they fired again, and again, because they wanted to keep him endlessly dying.

"It was a pleasant daydream," Chaim Zischer later said.

More than anything, the prisoners wanted the world to know they weren't going to their deaths passively, and even if an escape failed, even if they never made it beyond the barbed wire, perhaps they could destroy the engine that pumped carbon monoxide into the gas chambers. An escape attempt, even a poor one, meant the machinery of death might be slowed down for a few days. They didn't know what lay beyond the trees, and they didn't know who they could trust outside Lubizec, but it was a worth a try. Anything was better than doing nothing.

It was therefore decided that the newer prisoners shouldn't know about the plan beforehand because someone might betray them for a roasted chicken or the promise of oranges. The men in Barrack 14 began to speak in code, and they let secrecy be the order of the day. Once the fighting started, maybe others would join in.

They hatched a plan.

They shook on it.

They said, "Good luck."

It started when Avrom Petranker asked to sharpen three knives. He walked across the soggy ground and went to a toolshed near the gas chambers. Sebastian "SS" Schemise came from the other direction and took out his pistol. He held it playfully, at a sloppy and carefree angle. The bolt was oiled and ready for use.

"What're you doing here, friend?"

"I need to sharpen these." Petranker held up the knives and explained that a cow had been bought from a nearby farm. He was ordered to butcher the animal but the knives were too dull.

Schemise curled a long finger as if to say, *Let me see them*. He ran his thumb along one of the blades and looked doubtful.

"Make it quick." He dropped the knife point first into the ground. It stood for a moment before it fell sideways into the soupy sand.

"You a kosher butcher? I'd be interested in seeing that dying art."

Petranker shook his head—"No, sir"—then kneeled down for the knife. He backed away into the shed and let his eyes adjust to the dark. He waited to see if Schemise was following him but, no, he wasn't. Tools hung on the wall, and around each of them was a white silhouette to mark where they should go. In this way, the guards could tell at a glance if something was missing. Everything around him was covered in grease and sawdust.

Petranker reached for a sharpening stone that was gritty and smelled of oil. He began running it against a blade. A grinding metallic scrape filled up the shed.

It took half an hour to make the knives glisten, but he was pleased to see blood rise up from his thumb when he touched the blade. He reached for some needle-nose pliers and began to sharpen a notch that could be used for snipping wire. He tested it on a coil of barbed wire and smiled when he heard a soft *clip*. He tried it again. Success! He opened his coat, reached for several screwdrivers, and then stuffed them into his pockets. A hammer was snugged behind his back, gunlike. It fit neatly beneath his belt.

He jogged past a group of naked women on their way to the gas chamber and hid everything behind an enormous sack of hair. He still wasn't used to the smell and he felt something tart rise up in his throat, like rancid butter. He gagged and covered his nose. He spit on the floor a few times to clear his mouth.

When he ran back outside, the engine was clattertapping at

full speed. There were muffled screams for help from inside the gas chamber, and he knew that, soon, he would be dragging those bodies to the Roasts. He would have to grab wrists and ankles. He would have to pull, and tug, and yank.

While Petranker waited outside the chamber with the other prisoners, he glanced at Zischer. They looked at the gritty wet ground that swallowed up their shoes, and they tried not to think about what was happening behind the metal door. There was banging and yelling.

"Mommy, help me!" a child screamed.

They had already seen such terrible things that morning—haunting, lingering things—but it was no different from any other morning in this "Garden of Evil," as the prisoners were now calling Lubizec. Here, each sin was polished to a high shine. There were tears and screeching and deep-lunged wailing and stunned looks of disbelief. The world became a blur of wickedness and things that once seemed hideous—like when one of the guards, Christian Schwartz, hit a child so hard he broke her arm—became instead commonplace and unremarkable. And now that same child was dying in a gas chamber. In this garden of evil created by man, sin was bitten into hour after hour. A great serpent hissed out poison and still the trains kept on coming.

The shouting slowed behind the metal door as hundreds of hearts stopped beating.

Zischer readied himself for the hard work of pulling gold teeth. He glanced at Petranker and there was a brief nod between them that said, *Yes.*

It had taken several days but each man had gathered the things he needed, not only for the escape but also for the uncertain future that lay ahead of them. Dov Damiel stuffed a shaving kit, soap, some money, and several diamonds into a pillowcase. David Grinbaum had a razor, a toothbrush, a compass, and some ruby necklaces. Avrom Petranker had a can opener and four watches. Moshe Taube had these things plus a pair of boots.

When the gas chamber door was thrown open, banging and

vibrating against the opposite wall, the men dragged out the bruised bodies. Zischer saw the girl with the broken arm and he bowed his head.

Soon, he told himself. Soon.

They waited until dusk because they wanted enough light for the escape, but they also wanted enough darkness to hide in the woods. And so, after many long hours of anxiety—and after 2,057 souls had been snuffed out on the 2:00 p.m. transport—inky night was at last poured onto the land and the electrical lights near the gas chamber flickered on like spirits. The camp was quiet. At rest. Almost peaceful.

It started when Moshe Taube took in a lungful of air and yelled up to the heavens in Hebrew, "THE END OF THIS WORLD BEGINS NOW!"

This set everything into motion. Damiel and Petranker took out the knives hidden in their coats and they charged at the guard closest to them. It was so unexpected and fast that *SS Unterscharführer* Christian Schwartz didn't shout for help. He dropped to his knees and was shocked to find that he had been stabbed five times in the belly and once in the shoulder. He looked at the dark blood dripping like molasses on his hands and, when he tried to speak, only a low gurgling came from his lips.

Damiel and Petranker reached for his pistol and dragged him against a wall. They bound him with rope and stuffed an oily, sawdusty rag into his mouth. Instead of shooting him, which would draw too much attention to their position, Petranker spat on the Nazi. He dragged a tarp over the dying man and spat again. He kicked once, twice.

Then the two prisoners set off for the gas chamber. They felt a strange sense of power wash over them as they ran through the sloppy sucking sand.

The gas chamber stank of chlorine and the walls were damp. Petranker flattened himself into the dark while Damiel stepped outside to find another guard. He approached Gustav Wagner, who was busy trying to light a cigarette. He had a face like an anvil and he wore strong aftershave.

"Sir," Damiel said, snapping off his cap. "The drain in Chamber #4 is plugged. I'm sorry, sir, but could you come and look?"

Wagner shook his head. "Do I look like a plumber?"

"I don't know how to unblock the drain, sir. The next transport is due tomorrow and I don't want things to slow down."

"You Yids. So fucking useless. Okay, show me."

They stepped into the building and Damiel pointed to the center of the floor. "It's plugged with something. Hair maybe or—"

Before he could finish his sentence there was a tremendous flash of orange. His ears rang and Wagner crumpled to the floor. The smell of cordite hung in the air and this made the escape real in a way the knifing had not. Petranker pounced on the fallen body, he smashed the man's opened skull into the floor a few times, and then he patted the dead man's hips. He held up a pistol.

"Here. Take this."

Damiel took the gun with both hands and couldn't believe he was holding such a powerful thing in Lubizec. It seemed dreamlike. The metal was cold and its weight felt like an extension of his fist. All he had to do was point at something he didn't like and pull the trigger. It was simple. A hammer would snap down and the life in front of him would drop. His face hardened when he thought about this, and the two men stuffed the pistols into their coats. They walked out the door.

Prisoners were busy dragging bodies towards the Roasts and the guards shouted for them to move faster. Damiel and Petranker slipped around the back of the gas chamber and breathed heavily; they knew they'd run into at least one guard because no one was allowed behind the gas chambers—that's where the engine was. It looked like a swollen sea creature with monstrous tentacles, and it was always guarded by the SS because they worried about acts of sabotage. It was the SS who made sure the spark plugs fired properly, and it was the SS who made sure the gears were well oiled. They checked belts and hoses once a week; they guarded it like a loved one. A shadow paced beside the monstrous engine.

It was Rudolf Oberhauser. "Is that you, Schemise?"

Petranker tiptoed through the deep blue light. The pistol in his hand tugged him forward, forward, forward.

"Schemise?"

The shots drilled the air but the guard didn't fall to the ground. Instead, he ducked behind the engine and began to shout. "Attack, attack! We're being attacked!"

Petranker followed him around and fired again.

"Attack! We're being attacked! Sound the alarm!"

The air sizzled with confusion as other guards began to shout. Damiel found himself holding a pistol with both hands and when Rudolf Oberhauser ran around the engine towards him—he fired. The force of the gun surprised him and his ears rang.

The German who always yelled "Time to die" before the carbon monoxide was pumped into the gas chamber dropped to the ground and began to roll around. He ripped open his jacket, which sent buttons popping into the air, and patted his chest frantically. Blood leaked out of him.

"I'm shot," he half shouted. "I've been . . . *hurt*," he said this in wonderment as if something supernatural had happened.

Dov Damiel was later asked how he felt about this in an interview conducted in 1988. He shrugs. "Should I grieve for this man who yelled into the peephole of a gas chamber? Should I feel sorry for this killer of children? No."

The interviewer then asks Damiel if he wanted to say "Time to die" as Rudolf Oberhauser bled to death on the sandy ground.

Damiel's answer is worth noting because he looks at the interviewer for a long time. He squints and shakes his head. "That kind of thing is only done in the movies. I was more interested in escape than in theatrics. Time to die? Why would I waste my breath on such words?"

As Oberhauser went about the business of dying, the searchlights snapped on, but rather than point these shafts of light into the camp, where the gunfire was coming from, something unexpected happened. The guards aimed these huge cones of light into the woods because they assumed the Russians were attacking Lubizec. They thought the front line had somehow shifted and that the Red Army was closing in on them. It never occurred to them that Jews might be rebelling, so the guards opened up their machine guns in a hail of bullets. Hundreds of rounds were fired into the trees. Branches tumbled to the ground. Trunks were peppered with holes. Bark exploded into shreds. The searchlights jerked through the woods and this made phantom shadows seem to run across the forest floor. For the guards (at least in those first few minutes of the escape), the enemy had to come from outside of Lubizec. They just couldn't imagine the enemy was inside the camp.

Damiel stepped over the body in front of him and began to study the engine. The metal was cold as he searched for a way to start it. Petranker crawled under the iron monster and looked for the oil plug.

"Where is it? Can you see the damn thing?"

They only had a few minutes to destroy the engine before they had to snip the barbed-wire fence and meet up with the others. Time was ticking away as machine guns rattled long threads of light into the woods. Weird shadows were cast onto the ground as Damiel and Petranker searched for the oil plug. It had to be somewhere. Their hands groped the fat belly of the machine, sand got into their hair, and it was hard to see. Once they found the plug—*if* they found the plug—oil could be drained from the crankcase and then they could start it up. The pistons would ride up and down in unoiled chambers and the whole thing would shriek to an earsplitting stop. The engine would be wrecked, destroyed. Killed.

But first, they needed to find the oil plug.

"Where *is* it?" Damiel hissed.

While all of this was going on another group of prisoners (Moshe Taube, Chaim Zischer, and David Grinbaum) ran towards the lower end of camp. It was their job to burn Zurich to the ground and if possible shoot Guth. The ground was wet as they half ran, half slid, in front of the squat barracks. Their reflections appeared on the thin windows, and Chaim Zischer ran his fingers along the rough wooden clapboards. Keep going, he told himself.

The world was a blur of motion and he felt alive down to his nerve endings. Searchlights slashed the woods. Guards shouted. The whole world buzzed with noise and light and fear as Zischer opened a low gate that led to the warehouses. He and the others pushed into one of the buildings, and when the door was closed, when it was latched shut, they allowed themselves to catch their breath. They leaned against the wall and looked around.

Machine guns sounded like hammers knocking against a metal wall. They pounded and pounded the air.

"So this is war," Zischer whispered to himself.

Something shifted inside his bowels and he had to tighten his asshole to keep from soiling himself. "Easy," he told himself.

It is important for us to remember that none of these prisoners expected to live. They simply wanted to disrupt Lubizec for a few days and slow down the killing process. Yes, an escape had been planned, and yes, they wanted it to succeed, but they had no idea where they would go after they cut the barbed-wire fencing. They couldn't go home. They couldn't stay in the woods. Farmers would turn them in. And even if they reached major cities like Warsaw or Kraków, what then? Jews were being rounded up by the millions. The prisoners certainly hoped to live, but their primary goal was to slow down the genocidal gears of the camp. If the guards had to hunt them down in the woods, it meant they couldn't be running the gas chambers or sending gold back to Berlin. It's important for us to remember that the escape wasn't about escape: It was about rebellion.

Zischer and the others walked to the wooden shelving. A metal can of gasoline had been hidden in the barracks earlier that day and now they reached for it. They splashed it onto clothes and piles of money. They splashed it onto the shelving itself. They dumped the last of it on a pile of woolen caps. They found bottles of whiskey and vodka and cognac and smashed those against the walls.

"Ready?" Moshe asked, picking up a cigarette lighter. There were hundreds of them in a wicker basket and he underhanded several to David Grinbaum. "Here. Take these."

Machine guns continued to rattle and pound outside as the three prisoners put tongues of flame to wood. Blue and orange-yellow flared up the pine shelving. Shirts and caps and tables were soon burning. The three men (for in that moment they felt like men again) ran outside and left the front door open. Fresh air moved into the building and the flames grew and grew. Smoke began to cloud the windows.

They ran into another barrack and splashed yet another hidden can of gasoline onto piles of socks, corsets, dresses, and children's clothing. It was also set on fire and they went into a third barrack—this one was packed with enormous burlap sacks of human hair—and the men stopped in their tracks.

They looked at each other, wondering what to do.

There was an odd smell hanging in the space and the noise around them fell away as they stared at the harvest of hair. It was unsettling. There was something intimate and private about this. They had gotten used to dead bodies and sizzling corpses, but here were the last tangible remains of the living. Cells and roots. Tresses of black and blond and gray and red. There were long braids that had been snipped off close to the base of the skull. And it was all going to be woven into fabric, made into blankets. Each sack was the size of a file cabinet and they stood in ordered rows like huge cancerous tumors. The words REICH PROPERTY were stamped onto each of them.

"Come," Moshe Taube said.

He clicked one of his cigarette lighters. It was an older model that stayed lit until the hinged top was snapped back into place—only then would the flame go out—and he leaned it against a sack. The bag began to smolder as orange worms of light ate into the burlap.

Zischer and Grinbaum reached for their own lighters and they too rested little flames next to the dried hair. They went down the line, placing lighters here and there. The sacks grew into smoky balls of acrid flame.

The men ran outside and heard machine guns strafing into the woods. The first warehouse was now a raging fire, windows cracked and shattered, and a huge cloud of filthy smoke billowed out the front door. It lifted into the night like a dark tornado.

When the guards saw this, there was a slowing in the camp. A pause.

The machine guns stopped firing into the night and the searchlights rested on the tree branches.

Silence.

A moment of hesitation. Only the soft roar and crackle of the fire could be heard.

And then the searchlights wheeled around and illuminated the whole camp. Prisoners scurried away as bullets chewed up the Rose Garden. Clumps of wet dirt hopped into the air and prisoners began to shout.

"Stop!"

"Don't shoot!"

The men still had three more barracks to torch but if they wanted to kill Guth they needed to do it now. Time was running out. Moshe Taube had a sharpened knife in his jacket while Zischer and Grinbaum had screwdrivers. The moon was a dirty white rag rising on the horizon, and they ran towards an area of camp they had only seen from afar: the private barracks of the SS. A light was on in Guth's office.

Bullets splintered wood around them as they threw themselves into the wet, sandy muck to protect themselves. They breathed hard and wondered what to do. They spat sand from their mouths and looked at one another. Was Guth in there? If so, for how long?

Machine guns swept the other side of the Rose Garden. Everyone was shouting and moaning and screaming, the whole camp was a swirl of chaos, and that's when someone with a deep voice got on the loudspeaker.

"Achtung! Achtung! Jetzt antreten zum Appell!"

The voice ordered the prisoners to line up in the Rose Garden, but everyone knew there would be no salvation or mercy if they did such a thing. They would all die. Zurich was in flames and the guards would reap a terrible vengeance. Whether they were shot by machine guns now or whether they were lined up before the Roasts later didn't matter because, come morning, everyone would be turned into corpses. In that moment every prisoner in Lubizec knew what waited for them. They scattered from the searchlights. They ran. They hid.

"*Antreten, antreten.*"

As Zischer, Taube, and Grinbaum ran towards Guth's office, a string of SS sprinted towards them, their legs working hard. One of these officers was Birdie Franz and when he saw the prisoners in an area of camp that was strictly off-limits to them, he pulled out his pistol. He lowered the snout of his gun and took a few steps forward.

"What're you doing here?"

His green eyes were hard and piercing. Shadows of hellfire danced on the visor of his SS hat and this made the little death head's emblem seem bright and alive. He took another step and repeated the question.

"I said, what are you doing here?"

Moshe Taube clicked his wet shoes together and came to attention. "Sir," he said with a little Hitler salute, "I wish to report we have been sent to get buckets."

"Buckets?"

"To put out the fire, sir."

Birdie looked at the sooty cloud pouring up into the sky. It was a volcano of ash and spark. He lowered his gun, cocked his head back and forth as if weighing a thought, and then took off running with the other guards towards Zurich.

"Get those buckets," he yelled back. "Hurry!"

We should remind ourselves that Birdie was in charge of these buildings, and he was probably worried about how he would explain the fire. Was it arson? An accident? Did he do it on purpose to hide the true extent of things *he* had stolen? These are all questions Berlin would have asked, and since he had already been investigated once before for missing inventory, he must have been anxious to put out the fire. No wonder he didn't shoot any of the prisoners. This is almost certainly why he spared them and told them to get buckets.

"Antreten, antreten," came the voice over the loudspeaker again. It sounded nervous and human.

The machine guns weren't popping so often now, and Chaim Zischer took a moment to notice the bodies scattered around the camp, how the moon shimmered in invisible waves of heat, and how the barracks were being eaten alive. Something primal was devouring Zurich. The wooden walls were greased with fire and orange sparks drifted up. A window shattered and there was a sudden roar of flame.

"Antreten, antreten."

The three men ran towards Guth's office. A light was on and they moved down a brick path. Zischer was full of adrenaline when they came to the little wooden building. Two large flowerpots filled with melting snow and cigarette butts were on either side of the door. There was a sign that read, *SS Obersturmführer Hans-Peter Guth.* The prisoners looked at each other and got out their weapons. They turned the handle.

Avrom Petranker and Dov Damiel were happy to be under the engine when the machine guns began showering bullets into the camp. Their fingers danced on the cold metal until they found the plug. It was easy to unscrew because the oil was changed so frequently and because nothing was allowed to get rusty. If the engine went down for repairs it meant transports would get backed up on the line, and this in turn would make the higher-ups in Berlin furious. As a result, this engine, which ran for hours at a time, was in immaculate condition.

Petranker unscrewed the bolt and felt thick oil dribble onto his fingers. It threaded its way down to the hair of his forearm.

"Good," he said, wiping it onto his trousers.

Even in the murky dark with searchlights slashing all around them, Dov Damiel could tell his fellow prisoner was smiling. They were supposed to start the engine but it was now so black they couldn't find the ignition switch. Damiel slapped the instrument panel in frustration because they were running late to meet up with the others.

"Wait, wait," Petranker said, holding up a finger.

Wordlessly, he went around to the gas tank and began to unscrew the cap. Two guards huffed past them with guns but they didn't pay any attention, nor did they see the body splayed out on the concrete pad beneath the engine. Petranker threw the gas cap on the ground and went over to Oberhauser's body. He pulled off a leather boot and yanked on the man's damp sock—he stretched it out like taffy—and when it finally snapped free he bent down to sop up the oil. He stuffed it halfway into the gas tank.

"Got a lighter?"

Damiel shook his head. The men looked around for something to light the sock, and after a few seconds of cursing and patting their pockets Petranker glanced back at Oberhauser's body. He searched through the man's bloody clothes until he found something: a silver cigarette lighter.

"You okay with this?"

Damiel knew exactly what he meant. When the gasoline was ignited, the tank would blast apart and shrapnel would shred everything. Men on the other side of the camp would be knocked off their feet and an explosion, like a smoky exclamation point, would rise gently into the sky.

"I'm ready," he said.

Once again, it is important to remember that Lubizec was a place without hope or mercy, and because none of the prisoners expected to survive the escape we shouldn't view Damiel or Petranker as either heroic or fatalistic. They were just being realistic and they acted accordingly.

In an interview that was conducted in 1988, Damiel looks down at his gnarled hands and says about this moment, "It wasn't that I wanted to die. Who does? If I was killed in an explosion, so be it. If I was shot, so be it. Sure I wanted more minutes of life, everyone wants such things, but I thought my body would be on the Roasts that night. We all did. And if I died in an explosion or if I died later at the hands of the SS, what did I care? Dead is dead. It was a matter of *how* I died, not if."

Avrom Petranker flicked the thumbwheel of the cigarette lighter. A few weak sparks appeared in the dark. He tried again and again, but still nothing. He shook it next to his ear.

"Damn it."

When asked about this in 1988, Dov Damiel smiles. "Ironic, no? A fire is eating the warehouses of Lubizec but we can't light a stupid sock."

The two men stood there and watched five more guards run towards Zurich. All of the prisoners were ordered over the loudspeaker to scoop snow into buckets and toss it onto the blaze. The machine guns slowed down and the searchlights were no longer making wild figure eights over the camp. It was during this time that a shaft of milky brightness cut over their heads and landed on the Road to Heaven just behind them. Damiel and Petranker weren't in this beam but it was close enough to lift the darkness around them. Damiel saw the instrument panel on the engine and there, hanging above the keyhole of the ignition switch, was a little box with a white skull painted on it. He snapped it open and found a key tethered to a chain. The searchlight flicked away and the air around him was again doused with night. Damiel felt the instrument panel like a blind man until a little notched slot appeared under his fingertip. He pushed in the key. It clicked home.

"Stand back!" he yelled.

When he turned his wrist, the engine shook to life. The ground beneath his feet began to vibrate as pistons and valves clattered faster and faster. The moving parts inside the engine block were still bathed in oil but it was only a matter of time before the greased metal parts would shriek against each other and then, when this happened, everything would seize up. The whole crankcase would be torn up, destroyed.

"Do you have the clippers?" Damiel shouted over the noise.

Petranker nodded and they ran for the barbed-wire fence.

The door to Guth's office wasn't locked and when they stepped inside it was noticeably warmer. A song about homesickness was murmuring on the radio and the three men glanced sideways at one another. *Where is he?* they asked with shrugging shoulders.

A large oak desk, the very symbol of power, stood before them but they weren't sure what to do. It was odd being in a place that reminded them of their former lives because it was like entering a lost world where everything felt civilized and polite. They could have been standing in a banker's office or an accountant's, but instead, this place belonged to a serial mass murderer. There was a typewriter along with a stack of carbon paper. There was a slide rule, a dictionary, an ashtray, a teapot, a fern, a desk calendar, a potbelly stove, a series of file cabinets, and a wicker basket overflowing with toys. Framed photos huddled beneath a lamp, and it was very strange, wholly bizarre, seeing Guth's family. His wife looked like a movie actress with her long beautiful hair that splashed down around her shoulders, and his children smiled up from what looked like a camping trip.

So this was the epicenter of the camp?

Moshe Taube, Chaim Zischer, and David Grinbaum held their knives and screwdrivers. They stood on an expensive carpet and couldn't remember the last time they had done such a thing. Their shoes were muddy so they backed away to keep it clean. There were books on a shelf with titles like *Old Shatterhand, Applied Management & Systems,* and *A Short History of Barcelona.* Guth's diploma from the University of Hamburg was on the wall along with a photo of Hitler.

A machine gun sounded close to the window and this made them all turn around.

"We should go," Moshe said, getting out a pocket watch. "It's almost time."

When writing about this in *The Hell of Lubizec,* Chaim Zischer mentions something worth repeating. In his typically blunt fashion he states that "This escape is not an adventure story and our revolt should not be read as entertainment. Do not focus on what we did. Focus instead on those who died."

Later, in a 1985 interview, he added, "Hundreds of thousands were sealed into gas chambers and they watched a door swing shut on their futures. Whole villages died. Whole cities disappeared. That is the true history of Lubizec, not a handful of men running around with sharpened screwdrivers. People focus on our story but it is the story of nonescape that matters. I'm . . ." He stops here and waves his hand as if searching for the right word. "I'm such a tiny part of a much larger whole. I am nothing. I am like dust."

And so, as we turn our attention back to the camp and back to the sparking machine guns, we should remember that what comes next should not be given greater attention than the days of annihilation that came before it. The real story of Lubizec is "Gas and Burn." Not the wire cutters. Not the knives. Not the cigarette lighters. Not the running. No, none of it. The real story of Lubizec is about an engine coughing to life.

Before they left Guth's office they ripped out the telephone cord and looked around for any guns that might be lying around. There were none, so they turned back into the night.

The Rose Garden was full of slashing lights and voices by this time. The men skirted the barracks and made their way to the fence. Bodies were slumped over in odd positions—many of them had been shot while running away. The fire from Zurich was enormous now and flames towered up from walls that were bright orange and white. Roofs collapsed in and jets of crackling sparks shot high into the sky. The guards held machine guns.

"Quickly, quickly! Throw the snow on it!"

The escaping men had gambled that a fire would distract the guards because they knew it was a major weakness of the camp; they knew there were no water pipes to douse these flames and, although there was a huge water tank next to the SS canteen for cooking and cleaning, there was no way to get this precious fluid over to Zurich. The idea that Jews might set fire to the camp never crossed the minds of the SS, and now because of this blinkered oversight based upon bigotry, the prisoners of Barrack 14 had the diversion they needed. They sprinted for the fence.

What happened next happened very fast.

Avrom Petranker was already snipping the wire when the others arrived. He worked quickly and grunted as first one strand was cut, then another. The metal was shiny and when it was cut it made a dull noise. The searchlights were on the main entrance and a murky orange from the fire danced all around them. The smell of burning wood hung in the air and it seemed almost like perfume because it was so different from the meaty bonfires they were used to. These flames were not made from burning fat and bone.

The strands of barbed wire fell. Petranker grunted his way forward.

"Two more," he whispered. It was a triple-layered fence and he got down on his belly to clip the last strand. The ground beyond the camp was covered in untrampled snow.

"Hurry," Damiel hissed.

Zischer's hands were bloody as he pulled at the spiderwebbing of barbed wire. It ripped his coat and he got hung up in it. After a few tense moments they created a hole. Petranker crawled towards freedom and motioned for the others to follow.

"Let's go," he half shouted.

A group of prisoners throwing buckets of snow at a warehouse saw what was happening, and they backed towards the fence. Within a few seconds a steady stream of men were leaking out of the camp. The searchlights paced the front gate but, so far, the guards in the watchtowers hadn't noticed the shadows leaving the camp. All eyes were on the fire.

This changed when a tremendous geyser of sound blasted up from beyond the barbed wire. It was a landmine, one of the hundreds that had been sown into the ground after Guth's arrival in May 1942. The current prisoners of Lubizec knew nothing about the so-called "moat" because they arrived long after the explosives had been planted by previous prisoners. When one of these discs detonated, a cloud of fleshy dirt spewed into the air, and the searchlights immediately craned their necks towards the fence. Machine guns began shooting bullets into the night.

The men of Barrack 14 kept running. Zischer covered his head when falling clumps of dirt showered down onto him. The snow was soft and he tried to put his feet where others had stepped but it was hard to see with the searchlights following first this man, then that man. Zips of yellow flashed all around him and prisoners fell as if the machine guns were merely tripping them up. He was breathing hard and he expected bullets to spear his chest at any second. Someone next to him—Moshe?—Petranker?—stepped on a mine and was blasted into mist. A wet spray hit Zischer's face but he kept on running. Another mine went off—Damiel?—but he couldn't be sure. Dirt and body parts rained down onto his shoulders and he was certain, absolutely certain, that David Grinbaum had been turned into jagged tissue. Bullets winged around him and he knew men behind him were being shot dead at a dizzying speed. It was total confusion, naked fear, and as he ran deeper into the woods, it felt like he was running through wax.

After several long minutes, he pushed himself against a tree and tried not to breathe too loudly. His tongue was dry and, while panting, he peeked around the trunk to look at the camp. Bullets flitted from the towers in strange slow arcs and a second later he heard their sound.

The voice on the loudspeaker echoed as if underwater. "Attention. Attention. Return to your barracks immediately. Any prisoner not in his barrack will be shot. Repeat. Any prisoner not in his barrack will be shot."

The snow around him was slushy and he bent down to wet his lips. He chewed, he swallowed. It felt good to have something in his belly and he glanced around the woods before he broke into a wild run once again. Another explosion went off far behind him, and again there was the distant rattling of machine guns.

Zischer tumbled down a hill, hitting a large rock at the bottom, and he wondered where the others were. He paused to listen and during this moment he heard something behind him. It sounded like snapping branches and he flattened himself against an oak tree. The bark dug into his back. Blood pulsed in his eardrums.

"... m?"

Footsteps crunched over the snow.

"Chaim?"

It was Dov Damiel. They embraced and allowed themselves to weep for a few seconds. They were alive, they were free, and they weren't wounded. They slipped to the ground and held each other.

What sounded like an air-raid siren came from the camp. They sat there for a long moment wondering what to do. They buttoned their wet coats and adjusted their hats as the wind made the branches sway and clack overhead. The air-raid siren whined on and a little farmhouse on the horizon snuffed out its lights.

"What now?" Dov whispered.

Zischer shrugged.

They crouched behind a tree and spoke with their hands.

Let's go this way.

No, this way.

Is that a road?

I think so.

The night was salted with stars as they trudged through sloppy wet snow. Their ankles were numb, they were shaking, their stomachs popped and gurgled, but they kept moving away from the camp, always away from the camp.

They found a dirt road and whispered about what to do next. It angered Zischer that he had to remain motionless behind an evergreen bush as they discussed their next move. All he wanted to do was run and run. It felt like he was stuck in a world of slow motion. It felt like a thick moony paste was weighing him down.

The headlights of a canvas-topped army truck came toward them. It slid down the road and squealed to a stop just beyond where they were hiding. A door opened and a guard stood on one of the running boards. The yellow headlights illuminated the road ahead and the engine thrummed. Exhaust hung in the air.

"Prisoners of Lubizec," the guard shouted to the surrounding landscape. "Come home to warm food. We won't hurt you." A pause and then, "Prisoners of Lubizec, are you there? Can you hear me?"

Zischer and Damiel lowered themselves deeper into the snow.

"My Jew friends, where do you think you are? This is the Third Reich. The whole country is a prison for you. We will find you." The guard pulled out his gun and fired blindly into the woods ahead. The crack echoed through the trees like dying thunder.

"Do you hear me, prisoners of Lubizec? The whole *country* is a prison for you fucking Jews. The whole country!"

He climbed back into the truck, and as it gear-shifted away, a few more shots were fired out the window.

The yellow headlights rounded a corner and felt their way through the woods. A moment passed and an invisible blanket of silence settled back onto the road. High above, a shooting star burrowed through the night and an owl called from somewhere far away.

The two former prisoners stood up and brushed snow off their clothes.

They were free, but now what?*

---

*Now what indeed? Perhaps it is good to pause here and remember that successful escapes like this one also happened at Sobibór and Treblinka in 1943. Hundreds and hundreds of prisoners escaped from these two camps. A year later, there was even a doomed revolt in Auschwitz-Birkenau where prisoners managed to blow up Crematoria IV. In each of these cases, the prisoners staged an uprising because they saw themselves as part of a larger whole and they didn't expect to live. It wasn't about heroics. It was about making a statement and trying to slow down the genocidal gears of killing. Those that managed to escape were deeply surprised to find themselves still alive, so is it any wonder that Chaim Zischer and Dov Damiel glanced at each other, uncertain what to do next?

20

SHIFTING TO AUSCHWITZ

The buildings were still smoldering when the sun came up the next day and everyone was coated in a grimy layer of soot. Guards and prisoners alike looked like chimney sweeps because the whole camp was up all night shoveling snow and bending into the blazing heat. The gas chambers hadn't been set alight—they were made of brick—but immediately behind them, in a part of the camp the prisoners were never allowed to go, the guards found a pool of oil beneath the engine. The crankcase was bled out, it was dead and harmless, and when they couldn't find the plug Heinrich Niemann went into a rage.

"Go around until you find a goddamn engine like *this* one and take *that* oil plug. I'm not going to be slowed down because we can't find a stupid fucking part. Now go!" he barked. "I want to know if this fucking machine still works!"

The mood in Lubizec was now different. Not exactly free or changed, but the air was plump with a strange new feeling of hesitation. This camp, which had run on a strict timetable of gas and burn, was now as lost as a demagnetized compass needle.

Shoes and boots were everywhere because as the prisoners tried to get away from the bullets, many of them sprinted out of whatever they were wearing. In the landmine field, shoes lay higgledy-piggledy and a few of them still had a foot inside. Splotches of red mist dotted the snow. Jagged meaty pieces were near the blackened craters where the mines had detonated. It was, as one guard put it, "An unbelievable mess."

At least 130 prisoners escaped from Lubizec that night, and of that number, 70 were either cut down by machine-gun fire or they were blown up by landmines. Another 150 inside the camp had been killed by flying bullets or they were shot for moving too slowly with buckets of snow.

And of Guth? What of him?

He was at home enjoying a meal. We only know about his reaction that night thanks to Jasmine's unpublished diary, and according to her, he was enjoying cheesecake dripping with cherries. He had consumed an entire bottle of Châteauneuf-du-Pape and was working on another schnapps when a knock came on the door. He glanced at Jasmine and walked down the hallway, steadying himself with his fingertips.

"The Jews did what?"

There was a low murmuring.

"Show me."

He arrived to find much of his camp in flames. His face became a slab of concrete and he ordered the barbed-wire fence to be fixed immediately. He spoke to his guards through clamped lips. "I want no more prisoners shot tonight. One of these sons of bitches knows something," he said, looking around. "Find out who started the fire. Question them all."

The amount of damage couldn't be assessed until morning. Guth paced up and down the wooden platform of the train station and laughed.

"Ha! Everything looks fine here. Good, good."

He jumped down to the tracks and walked between the rails. The smell of creosote lifted up and he kicked a few pebbles. He pulled himself back up to the platform like a swimmer getting out of a pool, and he marched beneath the WELCOME sign.

"Follow me."

He breezed up the Road to Heaven, walked past the flowerpots, and looked into each of the four gas chambers. A smile and then, "No damage here either."

"Sir," Heinrich Niemann offered. "There's a bullet hole in Chamber #4. That's where Wagner was shot in the head."

"Paint it."

Guth walked around to the back of the building and spent a long time studying the engine. He put his hat on one of the protruding temperature gauges, got down on his knees, and looked at the hole.

"Can this be fixed?"

"We're searching for a plug now."

He stood up and slapped bits of sand off his trousers. "Did they ruin it?"

"We're not sure yet."

Guth rubbed his eyes with both hands and let out a long exhale. "Right. Okay. Listen. I want this machine tested before lunch and after that—" He cut himself off and started over. "Scratch that. Just bring me a new engine. Make it the largest one you can find, and I want it installed in the next twenty-four hours. Go. Do it now."

As for Zurich, most of it had been turned into cinders. Smoke from blackened stumps lifted lazily into the sky, and the charred warehouses looked like burnt rib cages from some prehistoric creature. As Guth walked through the smoldering mess, he picked up a blackened spoon. It was hot to the touch, so he dropped it. There were crinkled wallets, scorched coins, and a lumpy pile of melted eyeglasses. Jewelry had been fused together in glittering blobs. Whole steamer trunks of paper money had become nothing more than fibrous ash.

"It's not my fault," Birdie kept saying in a daze. "It's not my fault."

Guth was chain-smoking by now. "What a fucking mess," he said, walking across the scorched wasteland. His boots crunched over burnt wood. "It's like something out of Dante's *Inferno*."

"It's not my fault. It's not."

"Well, Birdie . . . someone has to pay."

Hans-Peter Guth saw the uprising as somehow linked to the larger lie of a global Zionist conspiracy to rule the world, and he went around the camp yelling about how he was "stabbed in the back." This of course was the fuel that made him a Nazi in the first place, and the fact that his prisoners were not going to their deaths passively was, in his mind, somehow linked to a secret Jewish council that wanted to control the world. What is astonishing about the escape, even mind-boggling, is that Guth felt like a victim. As he later noted to his wife, the rebellion happened on the Ides of March, and he thought of himself as Julius Caesar because he had been stabbed in the back.

"How could this happen?" he asked her. "It's like lice bringing down a healthy man."

Lubizec was temporarily shut down because the camp needed to be secured, damages needed to be assessed, new warehouses needed to be built, and the engine attached to the gas chamber needed to be replaced. Guth locked himself in his office and began to calculate how much voltage was needed to electrify the fence, and he ordered new slabs of concrete poured behind the gas chambers. He commandeered three tractor engines from local farmers.

"This won't slow us down," he told his men one morning as he walked past the ashy remains of Zurich. "On the contrary, these new modifications are going to speed things up. This little misadventure has hidden lessons in it. Hidden lessons, I say."

Over the next few days, a number of prisoners were found in the woods, and they were brought back to Lubizec with their wrists bound in barbed wire. A huge gallows was erected on the north end of the Rose Garden, and these men were all hanged with piano wire. It was a slow and painful death, made all the more heartbreaking by Guth's decision to have piano music played over the central loudspeaker. As the men dropped, one by one, Chopin's "Nocturne in C-Sharp Minor" floated and danced around the camp. The music waltzed on, spritely and light, as the throats of these men were cinched shut.

Avrom Petranker died in this way. He had been found hiding in a hayloft, and a farmer turned him in for two bags of sugar. According to eyewitnesses, Petranker said something before the stool was kicked out from underneath him, but no one knows exactly what it was. Some heard him say, "Free Poland." Others heard him say, "I am going to Israel now." We don't know exactly what he said before the piano wire cinched his airway shut, but since he chose to fight the Nazis when they first invaded Poland, and since he was a key organizer of the escape, it stands to reason that his last words were full of defiance.

Moshe Taube, the same man who stood up during the mock Seder and sang about his murdered wife, was also captured. It happened in a field and he was badly beaten as they dragged him back to Lubizec. He too yelled out something before the stool was kicked away, but this too has been lost to the ether of history.

Equally, we don't know what happened to David Grinbaum. His body was never found and he wasn't hanged, so maybe he escaped. Maybe he wasn't blasted into mist by a landmine and maybe he survived the war. Maybe he started life over again and erased the word *Lubizec* from his vocabulary. This is possible. Anything is possible. Is it very likely, though? How we answer this question says much about our sense of hope.

As for Guth, he had to write a report about the escape. He went into his office, rolled a sheet of paper into his typewriter, and stared at it for a long time. He lit a smoke and rubbed his forehead. He started biting his fingernails again.

Thanks to the Nazi mania for documentation, we have this report today. It is brief, very businesslike, and the first page is in paragraph form. The second page (marked "Addendum") is a long list of damage to the camp. Guth suggests that no one could have foreseen the escape and he writes that "all culprits have been caught and hanged." There is a short paragraph praising the guards who were killed in the escape, and he mentions that Christian Schwartz was "ambushed with a knife" and that Gustav Wagner was "shot in a cowardly surprise attack." He also talks about how Rudolf Oberhauser was "murdered while defending a vital sector of the camp" and that Kurt Hackenhold was "beaten to death by unknown enemies." Guth concludes the report by saying, "They died in service to the Führer."

There is one final line before his signature. We can almost imagine Guth sitting in his oak chair and staring at a wall calendar for March 1943. Sunlight flitters through a dense haze of cigarette smoke as he leans forward and types the last sentence. His fingers work quickly and the snapping keys sound like bullets being fired into a wall.

"Lubizec must temporarily cease operation."

What isn't mentioned in the report is what Guth told his wife later that night. He fully expected to be taken to Lublin Castle, and shot.

Chaim Zischer and Dov Damiel hid in the forest for three days. They crouched in a ravine and listened to truckloads of Germans searching for them. Dogs were sent into the woods, but they always seemed to sniff in the opposite direction and round up other prisoners. The newly freed men tried to sleep during the day and follow the milky moon at night. They shivered with damp and fantasized about eating huge meals in front of a roaring fire. After several nights of walking southwest towards Kraków, they felt as if they had finally moved beyond the gravitational field of Lubizec, and they began to see things, normal things, things they had almost forgotten about, things like cars on the roads, and farms, and trains loaded down with something other than people.

Hunger gnawed at them. It nibbled at their bowels and made them burp ceaselessly. They produced an unbelievable amount of saliva, as if their mouths were working on invisible chunks of food. Zischer and Damiel marched through sloppy wet snow and talked about eating loaves of rye bread with fat squares of melting butter. They licked their lips at visions of grilled cod and potatoes. They talked of mutton and carrots. Their stomachs were fleshy sacks of emptiness, and these unfilled gurgling spaces at the center of their being finally got the better of them when they stood near a farmhouse and watched a woman feeding chickens. They dreamed of drumsticks, wings, and warm yolks. They still had the diamonds from Lubizec and they held out their hands as if these precious rocks might turn into eggs.

Dov wanted to wait until nightfall and steal two chickens but Zischer said they couldn't cook it with a campfire.

"We can't risk the light," he said.

They argued in whispers about what to do and decided to approach the farmhouse at dusk. If the woman agreed to help, great. If she didn't agree to help, they could always run into the woods and zigzag through the trees.

They crouched behind a large bush and watched the sun go down. A blanket of ink was pulled across the land and when it was completely dark they gingered their way towards the farm. The road was rutted and pools of melting snow reflected the stars above. A light was on and muffled music came from the kitchen. The two men were soaked. They shivered and smelled of the outdoors.

Dov knocked on the door with a single knuckle.

Nothing happened, so he knocked harder—this time, using his fist.

There were footsteps and the sound of a lock being undone. The door opened an inch and a woman with thick wiry hair, glasses, and a worried face stood before them.

"Yes?"

"We're soldiers, in the former Polish Army, and we're wondering if you have something to eat." Dov put his fingertips to his mouth and pretended to chew.

Before the woman could answer, a car came down the road and they all turned to look at the headlights. She adjusted her glasses as the car got closer and closer.

"Wait here," she said, shutting the door. A deadbolt snapped shut.

The car rolled over the dirt road. Puddles splashed up into its wheel wells and the radio blared out a German song about farming the land. It came over a low rise with its headlights reaching into the air and it slowed as it passed the farm entrance. It kept moving away, dragging the music behind it.

A few chickens clucked in the yard as the men looked at each other. They held their stomachs and glanced into the woods. Zischer peeked into the window and saw that it was warm and pleasant inside. A fire was going and something was steaming in a large enamel pot—the top quivered. He had forgotten that people still lived in this way. It seemed impossible, like a fantasy, and he stood there in wonderment.

The door opened suddenly and she held out a quilt. "Here," she said. "I've also packed a loaf of bread, some honey, and some tinned herring. You can't stay here, though. Leave now."

Dov had tears in his eyes because it was the first act of kindness he had experienced in years. Something fluttered in his throat and his knees buckled. He fell to the ground and covered his face.

"Please," Zischer interrupted. "We're both tired, as you can see. Can we sleep in your barn? We'll leave when the sun comes up."

"Are you Jews?"

"No, no. Not us."

She studied them for a long moment. A kink appeared in her eyebrow and she finally said, "The hayloft's out back but . . . if the Nazis find you . . . I'll deny everything. Understand? I'll say you broke into my barn and stole my chickens."

They nodded.

She started to close the door but stopped. She looked at them and added, "I've seen things happen to your people. Terrible things and . . . I'm sorry. I just wanted to say that. It's not right what's being done to you. It's not right."

The three of them stood in the lemony shaft of light that spilled out from her house until, at last, the middle-aged woman closed the door. It clicked, softly.

Zischer and Damiel stayed in the hayloft for three days and the woman (who never gave her name) made up backpacks of canned vegetables for their journey.

The former prisoners of Lubizec walked at night towards Kraków. They got the idea of acquiring forged identity cards with the diamonds in their pockets, and they hoped to slip into society, where they would pretend to be gentiles. In this way, they might survive the war. They might live to bear witness.

A reply to Guth's report came a week later, and it was from none other than Heinrich Himmler. The twin lightning bolts of the SS were embossed at the top of the letter, and beneath it were stamped the words "From the Office of the Reichsführer." No one except Hitler was higher in the Nazi universe.

Guth sat at his desk and read it a few times before the words really sank in. He lit a cigarette and leaned back in his chair. He spoke to his second in command, Heinrich Niemann.

"It's all over. We're being shut down," he said.

"You're joking."

"Not at all."

"That's funny. You're being funny."

"Here, let me read a few lines. *Lubizec is primitive . . . Zyklon-B is more effective . . . all operations are shifting to Auschwitz. Your camp is to be dismantled.*" Guth looked up and groaned. "Plus there's this line: *Report to Berlin immediately.* What on earth does that mean?"

Niemann shrugged.

A moment passed before Guth stubbed out his cigarette. He looked out the window and added, "Well, begin dismantling the camp. It's all over."

He got on a train the next day and made the long journey to SS headquarters in Berlin. He was made to wait in an enormous marble room for several hours while a bust of Adolf Hitler glowered down at him and trolleys outside the tall windows clanged on the street below. Sunlight spilled into the room and a large swastika banner rippled in light gusts of wind. He could hear the faint ticking of typewriters and the buzz of telephones.

To his great surprise—astonishment, really—he was not only promoted but ordered to Frankfurt where he would assume control of the SS stationed there. Everything happened so dizzyingly fast. One month he was in charge of a death camp and the next he was signing paperwork in a huge private office. It was his job to make sure political dissent was squashed and that trainloads of "special cargo" moved through his region of control without problem or hindrance. Most of these trains, of course, were packed full of Jews bound for the east. As for Jasmine, she was delighted to return to Germany. She began to decorate their new home in Frankfurt and her diary is full of entries about fancy parties and dresses. She writes about what was served at restaurants and who danced with whom. There is no more mention of Poland. It's like it never happened.

Most of the guards at Lubizec were transferred to Auschwitz-Birkenau where murder was so routine it was clockwork. Men like

Heinrich Niemann, Birdie Franz, and Sebastian Schemise quickly rose through the ranks because they had hearts of granite and they knew how to run a gas chamber. While they were at Auschwitz they helped make it the largest site of mass murder in human history, and they were well liked in the SS canteen because they often told stories of the "good old days at Lubizec."

As for the camp, it was plowed into the ground. The wooden barracks were knocked down and the entire area was planted with firs and lupins. By July 1943, nothing was left—even the rail tracks were ripped out. Wildflowers were sown into the ground and a farmhouse was built. Bricks from the gas chambers were used to make the foundation, and the whole thing was painted a bright pistachio green. A stone fireplace was added a few months later.

A Polish man was paid to live in this quaint little farmhouse and tell people it had been in his family for generations. And what did this man do for a living?

He raised cattle for slaughter.

PART III

— 21 —

ENDINGS

Most of Poland's Jews were gone by the end of the war, and even today, even in major cities like Warsaw, Kraków, and Lublin, their marks are barely visible. Empty synagogues line the streets and leafy parks exist where thriving communities of human beings once went about the business of life. To visit Poland today is to realize they are all gone. It is to walk with ghosts.

From a Nazi perspective, Operation Reinhard was a stunning success because it wiped out a perceived threat to Aryan blood and it made Poland almost entirely *Judenrein* (cleansed of Jews). It is frightening indeed to realize that what the Nazis learned between 1941 and 1943 in camps like Lubizec allowed them to kill at an even faster rate, and they subsequently began to streamline the process of death. Because of Operation Reinhard, Auschwitz became an unrelenting drain, and the remaining Jews of Europe were pulled toward its deadly center. Today this massive camp symbolizes a profound evil, and it defies our belief in a compassionate universe.

In an interview with National Public Radio that was conducted in 1998, Dov Damiel described what it meant to survive the Holocaust. He said whenever he should have been happy—on a warm summer day, for example—something always shook awake in his brain. The thunder of Lubizec rumbled down the days of his life, and he was never able to feel lasting joy. Laughter became a foreign language to him and horrible images echoed in his head whenever he saw trains, uniforms, or barbed wire. Movies with machine guns made him wince, the German language made him shudder, and, worst of all, he had trouble falling asleep because that's when the demons crawled out from his imagination. Today we call this "posttraumatic stress disorder," but that psychological phrase only begins to scratch the surface of his deep, lasting pain.

"The nights are a torment to me," he told National Public Radio. "Why did I survive? I wasn't any faster or smarter or better than the others. Why me? Imagine if everyone you knew, your family, your friends, your coworkers, people you see in the grocery store when you buy eggs . . . imagine them all dead. But you, you survived. And how did this thing happen? How did you make it out alive when so many others did not? This is why Lubizec is an unhealable wound for me. It remains open and raw."

It is here that Damiel stops and coughs. There is a pause before he adds, "Lubizec is burned onto my eyes. Onto my *eyes*, I tell you. The past is never going away for me. Ever."

When pressed about this, Damiel goes on to talk about what he calls his "second life."

"Sometimes when a man holds a door open for me, or a woman in a shop picks up some coins I have dropped, or a stranger gives me directions in a city, I walk away and think, 'Such nice people.' But a moment later I find myself thinking, 'Yes, they are nice now but how would they be in Lubizec?' Do you understand what I mean? My world is not nice and smiling as it is for other people. This is my second life, my life after Lubizec. I try to fight against this but the camp has become a part of the texture of my being. I . . . I have thought about suicide many times. I want my mind to stop working. I just want these memories to go away."

Damiel moved to Israel after the war. He eventually remarried and had four children, but he rarely talked about what he saw, especially during the first few decades of his second life. He kept the pillowcase he escaped with along with the shaving kit and the little slice of yellow soap. He stockpiled enormous rows of canned vegetables and fruits. His cupboards groaned under the weight of sugar and flour. He kept dishes of sweets in every room, and he had three locks put on his front door. At night, he slept with the lamp on.

He worked with troubled teens in Tel Aviv because it made him feel useful, somehow more whole, and he had pictures of his grandchildren scattered all over his little apartment. His face lit up whenever he saw them.

"You are such beautiful creatures," he sang. "You are sunrises. Sunrises."

When he died in 1999, his funeral was attended by over 1,500 people, and as his obituary suggests, we can only hope that he has finally "found peace beneath the shade of a date palm."

Although many survivors fell into a deep silence about what they saw and never spoke about it, others, like Chaim Zischer, tried to put their pain into words. In *The Hell of Lubizec*, he reminds his readers that their families are not in any immediate danger nor do they have to worry about being shot. He also reminds us that, when we read, we shed our bodies and travel elsewhere. Reading is essentially an out-of-body experience, but Lubizec, by contrast, was firmly rooted *in* the body. Because it was a place of physical pain, what does it mean to read about crippling thirst? What does it mean to read about standing at attention for hours or to feel the heat of a thousand burning corpses on your face? How can anyone understand what it means to wake up in the middle of the night because you've just heard a gunshot that was fired in March 1943?

In his book, Zischer explains that the past is never really over, and he writes about living in multiple time zones where the past, the present, and the future all get spun together like rope. One minute he is strolling through New York and the next, when a car backfires, he is immediately back in Lubizec again. A clattering subway train becomes the 8:00 a.m. transport chugging into camp. Children screaming with laughter on a playground are suddenly in the Rose Garden. A police officer reminds him of Birdie. The past, Zischer reminds us, is not about clocks and dead years. It isn't about dust and documents. It isn't about looking backwards. No, not at all. The past spills out of memory and demands a future.

Zischer spends several pages thinking about the ashfields of Lubizec. As he imagines a grassy expanse stretching out before him, all of these ghosts begin to climb out of the ground. It is worth quoting the entirety of this dream passage because it hints at two things: 1) Zischer's attempt to make the interior landscape of his skull real for the readers and 2) his obvious feelings of survivor's guilt.

As I dreamed about this place that killed my former life and robbed me of all that I once loved, I was aware that my feet were once again on wicked soil. Beneath my wingtip shoes were the ashes of my people. The grass moved and swayed in the wind, and I looked around, hoping to feel the pull of my wife Nela and my son Jakob. Where were their ashes? Could I sense their final resting place as if I were divining water?

I gathered up a handful of soil and pressed it to my cheek. I wept in this dream and as my tears fell to the ground that's when all these ghosts began to rise up. There were thousands of them and they were made entirely of ash. Their clothes were ash, their faces were ash, their skin, their hands, their lips, their chins, their eyelashes, their belts, their shoes, their dresses, and hats, their Star of David armbands and suitcases. It was all ash. They were all made completely of flaky ash.

Then these ghosts, these suggestions of happy former lives, moved around as if they were lost. *What happened to us?* they asked. I wanted to help but they couldn't hear me. I yelled until my throat was sore but they paid no attention. Bits of ash flittered off one man when I tried to grab his shoulder. My hand went right through him and my palm was covered in soot. Thousands of ghosts rose up from the underworld in an endless dry birthing and I saw before me a huge crowd of these ashpeople. Men adjusted their hats. Women reached out with their gray powdery hands for their children. They walked towards the barbed-wire fence and passed right through it as they went off into the murky forest. They left crumbled foot-prints behind them.

Nela and Jakob had to be among these dead so I yelled out and ran through ghost after ghost. It was like running through grainy fog but I found them after much searching. My clothes were covered in ash and I wept at the sight of my family. My wife looked beautiful even though everything about her was ash. Her hair. Her lips. Her eyes were little gray cinders, and when she smiled, the corner of her mouth flaked off. When I tried to hug her, it was like embracing coal smoke. My forearms passed right through her. When I looked at my hands, they were covered in her remains.

A sudden wind swirled out of a clock (it looked like the old clock on Jateczna Street in my hometown of Lublin), and a fearsome hurricane carried away these ghosts. Thousands of powdery spirits dissolved into air and I looked around, helpless to stop it. My wife and son scattered into nothingness and I found myself transported to a bustling city. New York. Car horns blared. Buses rumbled. People ate food on the go. My body was covered in human soot, but I was not one of these ghosts. I, I was condemned to live. And the world continued on around me, unable to see that I was clothed in ash and burning with agony.

Zischer goes on to explain that literary and artistic mediums break down when we approach the Holocaust. He reminds us that words like *appalling* and *horrible* only take us so far when we try to understand these camps. It is a story without hope because people came in one end and truckloads of ash came out the other. But how can we explain such things through words? Whenever we try to do this, we find ourselves in a world where the old ways of storytelling do not apply. Any Holocaust story that makes us smile at the end is full of the false belief that something can be learned from all of the murder, that there is some scrap of goodness amid the ash. Perhaps this is human nature, this search for the good, but to focus on acts of kindness or on moments of enlightenment is to turn away from the horror of the Holocaust. It is to search for the flickering candle in the darkness when, really, the darkness itself is the story.

But as Zischer notes in *The Hell of Lubizec*, "Who wants a story like that?"

Who indeed? No one wants to sink into despair, and yet if we are to engage with the death camps in any meaningful way, we need to understand that traditional modes of storytelling fail us. The villains outnumber the heroes. Resolution cannot happen. The Nazis do not have a moral awakening, and we should not feel uplifted at the end of such stories, but wounded.

Before we move on, it is worth mentioning one final sobering fact. Of the thirty-five guards that were stationed at Lubizec, only four received jail time (a paltry 11 percent conviction rate). Most of them were never punished in any way. They became, instead, bank clerks, electricians, carpenters, accountants, insurance salesmen, and bartenders. One became a priest. Another became a judge.

As for Guth, he fled to Barcelona. He decided to go to Spain after the war because everyone else in the SS was fleeing to South America, and he thought there would be safety in isolation. Go against the grain, he thought. Go against the crowd. Be anonymous. Hide.

He ended up washing dishes in a grubby little restaurant and eventually worked his way up to managing it. He called himself "Hans Bauer" and lived in an area of the city populated mostly by foreigners. Barri Xinès was a drug den, a warren of prostitution, and it was easy to hide in its narrow streets where landlords asked few questions as long as the rent appeared on time. Jasmine and the children joined him, and after a few years of pinching pesetas, they bought a rooftop flat in a safer area of the city, on Carrer de Marlet. Guth sold jugs of sangria at the restaurant while his children became fluent in Spanish.

"I didn't like it," Jasmine later recalled. "Barcelona was a cold bath. There were no more parties in the evening, money was very tight, we had to keep a low profile, but I got used to the situation.

I had to. Hans got into the habit of taking long walks through the twisting streets of the city. He walked for *hours*. Ribera, Eixample, Raval. He walked every part of the city and made Barcelona home. As for me, it took much longer. Our new life was . . . hard."

The world quickly moved away from the Holocaust as it began to worry about the cold war. Visions of mushroom clouds filled up the newspapers, and everyone built fallout shelters in their backyards. There was talk of whole cities disappearing beneath mighty eruptions of atomic fire. Human civilization could be wiped out by pushing a button. Rockets would then fire up from the ground and arch their deadly payloads across the globe. In a flickering pulse of time, shockwaves of light would obliterate the world, and because of this, no one seemed to care much about the ashfields of Poland. By the early 1960s, Guth even talked about moving back to Germany. After all, it had been twenty years and no one—not a single person—had knocked on his door to ask any questions.

All of this changed on November 2, 1965.*

The morning was cold, overcast, and Guth was caught near the massive unfinished church of Sagrada Família. Just as Big Ben symbolizes London, and the Eiffel Tower symbolizes Paris, this church symbolizes Barcelona. Sagrada Família launches itself into the sky and at night its eight steeples poke the stars like dripping wax candles. Its architect, a cranky genius named Antoni Gaudí, believed it would "expiate sin" from the city. In other words, the act of building Sagrada Família was an atonement to God, and it was designed to purify the city of evil. Whether Guth believed this or not is unknown, but we do know he visited this church every week because he liked watching the stonemasons chisel out chunks of rock. He brought along breadcrumbs for the pigeons, and he smoked cigarettes as building cranes and cement trucks went about the business of constructing something good and holy.

---

*Appropriately, it was All Souls' Day. When this was pointed out to Dov Damiel, he shrugged. "And so? This is a Christian idea. I do not think Christians believe it is for Jews. I do not understand Christians. They love a Jew that was killed two thousand years ago, but still they hate the rest of us."

It was at Sagrada Família that he was finally caught. In his wallet were several thousand pesetas, a Metro pass, and pictures of his family. The famed "Nazi Hunter," Simon Wiesenthal, spent five months tracking him down but it was worth the effort. Hans-Peter Guth, the Commandant of Lubizec, was finally under arrest. He was rushed to the airport in an armored truck and flown to West Germany where he was put on trial for the murder of 710,000 people.

The proceedings began on July 5, 1966. It was the first time he had been in a courtroom, and he looked nervous. In video footage, we can see him fretting with his tie and adjusting his cufflinks. He smoothes his graying hair with both hands and clears his throat. When asked about his role at Lubizec, he said the deaths were "regrettable," but he didn't see much difference between what happened in the camp and the massacre at Katyń or the firebombing of Dresden or the miniature suns that exploded over Hiroshima and Nagasaki.

"Civilian death happens in war," he said to the judge. "I was following orders and I never personally laid a hand on anyone. In fact, I didn't fire a single bullet in the last war. Not one. Not one single bullet. I didn't personally murder anyone."

The prosecutor shook his head in disbelief.

"But Herr Guth, the genocide of the Jews had nothing to do with war. You would have happily murdered them in peacetime. No sir, war and genocide are two very different things. Let us say Nazi Germany *won* the last war. You would have carried on killing the Jews anyway, wouldn't you? Well, wouldn't you?"

Silence.

"The whole world is waiting for your answer."

Guth shrugged. He looked annoyed.

It is worth quoting the remainder of this exchange as it appears in the court transcript because it sheds light on his emotions at the time.

> *Question*: Did you hate the Jews?
> *Answer*: No, I didn't hate anyone. I was doing my job.

Question: Doing your job. I see. Weren't you disgusted by what was happening?

Answer: At first maybe but you got used to it. We all got numb to the realities of our job.

Question: You keep calling it a "job."

Answer: It was a job.

Question: No, Herr Guth. It was murder. It was genocide. To oversee the destruction of hundreds of thousands of people is nothing short of demonic.

Answer: I was following orders.

Question: Orders?

Answer: Yes.

Question: Whose orders?

Answer: Odilo Globocnik's [lead administrator of Operation Reinhard].

Question: But it was *you* who watched the trains come in. It was *you* who gave a welcome speech. It was *you* who made sure the engine worked and the gas chamber sealed shut. *You*. Not Globocnik. Not Himmler. Not Hitler. *You*.

Answer: Let me ask you a question.

Question: No, I'm asking the questions today, Herr Guth.

Answer: That hardly seems fair.

Question: You're a man that's used to being in charge, aren't you? I think you liked being commandant because it made you feel important and puffed up. It made you feel like a god to decide who lived and who died. That's what you liked most about Lubizec, wasn't it? The power?

Answer: It was a job.

Question: A job that required you to kill 710,000 people?

Answer: No comment.

Question: No comment? Sir, the people you killed deserve better than "no comment."

Answer: It happened a long time ago.

Question: Crime doesn't melt away. You're a murderer.

Answer: I was an officer. I was doing my duty.

Question: Doing your duty. [Long pause.] Tell me . . . didn't you feel anything? Didn't you feel anything at all when women and children were being shut into your gas chambers?

Answer: They were cargo.

Question: Cargo.

Answer: I kept myself busy with paperwork, and managing the train schedule, and making sure my guards were paid, and worrying about drainage issues, and planning what flowers should be around the SS canteen.

Question: Flowers? My God, sir. Flowers?

Answer: Listen, I never personally killed anyone. Not a single person.

Question: Herr Guth, you're a mass murderer. Why can't you see this simple fact?

The trial lasted two weeks, and the lawyers debated about whether or not Guth fired a gun, about whether or not he watched an orphanage of boys get locked into a gas chamber, and about whether or not he slapped an old woman. To Chaim Zischer, none of these things mattered because they were missing the bigger picture. Guth was in charge of Lubizec, and these tiny moments of crime weren't as important as the daily mass homicides he set into motion. Who cared if he whipped a teenage girl when as many as four thousand people were murdered under his command in the course of a single day? Why focus on one event when it was the landscape in which that event was set that mattered? Who cared if he pushed a lit cigarette into an old woman's face when far worse things were happening at the wrong end of the Road to Heaven? Guth ran a kingdom of death and, surely, Zischer thought angrily, *that* was more important. *That's* what he was on trial for.

When it was all over, the judge sentenced Guth to life behind bars in Frankfurt Prison. Many people wished that West Germany still had the death penalty, but since it had been abolished after the war, this meant Guth would spend the rest of his days in solitary confinement. He would live although hundreds of thousands had died.

IS THIS GERMAN JUSTICE? read one headline from an Israeli newspaper.

Guth became a model prisoner. He kept his cell tidy and there were pictures of his wife and grown children on his desk. He folded his clothes, he read books, and he enjoyed his hour of daily exercise in the yard. He was granted a pair of binoculars and he took up bird-watching.

In 1969 he was interviewed by a journalist about his role at Lubizec. They met in a small guarded room and sat on opposite ends of a metal table. A tape recorder was placed between them, and the journalist, Tobias Duval, took notes on a yellow legal pad. He asked about Guth's childhood, his service in World War I, the economic crisis of the 1920s, and why he joined the Nazi Party, and then they moved on to Lubizec. Duval asked about the 710,000 people and wanted to know if Guth ever thought about their ashes.

The commandant took a deep breath and held it. He looked at the floor and said, "In my estimation, that number is too low. The real figure is probably closer to one million."

"As many as that?"

"The camp was very efficient."

Throughout the interview, Guth referred to himself in third person. It was like someone else had committed these crimes. Tobias Duval found this curious and he brought it to Guth's attention.

"When we talk about Lubizec, you say 'Guth did this' or 'Guth did that' but *you're* Guth. *You* did these things, not some other person in history. Don't you feel guilty about killing these people? Whole generations were wiped out because of you. You murdered the future."

"I've had a long time to think about this," he said, lighting a cigarette. Blue smoke lifted up. "It was war, you see."

"No, it wasn't war. To kill men, women, and children . . . *children*. Don't you feel anything about that today?"

He took a long drag and used the standard line he had been parroting for decades. "I was following orders and—"

"No. You killed them. You killed them all."

Smoke from Guth's cigarette threaded its way up to the ceiling, ghostlike. His breathing grew ragged and he swallowed a few times before he spoke.

"Maybe I . . . I've thought about this a lot you see, and maybe I . . . maybe I . . . it could be that I'm . . ." His face hardened and he shook his head as if clearing something dangerous from his mind. He stubbed out his cigarette and stood up. The chair rumbled on the cement floor.

"We're done for the day. Goodbye."

Guth turned on his heel in military style and knocked on the steel door with a single knuckle. A jailor opened up and he was escorted back to his cell.

Hans-Peter Guth died of a heart attack twelve hours later. Tobias Duval believed that something shook awake in him during that interview and the revelation of what he had done finally overpowered him. Perhaps, in the privacy of his prison cell, he was on the verge of recognizing something terrible about himself. We can't be sure of this, of course. All we do know is that he died in the early hours of July 20, 1969, and that he never admitted to the scope of his crime. His body was cremated and his ashes were buried in an unmarked grave inside the prison walls.

A few months later, one of the railway signs from the little town of Lubizec was sent to Yad Vashem, that museum to the Holocaust housed in Israel. It hangs there today.

— 22 —

WINTER

Guth's children had different reactions to his legacy. His son, Karl, was horrified by what happened in the camp, and it so sickened him that, as an adult, he spoke out against what his father had done. He toured around high schools and colleges in Germany. He wrote articles about mass movements and hatred. He tried to help refugees. When genocide reared its ugly head once again in Europe, he decided to work for the United Nations. He went to Bosnia-Herzegovina in the 1990s and worked hard to stop the bloodshed. Later he found himself in Rwanda and Dafur. And, as he went from one site of genocide to the next, he felt the world had learned nothing at all from the Holocaust, except how to kill people faster. He especially felt this way whenever he stood before a trench that was bloated with bodies. Flies were thick in the air and mothers wailed all around him.

"Look at this," he told a reporter. "Look at it. How come this is allowed to happen? We say 'never again' but here are the dead right in front of us. When will we learn from history? When?"

Guth's daughter, Sigi, initially stayed out of the public eye. She turned inward and felt so polluted by her father's genes that she married the first man she could in order to change her last name. At seventeen, she became Sigrid Matthes. It was like a magic trick, it was like her father had never existed. She erased him.

But after he died, she went through a long spell of drinking. She began chain-smoking and her life spiraled downward as she focused more and more on the Villa and how interlocked her childhood had been to the camp. She told her therapist that her father was a loving man—he never hurt her—and that she couldn't reconcile this man with the monster that ran Lubizec. Whenever she thought about this too much, it was like maggots were crawling around inside her brain. She wanted to scoop her hands inside her skull and dump these unwanted memories of her father's Nazism on the ground. She wanted to walk away from them and focus, instead, on how he encouraged her and how he helped her solve thorny math problems. Her therapist suggested she write a book about these conflicting emotions, so Sigi sat down at an electric typewriter and began to peck at the keys. It took four years to write *The Commandant's Daughter,* but when it was finished, in 1985, she went on a book tour around England, Germany, and France. People asked her if she still loved her father.

"Of course, I do. Yes. He was my papa."

Chaim Zischer was living in New York at the time, and it renewed interest in his own book, *The Hell of Lubizec,* which was published a few decades earlier. When reviews of Sigi's book began to appear, he was asked to give a presentation at Columbia University. His speech was recorded, and towards the end, he shakes his head in frustration.

"We shouldn't forget that Guth is responsible for mass murder. Rather than focus on him and his family, we should remember the unknowns he murdered. Where is their time before the cameras of history? Who speaks for them?"

A student raised her hand. "Do you forgive what happened to you?"

In the video, Zischer looks at the podium for a long time. He shuffles his feet and takes a long drink of water. When he speaks, his voice is clear.

"I have no authority to forgive such a crime, but I have decided not to hate. Hate is a cancer. Hate will swallow you whole. Hate will haunt you. I cannot speak about forgiveness—we need to ask the dead if they forgive—but do I hate? The answer to that question is no. Resoundingly no."

Today Lubizec feels more like a state park than it does a site of mass annihilation. The woods are refreshing, birds chirp in the distance, and sunlight drifts down through tangled tree branches. Pine needles cover the sandy ground, and it is very hard to believe that

710,000 people died in this little rectangle of land. Nothing is left. Not even the green farmhouse, which was torn down after the war. The Rose Garden is overgrown with trees and shrubs. The barracks are long gone, and it is hard to see the layout of the camp. Pollen drifts in the air, and there is a heavy quiet hanging from the trees. Occasionally a bird sings or a pinecone drops.

Although the Road to Heaven was demolished by the Nazis in 1943, it has since been reconstructed by the Polish government. A wide path, covered in pebbles, runs towards the site of the gas chambers, and tall bushes have been planted on either side, which gives the impression of walls. White rocks the size of skulls edge the pebbly path. A stone monument with the Star of David stands where the gas chambers once stood. THIS IS THE GATE OF THE LORD, it says in Hebrew. A wreath leans against it.

All six roasting pits were located in the 1990s thanks to satellite imaging, and they are now marked off with concrete edging. These long rectangles have been filled in with tons of pumice (a volcanic rock that looks scorched and burnt), and the overall effect is very powerful because it looks as if the fires have only recently died away. The pumice looks warm to the touch. The ground appears charred and wounded.

The trees around the Roasts have been cleared away because the ground is swollen with human ash, and in an effort to make it feel more like a cemetery, which of course it is, a grassy field was created. It is easy to dig down into the gray sandy soil. It is like holding charcoal dust in your hands, and it is a sobering thought indeed to realize what is stuck to the ridges of your fingerprints. Hundreds of wildflowers sway in the wind, and since there are so few visitors to Lubizec, it is often possible to have the place entirely to yourself. If this happens, you become aware of the blood flowing through the delicate universe of your body. And, as you look around at the trees, an overwhelming sorrow settles upon your shoulders.

There is a small information center just beyond the boundaries of the camp. It shows a ten-minute documentary, and there is a display case full of barbed wire, rusty coins, bullets, and keys. In 1991, a doll was found near the gas chambers, and this little toy became something special because it was saturated with the history of the camp itself. The doll's face is badly discolored, its eyes stare out vacantly as if in shock, and most visitors to the museum stand before it, saying nothing. Some touch the glass as if wanting to reach in and cup the soiled face.

The last notable gathering at Lubizec happened in 2008 to commemorate the sixty-fifth anniversary of the uprising. A violin played. The prime minister of Israel and the president of Poland were there. Several reporters and historians stood in the melting snow, and Chaim Zischer, the last survivor, was the guest of honor.

"Am I really the last Jew of Lubizec?" he asked the press.

No one said anything as he shuffled towards the site of the former gas chambers. His sons, daughters, and various grandchildren were there holding roses. Everyone sensed it would be the last anniversary with a living eyewitness, and they crowded around Zischer. He was famous not for what he had done but because he was still alive. Somewhere far away a commuter train whistled in the woods. Then this old man, who once pulled gold teeth out of mouths and watched bodies get incinerated by tremendous flames, turned towards the sound. His face tightened. The sunlight around him seemed to have weight and substance. The air was dense with memory. For a flickering moment, it felt like two different worlds were being folded into each other.

Zischer stood before the stone monument for a long time. He touched it with an outstretched hand and he let out a long, low gasp. His shoulders bobbed up and down as he wept, openly and loudly. His family circled around him and placed their hands on his back.

This is where a happy ending should be. This is where all the lost threads are supposed to be woven back together. A story of the Holocaust cannot end with the dead coming back to life—we know this, we accept this, but we still want mothers to be reunited with their sons. We still want people who were separated in the Rose Garden to see each other again and weep for joy at their reunion. It would be wonderful to imagine the dead being sucked back towards the camp, back into the hot womb of the Roasts, it would be pleasing to imagine their bodies being unburned and the gas chambers gifting them with the breath of life, it would be glorious to watch them climb back onto the trains and roll back towards their lives, unharmed and beloved. Millions upon millions of people would be reborn, and the Nazis would march out of Poland, picking up their bombs and bullets as they went. If the Holocaust ran in reverse like some kind of old and magical newsreel, it would be the most beautiful moment in history. Beautiful.

But that is not the story of the Holocaust.

The story of the Holocaust can only run in one direction: toward the watchtowers, the gas chambers, and the fires. This might be why Lubizec isn't visited by many people today. Perhaps its pain is too raw and full of too much weeping.

Meanwhile, as the years tick by and the snow continues to fall, we are lulled into believing that peace has finally found the camp. On a winter's day, everything looks so innocent. A heavy blanket of white allows us to pretend none of it happened. And still the snow keeps on falling down, down, down. It gets caught in branches and shrubs. It covers the nameless memorial stones on the Road to Heaven, and in that moment, the world seems so gentle, so pure, so cleansed of wickedness. But hiding beneath the snow is a thick layer of human ash. It hides there as a silent reminder of what we are capable of doing to each other. It cries to us from the ground and haunts our understanding of what it means to be human, what it means to be civilized.

This is a work of fiction. Lubizec never actually existed, but it easily could have in the Nazi state. It is a synthesis of such real death camps as Sobibór, Bełżec, and Treblinka where at least a million and a half souls perished between the years 1941 and 1943 under what was known as Operation Reinhard. Virtually all of them were Jewish.

The genesis of this novel sprang from a class I was teaching on the Holocaust, and it startled me—deeply—to learn that my students had never heard of the camps mentioned above. I believe most Americans see no fundamental difference between the camps listed above and the more "ordinary" concentration camps of Bergen-Belsen and Dachau. The reason for this has much to do with Sobibór, Bełżec, and Treblinka resting far behind Soviet lines after the war. These death camps simply weren't as well known as the camps in the American and British sectors. Auschwitz is a special case, as well it should be, because even though it was behind Soviet lines, it was both a death camp *and* a concentration camp; it was also unforgivably massive, and we have testimonies from a number of survivors about what the place was like. The Operation Reinhard camps were only slightly larger than three football fields, and they were designed to murder thousands of people a day. Such factories of death had little need for prisoners, and this meant few survived to bear witness, which of course is why we know so little about them. By late 1943, these death camps were all plowed into the ground in an attempt to hide their existence, and this, too, has contributed to a general lack of knowledge. Hardly any photographs of these places exist, and there is no known video footage whatsoever. The arithmetic of loss at Sobibór, Bełżec, and Treblinka is so vast, so painful that it's hard to grasp what happened there. These tiny spots of earth extinguished life at a breathtaking speed, yet for most people today, these camps reside in shadow. This strikes me as very wrong. I hope this narrative might in some small way shed light and act as a kind of remembrance. More than anything, I hope it might nudge readers to find out more about Operation Reinhard.

A number of books have shaped my understanding of the Holocaust over the decades, but for the purposes of this novel I am particularly indebted to Chil Rajchman's *The Last Jew of Treblinka*, Yitzhak Arad's *Bełżec, Sobibór, Treblinka*, Gitta Sereny's harrowing interviews with Franz Stangl in *Into That Darkness*, Jean-François Steiner's *Treblinka*, Richard Rashke's *Escape from Sobibór*, Samuel Willenberg's *Revolt in Treblinka*, as well as Laurence Rees's *Auschwitz*, and *"The Good Old Days": The Holocaust as Seen by Its Perpetrators and Bystanders*, edited by Ernst Klee. A number of documentaries have brought the Holocaust into sharper focus for me over the years, but for this book I am most grateful for Claude Lanzmann's nine-hour masterpiece, *Shoah*. I first watched this as a teenager in the 1980s, and it has continued to burn in my imagination ever since. It is essential viewing for anyone who wishes to understand the Holocaust better. (Finally, I suppose I should mention I learned much from Rudolf Höss's memoir, *The Commandant of Auschwitz*; however, I simply cannot bring myself to say that I am indebted to this mass murderer in the same way I am indebted to the others mentioned above.)

The quotes that appear in the chapter entitled "Evidence" are authentic. They really were said by Adolf Hitler, Hermann Göring, Hans Frank, Josef Goebbels, and Heinrich Himmler on the dates specified. Equally, Odilo Globocnik really did oversee the genocidal gears of Operation Reinhard, and while I have fictionalized his words, the spirit of his hatred was very genuine and very real. This man was responsible for a tremendous amount of pain, and yet he is just a footnote in most history books. For the minutiae of Hitler's life and what he was like in private (that information which appears in "The Visit"), I am indebted to Ian Kershaw's exhaustive and brilliant biography, *Hitler*.

The escape in this novel was inspired by those at Sobibór and Treblinka, but it is important for me to mention that the orphanage director in "Numbers" is based upon Janusz Korczak. A compassionate and gentle man, Korczak turned down several offers to save his own life, and instead, he accompanied nearly two hundred orphans to their deaths in Treblinka. We don't know exactly what happened when they got to the camp, but we do know that he told the boys to dress in their best clothes, and he told them they were all loved. Sometime in early August 1942, he stepped into one of the gas chambers with them. A memorial stone bears his name at Treblinka today.

This novel could not have been written without the generous financial support I received from the Bush Artist Foundation. This grant allowed me to spend considerable time in Kraków as well as many, many, hours in Auschwitz. I am also grateful for the ARAF grant that allowed me to spend time in Lublin (known as the "Jewish Oxford" before the war began), and from there, I was able to conduct extensive research at Majdanek, Bełżec, and Sobibór. The latter camp played a key role in how I envisioned what Lubizec might look like today. A National Endowment for the Arts grant via the South Dakota Arts Council allowed me to visit Warsaw, study the uprising of 1943, and spend time in the rocky wasteland of Treblinka. Although no place shook me to my core as deeply as Auschwitz-Birkenau, there is something about the jagged desolation of Treblinka that has never really left me. To visit these sites of mourning made the Holocaust rise out of history and become something very physical, colored, and real. It is one thing to study these places. It is quite another to walk their soil.

This project was very difficult to write—it gave me frequent nightmares—but I am unfairly blessed with family and friends who asked about it, kept me on track with their gentle questions, and offered suggestions on how to make it better. This includes the English and Journalism Department at Augustana College, the good people at the South Dakota Humanities Council, Saint John's University, Lynne Hicks, Jim Hicks, Sheila Risacher, Erin Crowder, Jayson Funke, William J. Swart, David O'Hara, Joe Dondelinger, Geoffrey Dipple, Jan Brue Enright, Christine Stewart, Jim Reese,

Jeannie Wenshau, Nick Hayes, David McMahon, Jon Lauck, Jeffrey Gustavson, Michael Trudeau, Kent Meyers, and Brian Turner. I'm totally beholden to Roland Pease and Chip Fleischer at Steerforth for believing in the project, nudging me with editorial questions, and helping me to tell this story—thank you so very much, gentlemen. My additional thanks to Peter Black at the United States Holocaust Memorial Museum as well as the many anonymous souls who answered my questions throughout my time in Poland (I am particularly grateful to the man who gave me his umbrella at Bełżec because he didn't want me to get wet; such a small act of generosity in such a terrible place). I am also thankful to Murray Haar for his guidance with Judaism, Stephan Lhotzky for his help with German, and Philip Gans (#139755) who survived Auschwitz and was enormously gracious not only with his time but also with access to his painful memories.

Most of all, I am grateful to my wife, Tania. She offered insightful comments, gave me unwavering support, and understood my need to write as well as my need to visit Poland so many times. Thank you, Tania. Thank you for this and for so very much more. Without you, none of this would have been possible. None of it.

READING GROUP GUIDE FOR
The Commandant of Lubizec
by Patrick Hicks

1. Although Lubizec didn't exist, were there times when you thought that it did? When did this happen?
2. What were your feelings about Hans-Peter Guth? How could he murder thousands of people a day and then go home to love his children? Is this believable?
3. Throughout the narrative, Hicks often blends fact and fiction. Why did he use footnotes that refer to real historical documents? What effect did this have?
4. What did you think of the relationship between Guth and his wife, Jasmine? How did living so close to a factory of death influence their marriage?
5. Hicks often interrupts the action to offer comments from Zischer and Damiel—these comments are all taken from fictitious interviews recorded years after Lubizec was destroyed. What interruptions were the most powerful for you? What did you think of the chapter called "Evidence"?
6. When Erich Bolender, an SS judge, shows up at Lubizec to investigate criminal activity in the warehouses of Zurich, were you surprised by his reaction? Is it likely that a high-ranking Nazi officer would be startled by the reality of a death camp when he sees one for the first time?
7. After the escape, why was the camp plowed into the ground? Why were the real-life "Operation Reinhard" camps destroyed in 1943?
8. How did having Guth as a father influence Sigi and Karl as adults? Which one of them has come to terms with their father the best? What would it mean to have a father like Guth? How would you react?
9. Did Guth ever acknowledge the scope of his crime? If yes, when did this happen? If no, what does this mean and why doesn't he admit his guilt?

10. Hardly any of the guards at Lubizec were put on trial after the war. In fact, Guth lived a comfortable life in Barcelona for many years. Why was justice so lax?

11. Chaim Zischer and Dov Damiel are haunted by what they saw at Lubizec. How do they cope with their memories? Who suffered more after the war: the victims or the perpetrators?

12. History itself is a story. What is Hicks saying about memory and documentation and how we remember the past? What will happen to our understanding of the Holocaust when our last living eyewitness passes away?

13. The final scene in the novel takes place at Lubizec, and we see what the camp looks like today. The novel closes with Zischer standing before the gas chamber site. How do we commemorate genocide? What have we learned from the Holocaust? What are you likely to take away from this book?

ABOUT THE AUTHOR

Patrick Hicks is the author of several poetry collections, most recently *Finding the Gossamer* and *This London*. His work has appeared in some of the most vital literary journals in America, including *Ploughshares*, *Glimmer Train*, *The Missouri Review*, *The Briar Cliff Review*, and many others. He has won the Glimmer Train Fiction Award as well as a number of grants, including ones from the Bush Artist Foundation and the National Endowment for the Humanities. After living in Europe for many years, he now lives in the Midwest where he is the Writer-in-Residence at Augustana College and also a faculty member in the low-residency MFA Program at Sierra Nevada College.

∾

STEERFORTH PRESS is committed to publishing quality works of fiction and narrative nonfiction. Our tests of a book's worth are whether it has been written well, is intended to engage the full attention of the reader, and has something new or important to say. Please visit us and explore our list at www.steerforth.com.